The Jig Is Up

June rolled her head in a way that seniors like me are warned not to. "My best friend, Zoe, she came here from Chicago right after I did. We've been friends, like, forever." She took a deep breath. "She's in jail."

What to ask first? Why? Where? I settled on "When did this happen?"

June looked around the living room. "Where's Skip?" she asked, accusingly, as if we were hiding him from her.

"I assume you tried all his numbers, June?" Richard asked.

"I left messages everywhere," she wailed.

"What can we do to help?" I asked.

June's head jerked up. She gave me a wide-eyed look. "Gerry, you have to look into this. You know, the way you and Maddie are always solving cases."

It was Richard's turn for a wide-eyed look.

Busted.

Malice in Miniature

Margaret Grace

BERKLEY PRIME CRIME, NEW YORK

THE BERKLEY PUBLISHING GROUP
Published by the Penguin Group
Penguin Group (USA) Inc.
375 Hudson Street, New York, New York 10014, USA
Penguin Group (Canada), 90 Eglinton Avenue East, Suite 700, Toronto, Ontario M4P 2Y3, Canada
(a division of Pearson Penguin Canada Inc.)
Penguin Books Ltd., 80 Strand, London WC2R 0RL, England
Penguin Group Ireland, 25 St. Stephen's Green, Dublin 2, Ireland (a division of Penguin Books Ltd.)
Penguin Group (Australia), 250 Camberwell Road, Camberwell, Victoria 3124, Australia
(a division of Pearson Australia Group Pty. Ltd.)
Penguin Books India Pvt. Ltd., 11 Community Centre, Panchsheel Park, New Delhi—110 017, India
Penguin Group (NZ), 67 Apollo Drive, Rosedale, North Shore 0632, New Zealand
(a division of Pearson New Zealand Ltd.)
Penguin Books (South Africa) (Pty.) Ltd., 24 Sturdee Avenue, Rosebank, Johannesburg 2196,
South Africa

Penguin Books Ltd., Registered Offices: 80 Strand, London WC2R 0RL, England

This is a work of fiction. Names, characters, places, and incidents either are the product of the author's imagination or are used fictitiously, and any resemblance to actual persons, living or dead, business establishments, events, or locales is entirely coincidental. The publisher does not have any control over and does not assume any responsibility for author or third-party websites or their content.

MALICE IN MINIATURE

A Berkley Prime Crime Book / published by arrangement with the author

PRINTING HISTORY
Berkley Prime Crime mass-market edition / February 2009

Copyright © 2009 by Camille Minichino.
Interior text design by Kristin del Rosario.

ISBN: 978-0-425-22558-5

BERKLEY® PRIME CRIME
Berkley Prime Crime Books are published by The Berkley Publishing Group,
a division of Penguin Group (USA) Inc.,
375 Hudson Street, New York, New York 10014.
BERKLEY® PRIME CRIME and the PRIME CRIME logo are trademarks of Penguin Group (USA) Inc.

PRINTED IN THE UNITED STATES OF AMERICA

10 9 8 7 6 5 4 3 2 1

Acknowledgments

Special thanks as always to my dream critique team: mystery authors Jonnie Jacobs, Rita Lakin, and Margaret Lucke.

Thanks also to my sister, Arlene Polvinen; my cousin, Jean Stokowski; and the many writers and friends who offered critique and inspiration, in particular: Judy Barnett, Sara Bly, Margaret Hamilton, Maureen Kaplan, Anna Lipjhart, Carole Price, Mary Schnur, Sue Stephenson, and Karen Streich.

I'm grateful for advice from law enforcement's superb Inspector Chris Lux; my friend and artist, Betita Gamble; and from my cousin and teacher, Susan Durkin. My interpretation of their counsel should not be held against them.

My thanks to Kathy Cordova and Jim Ott, of TV 30, Tri-Valley Community Television and the TV 30 staff, who provided generous advice and access to their studio. Readers should in no way confuse the real Kathy Cordova with Nan Browne, her ill-tempered fictional counterpart. I simply took Kathy's beauty, warmth, and wonderful qualities and twisted them for dramatic purposes.

My deepest gratitude goes to my husband, Dick Rufer,

the best there is. I can't imagine working without his 24/7 support. He's my dedicated Webmaster (www.dollhousemysteries .com), layout specialist, and IT department.

Finally, how lucky can I be? I'm working with a wonderful editor, Michelle Vega, and an extraordinary agent, Elaine Koster.

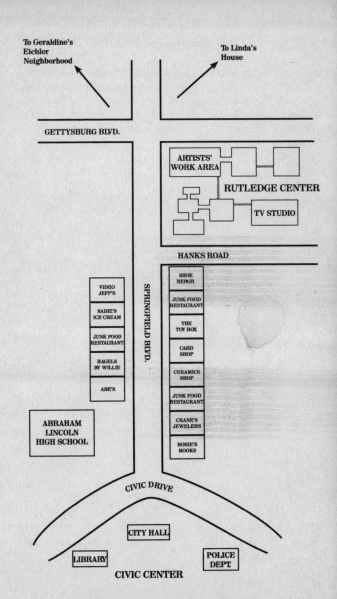

To Geraldine's
Eichler
Neighborhood

To Linda's
House

GETTYSBURG BLVD.

ARTISTS'
WORK AREA

RUTLEDGE CENTER

TV STUDIO

HANKS ROAD

SPRINGFIELD BLVD.

VIDEO
JEFF'S

SADIE'S
ICE CREAM

JUNK FOOD
RESTAURANT

BAGELS
BY WILLIE

ABE'S

SHOE
REPAIR

JUNK FOOD
RESTAURANT

THE
TOY BOX

CARD
SHOP

CERAMICS
SHOP

JUNK FOOD
RESTAURANT

CRANE'S
JEWELERS

ROSIE'S
BOOKS

ABRAHAM
LINCOLN
HIGH SCHOOL

CIVIC DRIVE

CITY HALL

LIBRARY

POLICE
DEPT

CIVIC CENTER

LINCOLN POINT, CA

Chapter 1

My new house didn't have western exposure in the kitchen. It was almost criminal. I couldn't imagine working at the sink or stove without benefit of the late afternoon sun.

Fortunately, it was an easy problem to fix. I picked up the house, rotated it about ninety degrees, and set it down in its corner. Only a couple of items fell over in the operation—a small lamp and a vase of flowers that apparently weren't glued down properly. I righted them and peered through the picture window.

Much better.

Now I had four dollhouses, spread throughout my life-size home, with picture windows that framed the setting sun, especially brilliant this February afternoon.

"You should have asked me to do that, Mom," said my husky son, Richard (the orthopedic surgeon, as I liked to append to all who would listen). "That must weigh forty pounds."

"I've been moving houses like this since—"

Richard followed me from the dining room to the kitchen,

where I resumed dinner preparations. "Before I was born, I know," he said. "First in the Bronx, and now in Lincoln Point. Yada yada."

His smile, with his long laugh lines, prompted me to kiss him on his scruffy cheek (it was still a novelty to have my only child back home). "Thanks anyway for the offer."

The truth was I'd gotten used to being alone and doing whatever heavy lifting needed to be done. I'd been a widow for more than two years. As wonderful as my local family and friends had been to me, they weren't by my side twenty-four/seven, and at the end of the day, I was on my own. I wasn't one to sit around and wait for help or call someone when I wanted to install a shelf or rearrange my furniture—even the life-size versions—when I was perfectly capable.

Richard, his artist wife, Mary Lou, and the joy of my life, my granddaughter, Madison Porter, recently turned eleven, had moved back to northern California only a few weeks ago. They were staying with me while their home-in-the-making near the Stanford University School of Medicine, Richard's new employer, was being completed. I didn't say it out loud, but my secret hope was that the contractors would live up to the stereotype and be many weeks late. But no matter what, my son and his family would be only ten miles to the north of me now, instead of hundreds of miles to the south in Los Angeles, where they'd been since Maddie was two years old.

"How many dollhouses do you need, anyway?" Richard asked me.

"I think one hundred would be a good number," I answered.

Not easily bested, Richard gave me another broad smile. "Well, you're on your way."

"I like your attitude. I'm glad I'm serving your favorite tomato sauce tonight."

I hadn't yet owned up to my family that my true heroine was a woman featured in a documentary I'd seen on our local cable channel. She's been collecting dollhouses of all sizes for many years. On the video you can see houses everywhere. One-room cabins, shops, and barns lay on her windowsills; large Victorians and colonials sit on tables and along the walls of every room. An especially beautiful structure from 1840 (she'd rescued it from a trash bin in a Welsh village), lined with majestic Palladian windows, takes up a large area of her living room floor.

I thought of visiting her until I learned that she lived in England. Who knew that Channel 29, the Lincoln Point cable franchise, had such far-reaching contacts?

I couldn't remember the last time Richard and I shared a meal together by ourselves. Tonight, the rest of our extended family was otherwise engaged. It was Mary Lou's turn to pick up Maddie from the after-school program in their new neighborhood. They would then have dinner together, for a little quality mother/daughter time.

With my near and dear reasonably content and healthy, the only stress in my life at the moment was the looming deadline to finish a room box by February 12, one week from now, when Lincoln Point would celebrate "the Real President's Day," as we called it. In store for us was a reenactment of one of the 1858 campaign debates between Abraham Lincoln and Stephen Douglas, with all the trimmings of period staging. My foot-long room box, featuring an outdoor debate setting, was to be raffled off for the benefit of the library.

I focused on the task at hand and stirred my special marinara sauce.

"Do you know where your wife and daughter are eating?" I asked Richard, handing over a hot shrimp for him to sample.

"It's a no-brainer. Mary Lou will suggest a salad bar or sushi or whatever, Maddie will bat her eyes and plead for pizza, and guess who'll win?"

"I'll count on a couple of leftover slices coming home," I said.

Richard stopped to lick his lips. "Mmm. The shrimp is perfect. Who needs pizza?"

What followed was more Maddie talk—especially about her adjustment to the move away from her Los Angeles school and neighborhood.

"She doesn't seem to have made many friends here yet," Richard said.

"It's hardly a month," I said. "Give her a chance."

If anyone but her father had suggested that my granddaughter was slow at assimilating, I'd have sounded even more put out. The only child of an only child, Maddie seemed determined to fill her life with surrogate siblings and cousins and had learned to charm both adults and other children.

Not that I was biased.

"I guess we'll see," said Richard, who knew enough not to belabor any hint of imperfection in his daughter in my presence.

He arranged dishes and glasses on the dining-room table. Probably I made too much of it, but I thought he looked more like his father when he was doing a chore that Ken often did, like setting the table or taking out the trash. My son had the Porter red hair and Ken's high forehead. I saw my genes only in his deep-set eyes. We couldn't trace his stocky build to either side of what were otherwise two families of long, lean men and women.

In his afternoon-off jeans and sweatshirt, Richard maneuvered around Mary Lou's paintings, stacked three and four deep along the walls and in front of the hutch, and found our favorite wineglasses. His wife's artwork, finished and unfinished, filled the house, giving my dollhouses and miniatures hobby competition for space. A four-bedroom house was no match for four people when one was a child with enough protective gear, bats, sticks, and balls to equip a small school, and two of the adults had clutter-based interests. Though this temporary company put a strain on my crafts rooms, Richard and his family lifted my spirits every hour that they graced my home.

At the front of Mary Lou's stack now was a work in progress, a rendition of a Lincoln-Douglas debate. She'd sketched out the two men, one short and round (Douglas), the other tall and lanky (Abe), in formal attire, addressing a crowd of people in an outdoor rally. American flags were draped across the stage; banners were hung on the large, full-leaved trees. I could feel the excitement of the event in the swirls and shades of the sketch. The scene was on its way to becoming a spectacular watercolor.

Like Maddie, my daughter-in-law could charm people even from a distance, and she'd gotten herself a commission to do the painting even before moving here. Mary Lou had the same deadline I did for my room box—the painting had to be finished, framed, and hanging in the lobby of the Lincoln Point City Hall on the morning of February 12.

But now it was dinnertime for Richard and me. I took a steaming bowl of spaghetti and sauce to the table, leaving a richly aromatic trail behind me. Richard added the bread basket, then held my seat for me. "I'm not being sexist, Mom, just honoring the cook. No offense."

"None taken."

He took his seat across from me. "This is nice," he said. "Not sharing you."

We toasted with wine Richard had brought home from a recent family outing to the vineyards of Napa Valley.

I heard the pleasant clink of my parents' sixty-year-old wedding crystal.

Then, quickly afterward, a demanding *bzzz, bzzz, bzzz.* My front doorbell.

Richard and I looked at each other, eyebrows raised all around. Then we laughed.

"It *was* nice," Richard said.

If it had been a single buzz, like the signal from a delivery person warning us there was now a package on the doorstep, we might have ignored it. But this was an insistent ringing, as if someone were desperate to get to me.

Bzzz, bzzz, bzzz.

"I'll get it," Richard said. "Before I have a doorbell to repair."

As if he could. Richard was handy in the operating room and laboratory (I assumed, since Stanford had paid a lot to woo him to northern California), but he had none of his architect father's handyman skills.

He snatched a crust of Italian bread to eat on the way to the door.

"Is Skip here?"

I heard the distraught voice of June Chinn, my thoughtful next-door neighbor and my nephew Skip's girlfriend. A family favorite, I might add. I wondered why she hadn't simply hoisted her tiny body over our back fence into my yard and knocked on my glass patio door, as she usually did, day or night, in all seasons.

She was much too light to knock Richard over, but her entrance this evening was energetic enough to have made an impact as she pushed past him with a quick, "Hey, Richard," and landed in front of me, at the dining-room table.

"Gerry, something awful's happened." June stood at her full five feet, two inches and flailed her arms. The gesture, plus the intensely orange fleece vest she wore, gave her the look of a Caltrans worker on a freeway instead of the Silicon Valley tech editor that she was. "I can't find Skip."

I put down my fork and swallowed hard. I'd seen my nephew at noon when he stopped by for a quick bite. How could he be missing now? Frightening images went through my mind. Skip was a homicide detective on the Lincoln Point police force, and in my opinion, at risk every hour that he was at work. I remembered he'd mentioned a new case that was "touchy." My mind ran amuck. His mother, my sister-in-law, Beverly Gowen, was in Hawaii on vacation with her new beau. What if—?

I stood up, dropping my napkin, and looked at June,

who must have seen my concern. "No, no. I mean *I need to talk to Skip* and I can't find him."

I felt my shoulders loosen up, but not completely. June was not a drama queen, so I knew this must be serious. Richard used his best doctor manner to lead her to a chair in the living room part of our combined living/dining room. I followed, still not able to allow myself to relax fully.

June rolled her head in a way that seniors like me are warned not to. "My best friend, Zoe, she came here from Chicago right after I did. We've been friends, like, forever." She took a deep breath. "She's in jail."

What to ask first? Why? Where? I settled on "When did this happen?"

June looked around the dining room. "Where's Skip?" she asked, accusingly, as if we were hiding him from her.

"I assume you tried all his numbers, June?" Richard asked.

"I left messages everywhere," she wailed.

"What can we do to help?" I asked.

June's head jerked up. She gave me a wide-eyed look. "Gerry, you have to look into this. You know, the way you and Maddie are always solving cases."

It was Richard's turn for a wide-eyed look.

Busted.

Chapter 2

June's overwrought state kept Richard's questioning me at bay, though I knew eventually I'd have to submit to an interrogation on my grandparenting practices.

Usually a calm young woman, June had been an ideal neighbor and sometime babysitter for Maddie even before she and Skip started going steady (if that was still what they called it) a few months ago. Now she was dissolved in tears and barely understandable.

June chose tea over wine and calmed down enough to get started. I managed to hear that Zoe Howard, whom June had known "like, forever" (a lot of language usage had changed since I'd retired from teaching high school English only a couple of years ago), had a boyfriend, Brad Goodman, who was an artist. He was currently working on the stage set for the Lincoln-Douglas debate.

Richard and I sat at attention on the sofa, across from June. A few sips of tea, and she seemed ready to continue. "Zoe was really happy that Brad got this paying gig," June said. "I guess there was a lot of competition. The losers . . .

well, I guess that's not a nice way to put it, but that's what they say . . . the losers work on a big mural together, but the winners get commissions to do individual paintings."

"My wife got one of the commissions," Richard said, with unmistakable pride in his voice. His praise of Mary Lou was unnecessary, since I already knew she was a wonderful painter and June paid no attention.

"They'll all be on television on our Channel 29. The crew there are all caught up in the debate because they're going to video it, then show it over and over all month. It's great exposure for an artist."

"We know. My wife is painting . . ." Richard began, but June still wasn't interested in anyone else's story.

Until she turned to blow her nose and came eye to eye with the dining-room table and two heaping plates of congealing spaghetti marinara. "Omigod, I barged right in on your dinner. I'm so sorry."

"Don't worry about it. Unless you're hungry? There's plenty—"

June held up her hand and shook her head, a deep frown forming, as if the sight of my best meal all year had turned her stomach. I couldn't blame her since my specialty had lost its appeal even to me. How could a few degrees—from steaming hot to room temperature—change an aroma from mouthwatering to distasteful?

"I'm fine," June said.

"Please, go on," I said. "Zoe's boyfriend, Brad, has a commission to do a painting, and . . . ?"

Bzzz, bzzz, bzzz.

I was sure June had no idea why the doorbell brought laughs from Richard and me as our quiet evening was turning into one of the busiest of the week. Not to mention traumatic for our sweet neighbor.

Richard opened the door to his cousin, Skip Gowen, another redheaded Porter (on his mother's side), safe and sound, I noted. Like Maddie, Skip was an only child who did an extraordinary job of winning people over.

But not this evening. Skip wore his detective garb—neatly pressed slacks and a sports jacket—and a serious cop look that he seldom brought into my home.

Richard and Skip exchanged a brief round of "Hey, cuz" and "What's up?" No answers were offered on the walk from the front door, through my atrium, to where June and I were sitting.

I expected a pleasant "Hey, Aunt Gerry," but June rushed up to him as soon as he crossed the threshold into the living room. She crashed into his chest, her head reaching nowhere near his chin. "Skip, I've been looking all over for you, leaving messages." Her words were barely audible until she released her hold on him and we were all seated, across from each other, one more tense than the other.

"I . . . uh . . . I've been tied up all day," Skip said.

"I wish you'd called me back," June said. "I've been so frantic." She twisted a tissue in her hands, tiny white shreds dropping onto her black spandex tights. "There's been a terrible mistake. They've arrested Zoe. She's in jail. Did you know that?"

I caught Skip's expression. I knew my nephew well enough to tell that this wasn't a surprise to him.

He pointed in the direction of June's house. "I went over to talk to you. When you didn't answer the door, I figured you were here," Skip said.

Hmmm. This was Skip's usual technique of not answering direct questions, as if the person asking were a prime suspect. But this evening more than that was going on. Memories of my nephew when he was about Maddie's age came to me. "I don't know who broke that [fill in the blank], Aunt Gerry. Maybe it was Richard," he'd said on more than one occasion. My nephew had always been transparent when he was being less than honest—at ten years old it was excessive blinking that gave him away, as if he wanted us to know he was not telling the truth—and I saw through him now. I knew he must have a good reason for not admitting what I suspected were the facts, that he hadn't tried to reach June, and that he'd been hoping to avoid her until he could talk to Richard and me about whatever was on his mind concerning the arrest of her friend.

I tried to ignore the odor of the spaghetti and shrimp, rapidly going downhill. It didn't seem the right moment for housekeeping chores. I did, however, prepare a cup of coffee for Skip and put a few of his favorite ginger cookies (from my special recipe) on a plate. I'd kept my ear tuned to the drama unfolding a few yards away as I stood in the kitchen waiting for the whistle of a very slow kettle. I'd heard not a word from Richard, and only a syllable or two from Skip.

As I came back into the room, June was still holding forth about her friend. "I've told you how bad it's been for Zoe lately, like she's had this cloud over her head the past month or so. Don't you remember?"

Skip nodded, patient. "I know. She had a flat tire—"

"*Four* flat tires," June said, holding up her fingers.

"Four at once? That *is* odd," Richard said, but neither June nor Skip appeared to hear him.

"And then someone stole her identity and used her Visa in the Philippines."

"That happens a lot these days," Richard said.

I shot my son a look. He raised his eyebrows and gave a slight shrug that said he was doing his best to bring a sense of normalcy to the situation. I shot another look that said "not now." He smiled in acquiescence and I was glad we hadn't lost our ability to communicate nonverbally.

"Zoe doesn't even know where the Philippines are. And anyway, that's not my point. She even thought she was being followed a couple of nights. And her purse was stolen, remember that? Now this. You've got to tell them she's innocent, Skip."

He took her hand. It was his turn to speak. "June. You'll know this soon enough. I'm the one who brought her in. But—"

June stiffened and gave him a glaring look, made less

threatening by the tears escaping from her eyes. She
yanked away her hand. "You put Zoe in jail?"

"Well, not—"

"Skip, how could you do that? Zoe is my best friend.
We're basically family. I'm all she has."

"You need to let me explain. Can you calm down so we
can talk?" If the tone of his voice didn't work to bring June
down from her highly charged state, nothing would.

And nothing did. June stuffed her hands into her orange
vest pockets. "I won't calm down until you make a call and
get her out right now."

Richard and I, back in our seats across from them, listened intently, as if we were the audience at a great debate.

Skip's tone was soft, pleading. "June, honey, you know
I can't do that."

June was up and out the door before he could stop her
(in reality, any one of the three of us could have halted her
progress and scooped her up, given her tiny frame).

Skip threw up his hands, then buried his head in them for
a moment. He hadn't touched his coffee or a cookie. Bad
sign. He looked up at us, seeming surprised that Richard
and I were in the room. I guessed Richard felt as awkward
as I did.

"Sorry," Skip said. He got up and headed for the door.

"What's Zoe in jail for?" I asked his retreating back.

He called over his shoulder, "Murder."

Now I knew what Skip had meant by a "touchy" case.

Though curiosity had been nagging at me during the
commotion over Zoe's plight, I'd had a little time to mentally prepare my response to Richard's inevitable question
about my "solving cases with Maddie," as June had put it.

"It was nothing," I said. "I needed to do a little research
and Maddie helped on the computer." I snapped my fingers
and appealed to a father's pride. "She's a whiz at it, you
know."

"She is good, isn't she?" He beamed.

We'd been working together to clean up (optimistically storing the unappetizing meal away for another day), which gave the conversation the casual flair that I wanted, and Richard seemed satisfied.

Now we took our wineglasses to the living room area for another try at a little togetherness.

"So who do you think Zoe murdered?" Richard asked. Not our usual family chat agenda.

"Allegedly," I said, feeling compassion for a woman I'd met only once or twice in large gatherings. I was sure my feeling had more to do with good-natured, put-together (though not this evening) June Chinn. I couldn't imagine her being best friends with a murderer. "Anyway, it's not our business."

Richard raised his glass to me, his sly grin partly covered by the crystal. "Good one," he said.

If he'd been wearing reading glasses, I'd have sworn it was Ken on the sofa.

Not five minutes later, the living room came alive again. The door slammed, a heavy backpack thumped on the tile in the entryway, and thick-soled shoes sporting a soccer ball design on their laces hit the atrium floor at breakneck speed.

"We're home, we're home," Maddie shouted, running to kiss me, then her father.

"No kidding," said her father, ruffling her red curls.

"Pizza, anyone?" Mary Lou asked. She doffed her pink faux-satin baseball cap (which her daughter scorned) and held up a white plastic container in the manner of a waiter with a large, fancy tray.

Richard jumped up and in one motion kissed his petite wife on the cheek and grabbed the leftovers box. "Sweet," he said.

Mary Lou pulled at her hair, still not used to her new,

shorter do—a layered design with blond strands of different hues and lengths, no two alike it seemed, the longest of which flipped out slightly just under her ears. She gave her husband a confused look.

"I was being facetious about the pizza. I thought you two had a nice, quiet, grown-up dinner planned."

"Planned but not implemented," Richard said, his mouth juggling a large bite of newly microwaved pizza. Apparently, my poor boy was ravenous. I thought fondly of our days in the Bronx, when "slice" would have said it all, as when Ken would ask, "Shall we all go out for a slice?"

"What's facetious?" Maddie asked me. She addressed the word person in the house—her grandmother, who'd been giving her age-appropriate word-a-day calendars since she was able to turn the pages.

"It means your mom didn't know our evening was so exciting that your dad and I didn't get a chance to eat."

"What happened? What happened?" Maddie was in her Xerox phase, duplicating every exclamatory phrase. It was as unnecessary as two (or more) exclamation points at the end of a sentence. I would have taken points off a test if one of my freshman English students had done it, but in Maddie I found it charming.

I regretted my teasing remark, since I wasn't eager to involve Maddie in police matters.

"Oh, we had a little company. How was your day in school?" I asked her.

She managed to touch her nose with her upper lip. "It was okay."

"How about the after-school program? What do they have you doing?"

"Nothing much."

"Are you working on crafts?"

"Nothing much."

Her parents had enrolled Maddie in an expensive "nothing much" program near their future home so she could start to bond with her neighbors-to-be.

"I thought you were going to try to get on the soccer team. Do they know you have a shelf full of trophies?"

She reached for one of the ginger cookies meant for Skip. "Nah, nah."

"It sounds like someone hasn't had her ice cream yet," Richard said.

Maddie brightened a little as we all headed for the kitchen and took up our established dessert duties. I noted how quickly people get into a routine, especially one that gives pleasure. Richard stacked a tray with three flavors of ice cream: double chocolate chip for Maddie and me, spumoni for Mary Lou, and vanilla for himself (I often wondered whether these choices were clues to our personalities); Mary Lou heated the chocolate and caramel sauces from Sadie's, our local creamery, and emptied a bag of chopped nuts into a small dish; Maddie and I set the table with bowls, spoons, and a replenished plate of ginger cookies.

All went as smoothly as a well-rehearsed theater pro-duction, down to our taking the same places at the table, as if they'd been assigned by a stage director. We dug into our customized sundaes.

"Why can't I go to school in Lincoln Point?" Maddie asked me. I knew she'd exhausted her parents with that question already. "I don't know anyone in Palo Alto."

"You don't know anyone here, either," Mary Lou said, handing me the jar of sweet-smelling melted chocolate.

Big mistake, I thought, and I didn't mean the chocolate sauce.

Maddie didn't miss a beat. "I do, too. I do, too. I know lots of kids here." She ticked them off on her fingers. "Jason, Ariana, Abby, Melana, Noah, Natalie . . ." She stopped the roll call and gave an exasperated sigh, as if she didn't have enough fingers and toes to name all the friends she had in Lincoln Point.

Besides Jason, who was my friend Linda's adopted son, I recognized the names of children Maddie had met on her many visits here. I felt a little pride that I'd been a good enough grandmother to have taken her to library reading events and other children's activities while she was in my care. I hoped her father was taking note.

"Well, that just proves how easily you make friends," Richard said. "So in no time at all you'll have a long list of friends in Palo Alto."

"Nuts," Maddie said.

I handed her the dish of them, but she was not amused. At least she hadn't said, "Nuts. Nuts."

It was my turn to tuck Maddie in, though she'd bristle at the term. She'd insisted on sleeping in the corner room, the one that had been her father's, but was hers on her visits through the years.

"I don't think I can sleep without the baseball afghan Grandma knitted for me," Richard had told her when they first arrived.

"Neither can I," she'd said.

Game over.

Lest I think I'd gotten away with something, as soon as Maddie and I were alone in her room, the baseball afghan in its proper place on her bed, she revisited her earlier question. "I'll bet it was Uncle Skip."

"What, sweetheart?" I asked, to stall for time.

"Uncle Skip came by and you talked about a case. That's why you missed dinner."

Was my granddaughter that smart, or was I that easy to read? "What makes you think that?"

"If it was someone else, you would have told me. And if it wasn't about a case, he would have just sat down and ate with you."

"Eaten, sweetheart. Remember? It's *would have eaten*."

"Okay, never mind. I'm tired anyway."

And my miniature detective was off to sleep, giving me a little reprieve.

As Maddie had gotten older and stayed up later, adult conversation time got shorter, but Richard, Mary Lou, and I had developed the habit of having a current events and "how was your day" chat before we went to bed, no matter how late. Richard would share what he could about his new staff and duties at the hospital; Mary Lou seemed always to have an art fact of the day: a way to create a richer purple in watercolor, or the scoop on a new brush; I reported on odds and ends in the worlds of GED tutoring and teaching and doing crafts.

Tonight when I returned to the living room, Richard was briefing Mary Lou on the drama that had cost him his fresh shrimp marinara.

"We're waiting for the eleven o'clock news," he said to me, his fingers poised on the television remote. "Ten more minutes." He pointed the control at the screen and switched it on. "Now that the minor child is asleep, we can hear the story and the gory details of a murder in Lincoln Point."

"Is your life that boring, honey?" Mary Lou teased. In fact we all knew it was anything but, with his new job and new staff at Stanford, and the new house that took a lot of oversight from both him and Mary Lou.

With the television on mute while we waited, we did a remarkable job of pursuing the topic of the evening, considering how little information we had.

"Let me see if I have it right. It was this artist boyfriend of June's friend who was murdered?" Mary Lou asked.

"We don't know for sure," I said. "June was just getting started when Skip came in."

"How was the person killed?" Mary Lou asked.

"We don't know," Richard said. "June was just getting

started, et cetera, et cetera." He twirled his fingers in the air, Yul Brynner style, surprising me that anyone his age had seen *The King and I*.

"Where did the murder take place?"

"We have no idea," I said.

"What's the evidence against June's friend that got her arrested?"

"We have no idea," Richard said, a mimicking grin across his face.

"Do we know where the body was found or who found it?"

"No, we don't," Richard and I said together.

Mary Lou was the first to laugh. "Sorry to sound crass, but maybe we should move on to something we can actually discuss."

"Like your painting," I said, slightly dizzy from the impossible quiz. "How's that coming?"

Mary Lou could talk a long time about her passion, watercolor. She'd been happy to land a flexible-hours job at a gallery in nearby Mountain View so that she could carve out long periods of time for painting.

The problem was finding a place to work while her state-of-the-art loft was under construction as part of their Palo Alto home. The Rutledge Center, a city-owned complex of buildings, had offered space to the artists like the elusive (murdered?) Brad, of "Zoe and Brad," who were working on the Lincoln-Douglas project.

The Lincoln Point television studio, where local Channel 29 originated, was located in the complex also. It was deemed convenient to have the works-in-progress under their roof for easy access as they prepared their documentary.

"It's been neat having the television crew around, taping us working, or getting set up in my case, asking questions about my brushes," Mary Lou said.

"I'll bet," her husband said, his eyes on the television screen.

"Their anchorwoman, Nan Browne . . . she's also the one who's the narrator of the documentary . . . is something else, though. She has a daughter who's a painter, Diana Browne. She lost out on a commission, so I don't think either the mother or the daughter likes me very much."

"I don't know Diana, but I've heard that Nan doesn't like too many people anyway," I said.

Mary Lou's in-progress rendition of a Lincoln-Douglas debate, which Richard had almost tripped over in my dining room, would be on its way to the Rutledge Center tomorrow, at the hands of yours truly. I'd offered to drop it off in the afternoon.

"You always see Lincoln towering over Douglas in paintings and drawings," Mary Lou said. "That's why I put Douglas in front in my version. I'll bet half the population thinks Lincoln won that election, just because he's so tall and imposing in all the debate images."

"He didn't win?" Richard looked genuinely surprised.

"Did you learn nothing in the public schools of Lincoln Point?" I asked my son.

"That was a long time ago, and I don't remember hearing about a President Douglas. Do we get his birthday off?" Richard sounded defensive, as if one of his teachers had just suggested he wasn't applying himself hard enough to his history lessons.

Mary Lou cut him a little slack. "I wouldn't have known, either, if I hadn't studied up to get in the spirit of the painting. The debates were for one of Illinois's two U.S. Senate seats. Lincoln lost that election, but it did put him in the public eye nationally and he won the presidential election two years later."

"Interesting," Richard said, but his tone said otherwise.

"Anyway, I want to try to give Mr. Douglas a little stature in my painting, even though he was under five feet tall."

"Interesting," I said, and meant it.

"Another minute and we should have some local news," Mary Lou said. "Anyone for more tea? Mom?"

I raised my hand. "I'd love some."

"I'll have some wine," Richard said.

"Can I have some hot chocolate?" a small voice said. It came from behind us, from the direction of the corner bedroom with the baseball afghan. "I can't sleep."

Richard deftly pushed buttons and got a blank screen on the television set.

Maddie, still smelling of strawberry bubble bath, climbed on my lap. "What's wrong, sweetheart?" I asked, stroking her head.

She rubbed her eyes and laid her head on my chest. "I don't feel too well. I might not be able to go to school tomorrow."

"Oh, right," Mary Lou said, heading for the kitchen, not a trace of sympathy in her voice.

"Here we go," Richard said.

"What if she really is sick?" *Such cold parents* was in my tone. I put my hand on her forehead. It was also cold.

"Grandma, you're playing right into her little act," Richard said. He walked over to where Maddie was using me as an easy chair. He reached out and tickled her. She came out of her slump and the two of them ended up rolling on the floor.

Two servings of tea, one glass of wine, and one hot chocolate got us through an abbreviated version of *Clue*. Declared the winner, Maddie crawled back into bed and so did we.

The television news came and went without benefit of our scrutiny.

Chapter 3

Breakfast was one time of day that had changed drasti-
cally since my family arrived from Los Angeles and moved
in with me. As a single person, I usually took my sweet
time in the morning, starting with the newspaper and coffee and adding cereal or eggs later. I showered and
dressed only in time for the day's meetings, which might
include tutoring sessions at the library, crafts classes for
the residents of Lincoln Point's retirement homes, and
various committee work for Lincoln Point's fund-raising
programs.

Not a hurried life, for the most part. Plenty of time for
my new reading pleasure, contemporary fiction. I felt I'd
read and reread the classics often enough in my twenty-
seven years of teaching to branch out.

Now there was a mad scramble every morning while
four people tried to get along with two bathrooms. I'd
given Richard and Mary Lou the largest bedroom and bath
suite (small by contemporary standards, at only twelve by
fourteen).

"Only one sink in the master suite," Richard had said, in an "imagine that" tone. How quickly he'd forgotten his modest roots.

I took the bedroom between parents and child, and shared the second bathroom with Maddie.

We were not crowded by 1950s standards. But I'd been to their sprawling Los Angeles home and had seen the plans for the next-generation Porter homestead in Palo Alto, and I could see why they felt cramped.

This morning Richard left first for an early surgery, followed closely by Mary Lou, on her way to open the gallery where she worked.

"Thanks for taking the painting, Mom," Mary Lou said. At least, I thought that was her message as she held a piece of dry toast between her teeth and loaded her work-in-progress into my trunk. I kept my car outside in the driveway since Richard's new sports car trumped my little Ion for garage space. Mary Lou worked against a slight drizzle, keeping her portfolio close to her body.

Maddie knew she'd lost the "I'm sick" battle and buckled herself into my Ion only ten minutes later than the ideal departure time on Wednesday morning. She had the afternoon off to allow the teachers at her school to take a class in CPR. I won the privilege of driving Maddie to school and picking her up around eleven. In between I could shop in Palo Alto. Not a bad deal.

"Isn't CPR for old people?" she asked.

Unfortunately, not always, I thought. "I'm sure it's for when the teachers are visiting their great-great-grandparents," I told her.

"My teachers in L.A. were always taking professional days," Maddie said. "They had things like team-building, but not for sports, and other stuff. I think they just needed a break from us."

A very insightful comment, but as a retired English teacher, I felt I needed to speak up for my profession. "Someday I'll show you all the notebooks I have from my own teacher conference days. They're filled with information on special programs for reading, writing—"

I could see Maddie in the rearview mirror, signaling "time out." Her way of cutting off speeches about the old days. We moved on to planning the present day.

Maddie and I decided that the afternoon would include lunch, a session on a miniature project or two, a movie and popcorn at home. We also needed to drop off Mary Lou's painting at the Rutledge Center. A lot to crowd in before Richard and Mary Lou came home for dinner.

We headed north on the Bayshore Freeway, driving through heavy traffic and a light but steady rain. The hills around us were as green as they would ever get; the rest of the year they were "golden" (read: "dry"). Ken would have said, "It's our two green weeks a year, always in time for Lincoln's birthday."

In about a half hour, we pulled up to Maddie's new school, Angelican Hills Elementary, named for its location on Angelica Avenue in Palo Alto. "It's so funny," Maddie told every new person she met. "My Los Angeles school was called Stanford Elementary, and now my school near Stanford is named Angelican Hills, you know, like Angeles."

We all got it and laughed every time.

"We're going back to Lincoln Point for lunch, right?" Maddie asked me. She stood by the curb, hooking on her brand-new backpack.

"I thought we could eat in Palo Alto, maybe invite one of your friends here to come with us, and also her mother or whoever picks her up."

"Nah, nah. I'd rather have a Willie's bagel and a Sadie's ice cream. Yum, yum."

"Okay, okay," I said, but she didn't seem to get the parody.

This was unusual behavior. As her father said, Maddie had always made friends easily. I wondered what was holding her back this time. Surely the self-consciousness and self-doubt of puberty hadn't already set in? I never thought

I'd be wishing my tomboy granddaughter would get involved in sports, but the circumstances required it.

I wasn't so worried that I forgot what I'd set my sights on, however—an enormous superstore of crafts just one freeway exit away from Maddie's school. I headed straight for it once I let Maddie and her stiff, new backpack off.

It was harder and harder to find dollhouse and miniatures stores these days, but an hour or two in a large crafts and fabric store went a long way to providing inspiration and general supplies for my hobby.

Maddie was a recent convert to dollhouses and miniatures, having always preferred to hit and kick balls around a field wearing a team shirt. The project that had won her over was the model of the Bronx apartment Ken and I had lived in when we were first married. He'd built it to what we miniaturists called full-scale—one inch for one foot of "real" space—and Maddie and I were now decorating it, keeping as close as possible to how the real apartment looked at the time.

"I used to think dollhouses had to be all frilly with pink flowered wallpaper and all," Maddie had said, especially pleased when I'd agreed to a miniature hockey stick in the hallway, where Ken always kept his—a souvenir from his college days.

Today I was on the lookout for bookcase materials for the apartment. I thought of the decidedly non-frilly bookcases, constructed of plywood and cinder blocks, that Ken and I used during our first years in the apartment. The plywood part would be easy to model since I had an abundance of wooden crafts sticks in my storage bins. I cruised the aisles of artificial flowers and other "nursery" items and finally settled on a sheet of gray florist's foam that could be cut to look like cinder blocks. One thing a crafter knows: if you're looking for something shaped like a block, don't restrict yourself to the block aisles.

Before I was finished, I'd added several other items to my cart. I arrived at the checkout station with a three-inch pale green bathrobe (a puffy sticker that was part of a bathroom set) for the apartment; picture frames (gold filigree stickers) to have on hand; and a large book with pages that could be used for floors, wallpaper, and the occasional handmade greeting card. I also treated myself to a new paper scorer so I could keep one at each crafts station (they were legion) in my home.

A pleasant day so far. I enjoyed the rain, especially since it was never very cold by Bronx standards, and I still had an afternoon with my granddaughter to look forward to.

I saw Maddie standing at a bus shelter outside the school talking with another little girl. When Maddie saw me, she bounded across the parking lot, slightly bent from her backpack, waving both arms at me. I remembered times in Los Angeles when I'd pick her up at school and I'd have to pry her away from a circle of little girls and boys.

"What's your friend's name?" I asked her when she'd settled into the backseat of the Ion.

"Her? Kyra. She's not exactly a friend."

"What would make her a friend?"

"I don't know. I don't know."

I thought I knew the answer. Kyra would have to turn herself magically into Devyn, Maddie's best friend who was still "home" in Los Angeles.

Maddie had thrown her wet backpack onto the front seat today, so she wouldn't have to go around to the traffic side of the car. I noticed paper or cardboard sticking out of one of the dozens (it seemed) of zippers. A postcard.

"Have you heard from Devyn?" I asked, guessing the card was part of the reason for her bad mood.

"Yeah, she sent me a postcard from when my class went to Disneyland after the Christmas break."

Still *my* class. As if she were on a short vacation from where she should be. "How is she?"

"I miss her."

Uh-huh. Poor Maddie was having withdrawal pains from her early childhood friends, perhaps thinking to remain loyal to them by not making new friends in Palo Alto. Call me Grandma Psychologist.

"I'll bet she misses you, too."

Maddie nibbled on an energy bar—a product of Mary Lou's campaign to encourage healthy snacks.

"I guess. Are we going to drop Mom's painting off before lunch?"

Grandma Psychologist would call this avoiding the "homesick" topic.

"Are you starving? Would you rather eat first?"

"Nuh-uh. I'm happy with my nutritious, tasty snack."

A healthy laugh broke the tension that psychological analysis can bring.

About a half hour later, we reached the city limits of Lincoln Point. Checking Maddie's hunger level one more time, I drove past Bagels by Willie, on Springfield Boulevard, our main street of shops. Up ahead was Hanks Road, site of the Rutledge Center, the building that housed our local Channel 29 studio, a large workshop area, and many hallways and classrooms.

Rutledge Center comprised a complex of buildings that had been an elementary school at one time, and was now an all-purpose city facility. It was common for Lincoln Point natives to still refer to it as the Rutledge School. I'd been to the center a few times, but never to the television studio.

I'd been a guest on Channel 29, as part of a documentary on the literacy project at Lincoln Point Library and on a couple of other occasions, but those programs had been taped off-site. A historic downtown hotel had provided a much richer backdrop than was possible in the studio. The same Nan Browne, whose daughter didn't get a painting commission and who didn't like Mary Lou, was the hostess on all of the occasions.

I turned the corner on Hanks Road and saw the familiar center buildings. They were all one-story, beige stucco with blue roofs. Some were connected by covered walkways and it was hard to tell where one building ended and another began. I didn't know exactly where the artists' work area was, so I pulled into the parking lot at the first opening. I drove a short way and braked. Harder than I needed to. Maddie jerked forward against her seat belt.

Along the southeast side of the property, yellow crimescene tape waved in the damp February breeze.

Oh, no. Could this be where the murder took place? In all the bustle of the morning, I hadn't even looked at the newspaper. I knew Zoe's boyfriend was an artist. Richard and I had only guessed that he was the murder victim since June began (and ended) her short story with his name. June had also said something about Brad's being part of the Lincoln-Douglas stage crew. It made sense that he, like Mary Lou, was working in the Rutledge Center. Still, that didn't mean the murder had been committed here. Except, apparently, it did.

"A case, a case," Maddie said, with inappropriate glee.

"Not again, not again," I said to myself.

My first impulse was to turn around and head back to Willie's, enjoy coffee and a cinnamon bagel, and forget I'd ever seen the streaming yellow decoration. Maybe it was left over from a party. Perhaps it was tape used by a construction crew. It might even be part of a set for a studio program on the crime fighters of Lincoln Point. I drove a little closer, Maddie now straining to see out the windows. "It says, 'police line, do not cross,'" she announced with exuberance.

No more wishful guessing. With all good intentions, doing an errand for her mother, I'd brought Maddie to a crime scene. I hoped all that was left of it was the rope. Once I allowed my attention to roam to the rest of the complex, I saw that the taped area was confined to only one set of concrete steps, those leading to the Channel 29 studio.

There was no officer stationed there or at the other entryways; people were coming and going through the other doorways as if nothing had happened.

From the backseat came Maddie's voice, pleading to be let out. "Let's see, Grandma. Maybe we can help."

"I think we should just go and have lunch and come back later, sweetheart." *After I drop you off at home.*

"No, no, Grandma. All the other buildings are all clear, see?" She pointed toward the west wing of the complex. "We can get in over there."

She was right about that. The rest of the buildings, where the offices, community outreach classrooms, and the workshop areas were located, were apparently open for business. "I don't know—"

I could see Maddie fold her arms across her scrawny chest. "My mom will be upset if she gets here later and the painting isn't where it should be."

She was good, no question. I gave in, not because of her persuasive reasoning, but because I saw enough people, including children, entering and exiting the other portals of the buildings.

I parked in the northwest lot, as far away from the yellow tape as I could get. The next question was whether to take Maddie inside the building. I could leave her in the car. It was a nice neighborhood. Except for the crime scene.

Definitely safer to have her with me, I decided, though I wasn't sure what I was protecting her from.

I knew Maddie wouldn't have been as thrilled to be inside a building that used to be an elementary school if it weren't for the potential mystery surrounding the colorful buffer zone.

"Is this what Uncle Skip came to talk to you about last night?" she asked.

"No," I said. Not a lie. Skip had simply uttered the word "murder" and, without a context, I had no idea if a few yards of "do not cross" around the east stairway had anything to do with what had sent Zoe to jail.

We walked down a long hallway lined with classrooms. Signs on the doors indicated that the children and adults inside were taking lessons in topics as diverse as portrait drawing, beginning computers, and the tax code. We walked up to one particularly noisy room, peeked through the small window in the door, and spent a couple of minutes watching student belly dancers, young and old, in bright, gauzy costumes.

I knew it wasn't unusual to see children in extracurricular classes on a weekday afternoon—Palo Alto wasn't the only school district where the teachers could have professional days.

"This place is big," Maddie said, running her hand along a brick interior wall.

"Can I help you?"

A short, thin young man in his early thirties, I guessed, wearing a blue-gray security company uniform, came toward us from a hallway to our right. Even stubble covered his whole head. Unless my memory was failing, this was one person between the ages of nineteen and forty-eight years old who had not been my student during my long tenure at Abraham Lincoln High School. A transplant, apparently.

"What's the yellow tape for?" Maddie asked, before I could answer.

"Oh, just some little problem the police have to look into," the young man said. "Nothing you have to worry about, honey."

I was grateful for his discretion.

"My uncle—well, he's really my dad's cousin, so he's *my* cousin once-removed—he's a Lincoln Point homicide detective."

"Wow, that's pretty impressive."

I broke in finally. "We're here to deliver a painting."

He looked at my empty hands and raised his eyebrows.

"It's in my car. I didn't want to carry it in until I knew where to put it."

"It's a painting by my mom, Mary Lou Porter, for the Lincoln-Douglas debate," Maddie said. "She's going to be finishing it in your work area."

Why hadn't I thought of saying that?

"Cool," said the young man.

I introduced myself belatedly and reached out to shake hands.

"Ryan Colson, Noble Security," he said.

"Were you guarding the place where the crime happened?" Maddie asked.

How embarrassing! Not that the question hadn't crossed my mind.

"Aren't you the little detective," Ryan said. "Following in the footsteps of your uncle?" He stepped back and held up his hands as if he were guilty of a grievous sin. "Whoa, I mean your cousin once-removed."

Maddie gave him a full smile, an expression she'd gone back to now that her teeth were all nearly even. "Maybe," she said.

I put my hand on Maddie's red curls. "Sorry to be so intrusive," I said to Ryan.

"No problem. Why don't you drive around the north side? It's closer to the workshop. Everything is unlocked until five o'clock, so you can do it later if you want. The rain might have stopped by then, too." He whipped out a business card. "This has my pager number. Give a call if you need help carrying it in."

"Thanks." I wanted to add, "Sorry about the little detective," but decided to let it go.

Ryan tipped an imaginary hat. A very pleasant young man.

But I noticed he didn't answer Maddie's question. Had he been on duty during the yellow-tape incident?

Chapter 4

Once we got back to the car, wet and cold, Maddie changed her mind about lunch.

"I'm starving," she said. "Can we go for bagels now?"

It sounded good to me, too, so we backtracked along Springfield Boulevard to Willie's. We could easily drop off Mary Lou's painting on the way home.

Bagels by Willie had a New York City décor that I loved. Depending on where you sat, you had a view of the Brooklyn Bridge, the Washington Square arch, the Wollman Rink in Central Park, or unidentifiable throngs on one tree-lined midtown street or another. I felt it was the only true environment for eating a bagel, though I'd read somewhere that the bagel was invented in seventeenth-century Poland.

Maddie always ordered the most artless items on the menu. Plain bagel, plain cream cheese, and potato chips with no added flavor. I liked to branch out; this afternoon, well past my earlier cinnamon craving, I tried an asiago cheese bagel with sun-dried tomato spread. Maddie pinched her nose as our waitress, Lourdes Pino, one of my GED students, pretended to get the order wrong and put my aromatic, spicy plate in front of my picky granddaughter. I knew if it weren't such a busy time, with a large lunch crowd, Lourdes would have teased Maddie further.

"What do you think happened there, Grandma?"

To save time, I skipped the pretense that I didn't understand the question. "I don't know. Maybe someone broke into the building. It could have been a poor person without a home who needed a warm place to sleep."

She gave me a doubtful look. "Right, right." She bit into her bagel sandwich and gave a self-conscious giggle when white cream cheese squirted out all around the circumference. "I think it's something Uncle Skip will have to solve and he'll need our help."

"Have you been reading that book I gave you on the Lincoln-Douglas debates?"

"Uh-huh. It's kind of beneath my reading level, though. It said ages ten to twelve, but I could have read it when I was eight, I'll bet."

"I'll bet you're right. So that must mean you finished it."

She shook her head slightly. "I know they were talking about slavery, though. And there were seven debates, all around the state of Illinois. That's between Iowa and Indiana."

Better than I could have done, geographically speaking. "Very good. Lincoln and Douglas traveled over four thousand miles in the course of that campaign. And you know traveling around was a lot harder at that time, more than a hundred years ago."

I knew Maddie's attention span for things that old was limited. Her gaze wandered around Willie's and then out the window behind me.

"There's that crazy lady again," she said.

"What crazy lady?"

"Me and Mom . . . oops, Mom and *I* saw her at the supermarket last week."

"Nice recovery," I said as we high-fived to celebrate the survival of correct grammar.

"The lady was crouched down near the bananas."

"Maybe she dropped one."

"Nah, she was, like, walking in a squat. I think she was hiding from someone. Now she's out there yelling at some other lady who bumped into her on the sidewalk."

I didn't want to turn to see what had drawn Maddie's attention. I wasn't happy about the idea that Maddie might be insensitive to a homeless person, or someone otherwise not "normal." Lincoln Point had its share of people who, for one reason or another, had fallen on hard times and wandered its public places. I wouldn't belabor it now, but I planned to make a bigger effort to see that Maddie grew up with compassion toward the disenfranchised.

"Maybe she can't help the way she is," I said. "And anyway, is that really more interesting than what Lincoln and Douglas were arguing about?"

She rolled her eyes. "When's Aunt Beverly coming home?" she asked. She didn't quite say that Aunt Beverly was more interesting than me, but I knew enough to move on.

"That reminds me," I said, pulling a postcard out of my purse. On one side of the card was a photo of a monkeypod tree, on the other a note from my sister-in-law and dearest friend, Skip's mother. "It's from Aunt Beverly. I forgot I had it. It came yesterday and it's addressed to all of us."

Maddie plucked the card from my hand and read. "Gorgeous sunsets here every night. Nick's teaching me how to snorkel." Maddie waved the card in the air. "Lucky, lucky Aunt Beverly. I've always wanted to snorkel."

Maddie often expressed desires like this, as if she were experiencing a midlife crisis, regretting that she hadn't fulfilled her lifelong dream. Whereas, she'd only known the meaning of "snorkel" for a couple of years.

"Maybe Uncle Nick will teach you." I was almost comfortable using "uncle" for retired cop Nick Marcus, whom

Beverly had been dating for a short while. She'd known him for years, however, working with him on a civilian volunteer program for the Lincoln Point Police Department, all of which made Aunt Beverly more interesting than me. The trip to Hawaii was a milestone in their carefully watched (by Skip and me) relationship.

Maddie grunted. "You can't snorkel in Palo Alto."

"I was thinking of San Francisco. Doesn't that sound like fun?" In fact, it didn't, to a landlubber like me.

"What did Uncle Skip's dad do?" Maddie asked, more or less out of the blue.

"He worked in electronics. You've seen his photos with all the equipment around him. Uncle Skip looks a lot like him, except for the red hair all you Porters have." I leaned over and moved one of Maddie's red curls off her forehead.

"No, I mean why did he die?"

Uh-oh. There were certain things I found it hard to talk about with an eleven-year-old. Among them were war, violent crime, and death. Eino Gowen Sr. had never come back from the first Gulf War. I didn't know how much Richard and Mary Lou had satisfied this particular aspect of their daughter's curiosity. We'd skirted around this information with Maddie in the past and now I wondered if it was time to tell her another fact or two.

"Uncle Skip's dad went overseas with the army," I began. "We don't know exactly what happened, just that he was missing and they were never able to find him."

"So he wasn't sick, like Grandpa?"

"No, not like Grandpa." Not the long, debilitating struggle against the leukemia that had killed Ken and nearly killed me from grief.

"And he wasn't just home and working, like my dad's doing now?"

Where is this going? "No, not like your dad is now."

"Uncle Skip said he was eleven years old when it happened."

And there it is. Maddie was doing some math, wondering if losing a father at eleven ran in the family.

I reached across Willie's black-and-white-tile tabletop and took her sticky hands in mine. She came around the table and leaned against me. I held her close. "Your dad is very young and very healthy, sweetheart, and nothing's going to happen to him."

Before Maddie came into my life, I wondered how adults could make such promises. Now that I was a grandmother, I understood.

I felt Maddie's deep breathing. What had brought this on, besides being eleven years old? Moving away from her familiar home and neighborhood? I'd read that moving was one of the top three or four activities to cause stress. Whatever it was, I resolved to help my granddaughter through it.

Maddie seemed to have bounced back to her normal ebullience on the drive back to the Rutledge Center. Maybe she was just hungry, I thought, and resolved to keep both nutritious and nonnutritious snacks handy at all times. She chattered on about a travelogue her class had seen, featuring the New Seven Wonders of the World. Maddie enjoyed being able to name them, whereas I stumbled after the Great Wall of China and the Inca ruins of Machu Picchu in Peru. I hoped her uplifted spirits weren't due to the prospect of revisiting a crime scene.

The Rutledge Center complex was as much a labyrinth as a set of buildings and walkways, taking up a whole block between Hanks Road and Gettysburg Boulevard. I drove around three times before I found the correct entrance, nearest where security officer Ryan Colson had pointed to as the artists' work area. I pulled up to the north door of the facility and retrieved Mary Lou's painting, encased in a flat black portfolio, from the trunk. As hoped for, the rain had stopped. Maddie and I and the oversize cardboard protector trundled up a few steps to a blue metal door marked simply A. From the worn-out black paint, I assumed the letter was left over from the days of the Rutledge School and its system of lettering classroom pods.

The door, which was unlocked as promised by Ryan, opened into an enormous warehouse-type room. The massive floor was covered with workbenches, easels, and piles of opened and unopened cartons. Tables were stacked high with tools and woodworking projects in progress. I recognized sections of the set for the debate stage, reminding me of my own unfinished, room-box political rally at home.

At some point in the next couple of days, I'd have to come back with my camera. If I'd been thinking clearly, I'd have brought it with me today. It was definitely harder to keep everything straight with three extra people, as wonderful as they were, in a house I hadn't shared in a long time.

I'd also neglected to get details from Mary Lou as to exactly who should take custody of the painting or where I should deposit it.

The few people in this wing were gathered into a far corner about forty yards away, apparently meeting around a watercooler (I could see the familiar shape of a five-gallon jug against the wall).

The door banged behind us, the noise causing only a slight stir among the members of the group.

"I'll go over there and ask them where we should put this," Maddie said, already breaking into a run. She was still delightfully awkward, with skinny arms and legs lacking graceful coordination. How she got to be a trophy-winning soccer player was a mystery, though I remembered Richard's telling me that everyone on Maddie's team won some kind of prize.

I propped the portfolio against my leg and waited, happy I'd worn my lined denim jacket. It was colder inside the building than outside. I stood near a pile of red-white-and-blue banners. More stage setting and another reminder—I needed flag fabric for my room box. I watched Maddie reach the group, turn, and point.

At the same time, I heard another loud bang as metal door A slammed again.

I turned to see who else had an errand in this hollow hall.

June Chinn, in jeans and a soft brown hoodie, was who.

In one hand she held a large cardboard box, empty, from the easy way she carried it. She stopped short when she saw me and tossed the box aside, sending it across the floor. A wide smile broke out on her face.

"Gerry, I should have known you'd be here. I knew you'd be willing to help."

"I'm surprised to see you, June. I'm just here delivering a painting for my—"

She came over and buried her head on my chest. Her arms closed tight around me. "I knew I could count on you to help Zoe out of this mess, Gerry. Thank you. Thank you."

She seemed to have picked up on Maddie's double phrasing. What could I say? That I wasn't in a position to help? That I wasn't a cop? That I had no information on the case? And absolutely no right to seek any?

I looked at June's sad, hopeful face, and at her hands, mostly covered by the long sleeves of her hoodie.

"You're welcome," I said.

We found two folding chairs against a close wall and took seats next to each other, knees almost touching. I had a stream of questions. I started with my top two.

"Who exactly is Zoe accused of murdering, June? Does it have anything to do with the crime-scene tape outside this building?" No time for smooth editing. I spoke in hurried whisper, aware that Maddie might be back at any moment.

"Someone killed Zoe's boyfriend, Brad Goodman, like I told you last night." June sounded frustrated, as if no one ever paid attention to her. In fact, she hadn't told us anything last night beyond the fact that her best friend was in jail. She pointed to the carton she'd thrown aside. "She wants me to pick up some of her stuff from his locker. They're outdoors in one of those covered walkways, but I can't get through from that side of the building. They have it all roped off."

June made no mention of the rope's being crime-scene tape. From the way she talked, she might have been stopped by silk cord like the kind used to reserve front-row seats at the opera or by white organdy bows to mark the first few rows at a wedding ceremony.

"I saw the tape," I said.

"They're sure making it hard for us."

There seemed to be no end to the inconvenience Brad's murder brought to June and her friend. I wasn't used to this facet of my neighbor and (I'd once hoped) potential niece-in-law.

"So Brad was murdered here?"

June nodded, with a "wouldn't you know?" look. "He wasn't at all well liked, you know," she said. "He was very pushy about getting ahead with his art career."

I did my best to dismiss the realization that my lovely neighbor might be implying that Zoe's boyfriend got what he deserved.

I looked across the hall to check on Maddie. She was no longer with the group of people by the watercooler. *A murderer had been (is still?) in this building, and I don't see my granddaughter.* I felt a shiver of panic.

Short-lived, fortunately, as I saw Maddie off to the side, engaged in animated conversation with a woman and a man from the group, benevolent staff members, I hoped. The woman was pointing out features on a life-size figure of Abraham Lincoln. (From this distance, my only clues about the identity of the likeness were the tall stature and the signature stovepipe hat.) How predictable that my granddaughter had become attracted to the various props and scenery scattered around the hall. The man seemed to trail behind them. If he was talking, it was gesture-less commentary since his hands were in his pockets.

I shifted my body so that I could face June and still see Maddie. False alarm or not, I had to be more watchful.

June's mouth was drawn, her lovely almond-shaped eyes puffy and ringed with red. Even on casual Saturdays, I'd never seen her rich black hair as it was today—pulled back in a runty ponytail with ends flying every which way.

"Brad's body was somewhere over there." June answered my pre-distraction question. She pointed to the east end of the complex and all but stamped her small foot. She pulled on the cords of her sweatshirt hood. I noticed another sign of her anguish and indifference to her appearance—no colorful lacy undershirt poking above the sweatshirt zipper today, just a white crew-neck T-shirt, loose and wrinkled.

I stood and held my arms out to June. She responded immediately, stepping into a tight embrace, then relaxing against me.

"I'm so sorry, Gerry," she said, between deep breaths. "I can't seem to approach this rationally. Zoe is like the sister I never had, and I'm hers, you know? I kept it together when I visited her in jail this morning, but now here I am lashing out at the only person who's offered to help."

Not that I actually volunteered anything but a hug. I assumed she was sneaking in a reference to her unhelpful boyfriend and the arresting officer, Skip Gowen. I patted her back, as bony as mine, but much shorter. "We'll get through this," I said. The line sounded familiar, as if everything I knew, I'd learned from television scripts.

Never has anyone promised so much on the basis of so little information.

As I pondered what I'd gotten myself into, still patting June's back, Maddie caught my eye. She and her new friends beckoned to me to join them at the far end of the hall. June mumbled about not wanting to talk to anyone and excused herself. But not before she extracted a promise from me to let her brief me on Zoe's case later this afternoon.

"I'm not sure I can offer anything but emotional support," I told her.

"Not true, Gerry. Just hear me out. Once you hear everything, you'll put it all together and help Skip see it. Zoe couldn't possibly have killed Brad. She was with me that night till well after midnight. We watched a bunch of *Sex and the City* reruns."

I had some experience with teenagers making up stories. "I left my homework in my other backpack" was very popular, as were "I dropped the floppy in a puddle on the way to school" and "My mom put my English folder in her briefcase by mistake and took it to work."

June was well past her teen years, but I thought I detected the same shifty-eyed expression.

I agreed to talk to June, but not in my home since I didn't want Maddie in on the discussion. Willie's seemed the best choice. I guessed June hadn't eaten in a while, and there was nothing wrong with two bagels in one day for me. My family and friends thought I still had some pounds to go to reach a healthy weight. I'd become almost as thin as Ken while he was in and out of hospitals. A therapist (I never took the advice to see one) might have said I wanted to drop as many pounds as he did.

I had to deposit Maddie somewhere. The usual lineup of sitters I used during Maddie's visits was otherwise occupied. My first call would have been to my sister-in-law, Ken's sister, Beverly, now in Hawaii. She was always happy to entertain or be entertained by Maddie, whom she considered her own granddaughter also. "Until my only son gives me one of my own," she'd say, but only when Skip was in earshot.

Number two, my friend Linda, was on duty today at the

Mary Todd retirement home. June was number three, and more unavailable than ever.

I'd have to move on to another typical scenario: drop Maddie off at Rosie's Books downtown. Rosie Norman, a former student, was bound to have a story hour in progress, plus a full candy bowl on the counter. Knowing Maddie's sweet tooth, I'd brought candy into the store several times when I picked her up, to replenish the supply.

June agreed readily to this arrangement; I doubted Maddie would. My only hope for a peaceful discussion was if Rosie had a group of preschoolers and Maddie could feel very mature helping out.

I wished myself luck in closing the deal with an eleven-year-old shark.

The watercooler group had broken up and people were returning to workstations throughout the hall. As I wove my way among them, carrying the large portfolio with Mary Lou's painting, I was greeted by "Hi, Mrs. Porter" a number of times from former students. A few offered to help but the package was lighter than it looked and I refused with a thank-you, sometimes even remembering the person's name.

Richard, and now Maddie, often teased me about how they had to behave themselves in public because I "knew everyone." Not quite true, especially since more and more people came to northern California for college and stayed, thus skipping over Mrs. Porter's English classes.

Maddie was waiting to introduce me first to Stephanie Cameron, a tall young woman wearing a long-sleeved black turtleneck and a pink quilted down vest. The rest of her appearance was of a kind with most of her generation, all of whom seem to have the same hairdo (layered in the extreme, with streaks of different colors), the same clothes (also layered, with all tiers showing, often including undergarments), the same perfect smiles (thanks to the availabil-

ity of braces and teeth whiteners), and a preponderance of
pink in their wardrobes.

The older (his elaborate mustache and beard had streaks
of gray) gentleman was Ed Villard, whose paint-splattered
denim shirt and pants placed him as another local artist. He
reached out to shake my hand.

Stephanie was of the age to have been my student, but
a transplant apparently, with a diploma from an institution
other than Abraham Lincoln High School. Ed looked familiar, but I couldn't place him except to say I might have
seen him around town.

Both were carrying water bottles, but if we were investigating who could carry the largest bottled water container,
Stephanie would stand out. Hers was at least quart-sized,
with a tiny red squirt top. The proportions of the container
were off, as when a doll maker lost the sense of scale and
put a too-small head on a torso.

"Nice to meet you, Mrs. Porter," said Stephanie and Ed
in turn.

"Maddie says you want to drop off a painting?"
Stephanie asked me. The question was accompanied by a
strange look.

"Gerry," I said and explained my errand. I lifted the
portfolio in support of my story.

"Okay, if you're sure."

"Why wouldn't I be?"

"Mmm, I don't recommend it."

Ed gave a loud grunt, the kind that would have been a
curse if it weren't for the presence of a child. "Stephanie
is overreacting," Ed said. "A few people are taking their
projects away today. I guess you didn't hear about . . ." He
looked at Maddie and stopped midsentence.

Maddie raised her eyebrows and put her hands on her
hips. Although she didn't utter a word, I heard her loud,
clear declaration: "You can't possibly leave me out of this."

"We know about the . . . uh . . . crime-scene tape," I said.

Stephanie took a drink from her oversize water bottle.

She had a long, thin neck with a hint of an Adam's apple. "Right, that's one of the things that happened. The other one was that a roomful of paintings were slashed. If I'm overreacting, I have good reason." She addressed this last sentence to Ed.

I winced. Were the paintings slashed with the murder weapon? I imagined a knife piercing not canvas, but a young man's skin. I worked against my dry throat. I wished I could ask Stephanie and Ed more details, but I needed to be careful in front of Maddie.

"Do the police have any clues about who did that?" I was embarrassed to have to ask, what with my own nephew on the force.

"Well, yes, and she's in jail," Ed said. He flicked his wrist as if he were banging a gavel. "Case closed."

"But still, everyone's nervous. I mean, you never know, you know?" Stephanie's comment came out with the tone of the "duh" I heard constantly these days.

I didn't know how to answer that question, so I simply nodded. "You think Zoe Howard slashed the paintings?"

Maddie had slipped behind me. I knew her tricks. If she was out of sight, I might not remember she was present. So far, there was nothing too offensive that I would regret her having heard. Not that *slashing* anything was an image I wanted to implant into her highly fertile mind.

Ed waved his free arm around, pointing in the general direction of the television studio. "We don't *think* she did it, we saw her do it."

"You saw Zoe cut up the paintings?"

"Uh-huh. On our security camera," Stephanie said.

Before or after *Sex and the City* reruns? I wondered.

The four of us deliberated for a few minutes.

"It's all safe here, now, Grandma," Maddie said, voting to leave the painting as planned.

Stephanie reiterated her "you never know" position.

"But if you want, I'll take it to where her assigned space is," she said. "Your choice."

I heard, *Don't blame me if something happens to it.*

Ed shrugged his shoulders, as if wondering what the fuss was about.

I felt the weight of the portfolio against my leg.

I called Mary Lou, but had to leave a message on her cell phone asking her preference. I had a good idea what my activist daughter-in-law would want. I could almost hear her. "Why would I let anyone intimidate me into giving up my work space?"

Richard and Mary Lou had met at the University of California in Berkeley—"Cal"—where tie-dyed shirts without designer labels still held sway at vendor booths on the streets around the campus. They loved to tell the story of their first meeting. Mary Lou was in a picket line, having joined the custodians and service workers on campus in their fight for better working conditions. Richard tried to cross the line to get to class and ended up carrying Mary Lou's sign and walking beside her.

I tapped my cell phone in my hand. Stephanie and Ed were waiting for my decision.

I handed the portfolio to Stephanie.

"Take the painting," I said.

Chapter 5

Maddie and I sat on a bench outside the Rutledge Center. Maddie leaned forward, kicking her feet as she always did when excited, either positively or negatively. Today I could tell that the energy was not good as she listened to my Rosie's Books plan.

I knew it wouldn't be easy, but I wasn't prepared for tears. Was this the way the next few years were going to be with my formerly sweet, mature-for-her-age granddaughter?

"I'm so bored," Maddie cried. Not the wailing kind of cry that I was used to at times like this, and that she'd bring out as a temporary measure to make her case. This was a sad cry, and I couldn't stand it. I nearly called June's cell phone and cancelled our meeting. I wished I knew whether this was a new tactic or a whole different phase Maddie was entering.

"You have homework to do, don't you? You can do it at the store." Going for simple problem, simple solution. "Or Mrs. Norman would let you sit in the back where all the new books are delivered and you can open the cartons. Or she might want you to help out with the little kids' reading program."

"That's not what I mean."

"What is it, sweetheart? I know you can't be this sad about missing a dumb meeting." (My own little device: throw her language back at her.)

She jerked her body toward me and landed half on my lap. She had to stop kicking to accomplish this, and I felt her relax a bit. "I don't know. I don't know."

I rubbed her head. "Are you sorry you moved up here?"

No answer. I looked across the road at the green hills to the east. Surely she didn't miss the ever-dry hills of Los Angeles? I had an idea what her problem was but I didn't want to press her if she wasn't ready. I moved closer and invited her to lean on me.

"You can tell me anything, you know that."

"I can't. You'll be mad."

I shook my head. "I can't imagine how you could make me mad, except to be sad about something and not tell me."

"I love you, Grandma. I'm glad I'm near you and Aunt Beverly and Uncle Skip."

"I know that, sweetheart. We can tell you're glad to be living here." (Or will be eventually, I added in silence.)

"Then how come I want to be back with my friends and my old school?"

"I would be shocked if you didn't miss them. It would mean you never cared about them all this time that you've known them."

"So I'm supposed to miss them?"

I nodded. "It's very normal."

She uttered a sound that was half whistle, half wail. "Do you still miss your friends in the Bronx?"

"Some of them, yes, even after all these years."

It never took much for me to time travel back to my life in the Bronx and my days at Hunter. I thought I'd never find anything as fulfilling as my daily interaction with classmates and professors. I could bring back everything

from my best friend's filling her bra with tissue paper before the prom, to the more serious gatherings in the assembly hall, about whether we should boycott classes after the
shootings at Kent State in Ohio.

"Did you have a lot of friends?"

"I did. But I have a lot of new friends here," I told Maddie and myself.

"It seems complicated."

"It is complicated. The older you get, the more changes
you'll make, and you'll make new connections. But you'll
still miss some things, and not others."

"I don't miss Mr. Duroucher."

"Aha. Tell me more."

"He's our soccer coach. He gives the best game dates to
the boys, and the best lockers, and new jerseys and us girls
get the leftovers. Like, who's going to come and watch us
on Wednesday afternoon?"

"There, you see. Maybe the Palo Alto coach will see
things differently. You might even have a woman coach."

Maddie laughed, as if I'd suggested something with as
low a probability as that school would be called off for the
rest of the year.

"You never know," I said.

"Then you're not mad that I wish I was with Devyn and
the other kids?"

"I'm not mad."

The next two passersby were older women who apparently saw nothing strange at the sight of a grandmother and
granddaughter embracing, both teary-eyed.

Not that Maddie gave up on a shot to go to the meeting
with June.

"I think June wouldn't be as comfortable with you
there," I told her, heading for Rosie's in my car. "This way
I'll find out a lot more and then I can tell you everything."

"You always say that."

"I do? Well, then it must be true."

The strains of "As Time Goes By" rang through the car. My latest cell phone tone, courtesy of Linda's son, Jason. Maddie refused to help me ever since I had Jason get rid of her favorite "Take Me Out to the Ballgame," which she'd surreptitiously programmed as my first ring tone.

Maddie dug my phone out of my purse and answered.

"Hi, Mom." Pause. "Yeah, yeah, my day is fine." Pause. "Okay."

She handed me the phone. After another round of "how's your day going?" I assured Mary Lou that I'd left her painting in capable hands at the Rutledge Center.

"Good choice, Mom," she said. "No way am I going to let someone intimidate me out of my work space."

I gave myself a mental pat on the back, proud of myself for how well I knew my daughter-in-law.

Maddie got her spunk from her mother and not her father, who was a much more cautious type. When it came down to it, I supposed we all wanted a surgeon who paid attention to details and followed the rules exactly, and an artist who made things up as she went along, and not vice versa.

Not that Richard hadn't engaged in typical teenage manipulative tricks, but when his clique of friends wanted to try bungee jumping off the Golden Gate Bridge, Richard volunteered to borrow a stopwatch from their physics lab and time the adventuresome jumpers. He also provided a cooler of drinks and took photos. Such was the extent of his risk-taking.

I saw Maddie work the muscles in her face now, trying to get something good out of this deal, wherein she'd be relegated to a bookstore while I was "on the case."

"Can I walk by myself from Rosie's to Sadie's and meet you for ice cream after your meeting?"

I thought about it. Rosie's was one long block away from Sadie's. Willie's was about halfway between. "Come to Willie's and we'll go to Sadie's together." After all, there might be a murderer loose in Lincoln Point. In fact, if I believed June, there *was* a murderer out there, since her friend was innocent.

"Okay, I'll meet you at Willie's in about ten minutes."

"Nice try. Let's say one hour."

"Deal."

Something told me she started low on purpose.

I'd called ahead to Rosie, my former student, who was waiting for us at the door. I waved to her from the car while Maddie went into the bookshop, with resignation, but no more tears. I knew she still had a long way to go to becoming acclimated to her new situation. I hoped I could help her through it.

I drove farther down Springfield Boulevard, festooned with American flags hanging from every light post—the February décor. Even Video Jeff's, our local arcade contributed to the theme, with a life-size caricature of Abe. I parked under one of the new banners in front of Bagels by Willie, announcing the events around next week's debate, and entered the shop's yeasty air for the second time today.

"Mrs. Porter. You're back already," Lourdes said. "I should have brought my homework for you to check."

"I'm sure it's perfect," I said.

"Yes, but you'll find something, huh?"

Lourdes was one of my most conscientious students. Approaching middle age, she had only one more exam to go and she'd have her GED and a chance for a full-time job at the Lincoln Point Library.

"We'll see on Sunday," I said, remembering that I'd promised Lourdes an extra two-hour session, two days before my room box was due. What had I been thinking?

Lourdes had already seated June at a table in the corner. I joined her, facing the large window onto Springfield Boulevard, intending to watch for Maddie. I had a clear view of our busy card shop across the street and one of several fast-food establishments that had survived an overhaul of the street a few years ago.

I noticed the woman Maddie had referred to as the crazy lady. This time she seemed to be pacing in front of Willie's, looking through the window (at me?), perhaps trying to decide whether to come in. From this distance, she seemed well dressed except for a stocking cap pulled low over her forehead so I couldn't make out her face. If she was trying to be inconspicuous, it wasn't working.

I ordered coffee and a brownie; June had ordered a bottled water. While I was at it, I asked for a dozen assorted cookies to go, to have around the house in case I didn't have a chance to replenish my supply of homemade ginger cookies. I was afraid June was going to be sick at the mere sound of my order.

I'd decided to let June talk before confronting her about Zoe's alibi.

"Tell me about Zoe," I began. "I've met her only two or three times and that was in a crowd."

June nodded. "At Irene's shower and then the wedding last year. Not her best moments."

I remembered Zoe's rich chestnut hair, how she was June's height but much chunkier (but then, nearly everyone but Maddie was chunkier than June). Mostly, I remembered how intoxicated Zoe had gotten. And how loud.

"You've been friends for a long time?"

Another halfhearted nod. "Zoe's a little younger than me, like three years. I was actually best friends with her older sister first, but she died. It was a car crash and Heddy and her parents were killed. It was awful." June took a breath and, I was afraid, a moment to relive that pain. "So we kind of adopted Zoe. Then Zoe went into tech writing like me and we got even closer and I got her her first job in Chicago."

Lourdes arrived with our order. It didn't seem right to eat my brownie while June was fasting and looking like even the smell of chocolate might turn her stomach, and the lady outside Willie's might be starving in spite of her normal attire. I wrapped the brownie in a napkin and took a sip of my coffee.

I wasn't trying to keep track of the "crazy lady," but she was smack in the middle of my field of view as I looked at June. I felt she was sizing me up, even trying to hear our conversation. I knew it was June's state that had me on edge, but I was glad when the woman finally wandered off to the left.

June went back to her story. "And then I came out here and then Zoe did, and now we're working at the same company again. So I guess I've kind of been her mentor as well as her family, except she's now in management. She's a go-getter, always knew she didn't want to stay in the ranks very long. She knows how to network, for sure. She's a lot like Brad in that way. They know how to get what they want."

Except Brad got himself murdered, which June seemed to have forgotten for the moment. "She sounds like an excellent resource," I said, staying as neutral as possible.

"Uh-huh. It's been great having her in Lincoln Point. She lives across Springfield Boulevard from you, a couple of houses down from where Linda lives, in those new condos."

The condos that Linda hated because they brought "loud young Generation Whatever Letter" to the neighborhood. "And Brad?"

"Zoe's had lots of boyfriends. Way more than me. But she was really in love with Brad. I could never figure out what she saw in him. He was very selfish. I got the feeling he'd do anything to get ahead in the art world."

I noted the difference—in June's mind, Brad was "selfish," but Zoe was "a go-getter" and admirably ambitious.

"But"—June made a helpless, palms-up gesture—"he said he loved her, too, and was over his ex. He came out here to be with Zoe, a few months ago."

"He was married?"

"For a short time, to this woman, Rhonda, who's still in Chicago. They were young."

They're still young, I thought. Never mind that I'd already been married to Ken a year by that age. We were exceptionally mature for our ages. I smiled at the idea.

I looked at my watch. It had been twenty minutes since I dropped Maddie off. I was sure she was well aware of the time and wouldn't be a minute late. I needed time to get my questions out to June, but she showed no signs of slowing down her narrative.

"You can't imagine how badly Rhonda took the breakup. She's Catholic and doesn't believe in divorce. In fact, she assumes they're still married. She writes him letters and signs 'your loving wife, Rhonda.' Hello? The divorce has been final for months."

"Do they have children?"

"No, and it's a good thing they didn't have any. Imagine putting kids through this. Zoe is very volatile, yes, but nothing compared to Rhonda. She went nuts, and threatened Brad several times. I was afraid she was going to go after Zoe, too."

If I didn't know June's Chicago origins, I'd be able to tell from the flat *a*'s (such as in "Brad" and "after"), all the more pronounced when she was under stress, as now.

"Have the police interviewed Rhonda?" I asked.

"I hope so. She might be connected out here," June said. I tried to picture a young woman named Rhonda in Chicago ordering a hit in Lincoln Point. Was divorce really worse than murder to Brad's ex? "Or maybe she flew out here and did it herself. She's the one they should be blaming, not Zoe."

Neither of us mentioned that "the police" and "they" really was Skip, my nephew and her boyfriend.

I wondered where that nephew was at this moment. Not interviewing other suspects if he was sure Zoe was guilty.

June seemed ready to answer anything, if not with a lot of energy.

"Will Zoe get bail?" (We won't know until later in the week.)

"Does she have family in Chicago?" (No. Maybe a cousin, but very distant.)

"Does she have a lawyer?" (She's broke and will probably have to have a public defender.)

Of course those were easy questions.

"June, were you with Zoe on Tuesday night?"

She bristled. No more cooperative demeanor. "Yes, I told you. We watched a bunch of *Sex and the City* reruns."

The same words she used earlier. I remembered Skip's mentioning how he could tell when someone was lying about an alibi. "No one says things exactly the same way twice unless they've rehearsed it," he'd said.

If that was true, then June should have said, "We watched television," or "We had popcorn and watched TV." Not the very same "bunch of *Sex and the City* reruns" she used last time. I doubted Skip would approve of this slapdash application of a scrap of dinner conversation.

I worked on my coffee, not as good as it would have been with a complementary treat. I fingered the paper napkin that was wrapped around my brownie. A whiff of chocolate rose up and I was tempted to eat it. Not the time, however.

I looked at June, who was sad-faced, having just re-alibied her best friend. I braced myself. "A security camera at the Rutledge Center says otherwise, June."

"Well, it's wrong." June's voice was louder than normal, attracting the attention of a table of four businessmen near us. They went back to their laptops and spreadsheets in a few seconds, except for one who couldn't seem to take his eyes off June. "Zoe was with me."

"You're not helping your friend by lying." I whispered this, hoping June's voice would come down in volume to match mine.

"I'm not lying," she said, with force. But I could tell her confidence was fading.

A moment later, forty minutes into my hour without Maddie, Skip walked in. Facing the door, I saw him first.

He took long strides and sat down before June knew he was there.

"Did you follow me?" June asked.

"In fact I did." A heavy tone.

June started to get up, but Skip put his hand on her shoulder, leaned over, and kissed her cheek. She sat back down and folded her arms across her chest.

"Don't I matter to you at all, Skip?" she asked, looking at her water bottle, squeezing the plastic so it popped in and out of shape.

"I wouldn't be here if you didn't matter. Now, do you want to hear what we've got?"

I certainly did. I wondered if Skip were going to tell us something not known to the general public. It was hard not to feel privileged as the only aunt of a homicide detective. I thought ahead to the long-term prognosis for Skip and June. Certainly she was getting a taste of what it might be like to be married to a cop.

"What about Rhonda? Have you questioned her?" June asked, without waiting for Skip's input.

"We're working on it. She's a real estate agent and works out of her house a lot. She calls into the office regularly but there's no telling from where."

"Her staff and colleagues don't know where she is? Doesn't that tell you something?"

"Not really. As far as they all know, she's calling from home."

"Hasn't anyone seen her?"

"Not in the last couple of days. Chicago PD are trying to locate her."

"Good. I hope they try hard. That's where you should be looking. Is Zoe going to get bail? Not that she could even afford it unless we have a fund-raiser, but is she going to at least have that chance?"

"You know that's not my call. It all depends on whether—"

June stood to leave, nearly knocking over her chair.

"Honey, I'd like to explain—"

But June stomped out, for the second time in as many days. Her last words were aimed at both of us. "Apparently I have to do this on my own."

I looked at my watch, and then at Skip. "Maddie will be here in about ten minutes," I said, allowing for the fact that Maddie would surely be early. If she knew her Uncle Skip was here, she'd race to his side.

"What am I going to do about this, Aunt Gerry? I have to do my job."

I offered him the brownie. When in doubt, *feed,* was my motto. The luscious treat was gone in two bites. Good. He looked forlorn, as last night, but wasn't so far gone today that he was fasting.

"What do you have on Zoe?" I asked. "If you can tell me," I added with elaborate deference.

He smiled. A welcome change.

"Brad Goodman was stabbed to death and Zoe's prints are on the knife. At least her prints are among many that are on the knife."

I cringed at the image. "The same one that was used to slash the paintings?"

Skip grinned. "Of course you'd know about the paintings. But, no, not the same knife. That knife was wiped clean."

I explained my errand for Mary Lou. "What kind of knife was the murder weapon, if I may ask?" I'd never been on such good behavior.

"It's an artist's knife, I guess you'd call it. The kind you'd have in a tool kit."

"Brad's?"

"Maybe. We don't really have the full story on whether the knife we found with the body is actually the murder weapon. It looks like it, but test results aren't back."

"If it belongs to Brad, Zoe could have handled the knife when she visited Brad in the work area, right?"

"There's more. We know she was in the building, from the security camera."

I gave him a weak smile and a slight nod.

"You know about that, huh?"

"I happened to run into a couple of the staff." Now that I thought of it, I didn't really know what "staff" function Stephanie Cameron performed at the Rutledge Center. I'd only guessed that Ed Villard was an artist from his paint-splattered clothes.

"And I suppose the timeline matches with the time of death and all." I was throwing jargon around, I knew, but my attention was still on the door and the inevitable curtailing of crime talk that Maddie's presence would bring.

"Their camera system is not that great, but there is one working that's focused on the work area. Zoe was in the building around eleven o'clock on Monday night."

"Did she enter with a key?"

"Hard to tell." Skip shook brownie crumbs from the napkin, into his hand, and then into his mouth. Suddenly I was hungry and dipped into the cookies-to-go bag, taking potluck: an oatmeal raisin with nuts. Good choice, but then I'd bought only my favorites.

"And by Tuesday afternoon, Zoe was in jail? That's pretty quick," I said after a healthy (or not) bite.

"Her prints were in our own local system from some substitute teaching she did. Otherwise we'd still be waiting. You know the state of crime labs."

I assured Skip that I did know the sorry condition of city and state forensics capabilities, and motioned him to get on with the story.

"We had the knife, the video, and several witnesses who said they'd been fighting lately."

That last was news to me, something June had neglected to mention. "What are you going to do now?" I asked.

"I guess I'll have to buy some candy and flowers."

"I meant with Zoe."

"I know," he said, and rose to leave.

He would have gotten away with the last word, except for the arrival of his first cousin once-removed.

Maddie's "Uncle Skip, Uncle Skip" brought another curious look from the businessmen.

Skip scooped her up. "Sorry, squirt, I just ate the last brownie."

"We're going for ice cream. Come with us."

"Gotta go to work," he said and was gone in a flash.

I knew what was coming. Maddie put her hands on her hips and gave me one of her comic glares, half kidding, half serious.

"Grandma?"

"He just got here, I swear. I was with June almost the whole time."

"You'd better tell me everything."

"Of course. Of course. Did you have a good time at Rosie's?"

"Yeah, she let me use her computer."

"That was nice of her."

I had a flashback to a newspaper article I'd read on how easy it was for kids to see inappropriate videos on the Internet. I made a note to ask Rosie if she had a way to filter anything offensive from her system. I longed for the days when Richard was little and all I had to worry about was whether he'd remember to wear his bike-riding helmet and look both ways crossing the street.

Maddie and I agreed that ice cream cones to go would be the best bet today since we had a lot of projects waiting at home.

"No time for table service," I told Sadie, who'd opened her shop right around the time Ken and I arrived in Lincoln Point, three decades ago. We thought she did it just for us.

"I thought you were retired," she said to me, her chubby hands digging into the freezer. "And you don't have time to sit for ice cream?"

"We hope *you* never retire," Maddie said. "We love it here."

I knew she was sincere, but it turned out to be a good move on her part—Sadie obliged her with an extra-heaping waffle cone. Maddie had decided to try a new flavor that Sadie called Honest Abe's Beard. It was a special licorice ice cream recipe, Sadie explained. I passed on it. Ice cream flavors were one area where Maddie was willing to branch out and I wasn't. I really wanted plain chocolate chip, but that seemed unpatriotic on a day so close to Lincoln's birthday, so I agreed to a small cone of "Galesburg" (for Galesburg, Illinois, the site of the fifth Lincoln-Douglas debate), which was French vanilla with strawberries and blueberries. In case anyone lost track of which debate would be reenacted in a particular year, Sadie named her special flavor for February to remind us.

During our walk to and from Sadie's, I'd brought out my usual thesaurus of euphemisms as I told Maddie about my meetings with June and Skip. All Maddie needed to know about the case that was striking close to home, I reasoned, was that a young man had died and her Uncle Skip had arrested a young woman who might have been responsible and she was now in jail. I threw in the last note in case she needed assurance that the killer wasn't roaming the streets. I wondered about that myself. If Zoe really was innocent, then . . . I looked up and down the side streets as we walked to the car.

For Maddie, I wanted the violence to sound more like a picnic gone wrong—due to a heavy downpour, a leaky cooler, or a takeover by an army of ants—but soon to be put right.

Buckled into the backseat of the car, Maddie continued asking questions. "Is that it?" she asked in an accusing tone when I'd failed to add new information. In the rearview mirror I could see her frown. I wondered if it were due partly to the taste of the awful-looking charcoal-colored ice cream.

"That's it."

"You're not telling me everything. I already knew

everything you told me and I know it's June's friend who's in jail."

"How do you know that?"

"I couldn't sleep last night when you guys were talking in the living room."

I feigned astonishment. "You eavesdropped?"

"You were talking too loud."

Maddie's bedroom was in the opposite corner of the house from the living room, on the other side of my large atrium. Even if we'd been shouting, she'd have had a hard time hearing us. I pictured her squatted down in her L.A. Dodgers (Tigers? Panthers? I couldn't keep the team names straight) pajamas, hiding behind my ficus.

"Then you heard everything there is to know. All that time in Willie's today, June was just telling me how sad she was that her friend is in jail."

Which was not far from the truth.

Chapter 6

I parked on the street in front of my house since we were the first ones to arrive. Later when the "good" vehicles were safe in the garage, I'd pull my car into the driveway.

June's house, next door, looked different today, its paint a duller green, her lawn showing patches of brown. What power the mind has.

What wasn't my imagination, however, was that her trash containers were toppled over, their contents spilled onto her driveway, two lawns away from mine. There hadn't been much of a breeze today, let alone a wind that could have forced the heavy containers to the ground. I envisioned a careless group of school children bumping into them, accidentally or through malicious mischief. I couldn't remember any other incident of this magnitude on our quiet street. Just occasional litter, like a soft-drink cup or candy wrapper I assumed had been dropped by a jogger or dog walker.

"What are you going to do about it?" Maddie asked, dragging her backpack to the front door.

"I'm going to change my clothes and clean up June's driveway," I said.

"I meant the case, Grandma."

"I know."

In truth, I'd almost forgotten what her question referred to. Maddie's earlier inquisition about the case had been interrupted by an accident in the car with her ice cream cone. A large portion of the ice cream had fallen to the floor and we'd spent some time cleaning it up at the gas station on the way home. I wondered how accidental it was. I'd seen her scowling face as she nibbled at the black globs. I did notice what a wonderful miniature tar pit she'd created on the floor of my car, and filed the image away for another project.

Maddie continued her negotiating after we'd changed clothes and started work on our second cleanup of the day, June's garbage.

"The case, Grandma?" she said, as if I were simply forgetful and not determined to get her mind off the crime.

"There's only one policeman in this family," I said. The declaration sounded hollow as I remembered my promise to June that I'd help Zoe. A somewhat coerced promise that I considered only partially binding.

"You know I like to help," Maddie said, as if she were offering to set the table for dinner instead of hoping to help solve a murder case.

"You can help by putting that recycle container right side up."

"I am." She lifted the container using both arms and one foot. "See? But you know I can do other stuff, like on the computer."

"I know and you're very smart. But the police don't need us right now."

"Do you know what I found out today?" she asked.

I walked toward her with a broom. "I can't wait to hear," I said.

"Yuck, yuck," Maddie yelled. I thought she'd merely thought my comment distasteful or insincere, but when I looked over she was scraping something off the sole of her shoe. Something that looked like blood. I dropped the broom and a bag of June's garbage and ran over. Had she cut her foot on a piece of rusted metal? Punctured herself with some kind of dirty needle? In my mind I was already rushing her to the emergency room.

But the bloody problem was not with Maddie. A dead raccoon was lying half on June's lawn, half on the sidewalk. It wasn't all that unusual a sight, though I would have expected June to call animal control instead of stuffing the carcass in her trash.

I noticed Maddie had been holding her breath. She'd taken off her shoes and thrown them onto a pile of rubbish. She seemed to be breathing in spurts. I'd never seen such squeamish behavior in my granddaughter and planned to tease her about it later.

She was pointing to the raccoon, to the side that was not visible to me. I walked around for a better view and saw the cause of her panic attack.

The raccoon had a knife through its chest.

"I'm on my way," Skip said on the phone.

I cut up a large plastic trash bag (no towel or other fabric that might pick up or leave fibers, I learned) and covered the messy corpse. Second best to the large piece of paper Skip had suggested, but which I did not have handy. I also sacrificed Maddie's sneakers, putting them in my own trash. I had no delusions that this would erase the memory of the stabbed animal.

It wasn't too hard to convince Maddie to wash up and throw her clothes in the washing machine while I waited for Skip. I paced the sidewalk between my house and June's, thankful that no neighbors came along.

Within a few minutes, Skip arrived in an animal control

truck, accompanied by a crime-scene technician. I assumed Lincoln Point didn't have much call for a specialist in murdered animals and Skip had thrown together this ad hoc group for the occasion. For once, I didn't argue when Skip sent me away while they did their jobs.

"**How can you be so blasé about a stabbed animal in** your girlfriend's driveway?" I asked Skip, who'd rejected my idea that this might have something to do with Brad's murder and Zoe's arrest.

"I'm here, aren't I?" he asked, standing in my living room. "And I sent the knife to be tested for prints. But truthfully, I think this was just a random raccoon casualty or—"

"The raccoon didn't fall on the knife, Skip."

". . . or a prank. You said yourself you thought at first it was some kids who knocked over the containers."

I thought it would be obvious to my nephew that that was before I saw the knife. "You don't think it's too much of a coincidence that it's June's house, that there has never been a prank this creepy, that the animal was stabbed, just as Brad Goodman and all the paintings were stabbed?"

"Hi, Uncle Skip."

A subdued Maddie, wrapped in her father's baseball afghan, came into the living room. She smelled of strawberries and cream, meaning she'd actually taken a bath voluntarily. I was glad she'd learned some coping skills, like the value of a relaxing, aromatic bath.

She put her arms, as best she could without losing the afghan, around me, and then around Skip and took a seat on my rocker.

Skip knelt beside her and smoothed her wet curls. "How are you doing? That was a nasty scene, wasn't it?" She opened her eyes wide and nodded. "How about some milk and cookies? Your grandma's cookies got me through some hard times."

"She just had ice cream," I said, without thinking. In reality, I was prepared to spoon-feed her from a half gallon
of any flavor.

She gave me the look I expected. "I lost most of it. You
saw."

Skip poured her a glass of milk and took two cookies
from the jar on the counter.

"Was the ice cream good?" I asked her, hoping for a
smile.

She obliged with a grin, on her way back to normalcy.
"It was something to tell Devyn about. Black ice cream."

"Black ice cream? No way," Skip said, aiming his finger
back and forth toward his mouth. "I'll stick to caramel
cashew."

I thought we'd moved on from the issue of junior police
investigators. But not quite.

"Uncle Skip, I can still help you, you know. I was just
freaked out for a couple of minutes. Will you tell me if
there's anything I can do to help you investigate?"

Good news, bad news, I thought. I didn't want her to remain "freaked out" but a little perspective would have been
nice.

"Sure," Skip said.

"I'm an outstanding researcher on the computer, my
teacher says. She even lets me help the kids who are a little
slower to learn."

"Well, I can certainly use a computer expert on my
side."

"I found out something already today at the computer in
the bookstore."

I remembered Maddie's announcement, just before she
exposed the raccoon.

"What did you learn, sweetheart?" I asked.

"I found out that Mr. Goodman, the artist who was
killed, won lots of awards for his paintings. He used to go
to Santa Fe and he beat everyone there."

I gulped. "Where did you see all that?"

"The Lincoln Point newspaper is online, Grandma," she said, as if she were teaching a class called Online for Dummies. "Does that help you, Uncle Skip?"

"Good work," Skip said. I knew he was as surprised as I was, but he covered it nicely.

"I can do more, you know."

"That was a big help already. I'll call you as soon as I need more from you, okay?"

"Promise?"

He hesitated. A promise made to Maddie was not to be taken lightly. After a moment of stalling, Skip found a way out. "If your mom and dad say it's okay."

"Nuts," Maddie said.

I noticed Skip hadn't included me in the approval loop.

The mailman had brought two postcards, one from Devyn from her home in Los Angeles and one from Beverly and Nick in Hawaii. They made a nice distraction from talk of crime and slain raccoons. I'd decided not to make too big a deal out of Maddie's online research, either with her or with her parents. My best bet was to get Rosie at the bookstore to show me what Maddie had read.

Beverly's card of the day had a photo of a whole pig looking very roasted, in an open barbecue, lying on a bed of wide lettuce leaves, with an apple in its mouth. Maddie read the greeting: "We went to a luau. That poor dissed pig! I'll never eat ham again. Love, Bev and Nick."

"Me, either," said Maddie, who hadn't eaten ham since she'd seen a video featuring a beloved pig named Babe.

Devyn's card showed a daredevil ride at Disneyland, with log-shaped containers holding screaming young humans. Maddie read, "Mr. Pierson, the new math teacher, is a dorkface. You should be glad you're not here." She smiled as she showed me the rows of *xoxoxoxox*, then ran off to her desk with its own stash of Lincoln Point postcards.

I tried to erase the image of my own students possibly writing to pen pals about dorkface Mrs. Porter.

Our town cards were no match for those of Los Angeles or Maui, but there was a small collection for sale in Rosie's bookstore. They were done by a local artist and featured such highlights as the buildings at civic center, the large redwood statue of Abraham Lincoln at the city limit, and a vineyard that no one could place. Maddie had nearly bought her out this month.

While Maddie was writing, I took the opportunity to have a cup of tea and think about my promise to June. My hopeful conclusion was that it was such an emotional time, she'd probably forgotten her impassioned plea or decided against it after our meeting at Willie's. No need for me to do anything but let my capable nephew and his colleagues do their job. I should just be grateful that she hadn't had to come home to her deadly trash. I made periodic visits to my patio door to check for signs of life around her property. It was clear that she'd spent the day on Zoe's problem—visiting her in jail, picking up her things at Rutledge Center, meeting with me. I was tempted to add: antagonizing Skip. I thought she might be home now, or even stop in at my house, but I saw no sign of her or her car.

It was time to bring crafts to the fore and forget about the often unpleasant large-scale world.

Although we were both eager to build cinder-block book-cases for the Bronx apartment, Maddie and I decided to leave that for another time. For now, we had to get to the project with a deadline—the Lincoln-Douglas debate room box.

I realized with some glee that when Maddie left my home with her parents this time, she'd be traveling only ten miles away, not all the way to Southern California. This meant she'd be able to see the project through, from its humble, un-painted beginnings to its placement in the civic center foyer.

We'd made the box over the weekend. I'd taken the easy way out, starting with a ready-made picture frame. As I set it on the crafts table now, the doorbell rang.

"It's Mrs. Reed," Maddie said. "I see her car. I'll open the door."

Nuts, I thought, noting how handy Maddie's expression was. Not that I didn't enjoy a visit from my best (after Beverly) friend, but I knew as soon as Linda saw how I'd used the bought frame for the front of the room box, thus eliminating the toughest part of the job, she'd have something to say about it.

Linda walked directly to where I was, in the crafts area beyond my kitchen. This was meant to be a laundry room, but all that was left of that plan were the washer and dryer. The counters and cabinets, plus the tops of the appliances, were filled with crafts materials and tools.

"Caught red-handed," I said, pointing with both index fingers to the box.

Linda gasped, clutching the front of one of her vast collection of oversize velour jogging outfits (not that she ever did any exercise beyond lifting pieces of wood to her table saw). An exaggerated effect, for Maddie's benefit.

"You are setting such a bad example for your granddaughter," said my only-from-scratch crafter friend. "It's the equivalent of using that refrigerated dough for your ginger cookies."

"Never," I said.

Linda picked up the frame-cum–room box and inspected it. I'd used an eight-by-ten picture frame, choosing one with a fancy edge, since the scene was a depiction of an event in Victorian 1858. Right side up for the scene would be with the long side of the frame as "the ground." I'd extended the whole frame eight inches out behind the glass, making the room box a foot along the front (counting the frame edges), eight inches deep, and ten inches high (again, an added two inches for the fancy frame). "I see what you did here." She examined the edges of the box through the bottom lens of her bifocals. "Not bad."

From Linda, that was high praise. She pitched in and helped us cut sandpaper to size for the ground and glue it to the floor of the box. An outdoor scene called for trees, and I had a box full of all sizes. We picked out trees suitable for rows along the back and side walls of the box. I'd already wallpapered the back section with a sky design I'd found in a scrapbooking store.

I knew Maddie would be daunted by the task of placing tree after tree along the sides of the box. She got bored, as I often did, with the rote aspects of crafts. It would take at least two dozen trees and bushes crowded together to give the scene a realistic appearance. Like me, Maddie enjoyed the creative part but easily tired of the repetitive cutting, painting, and gluing that some scenes required.

"I'd better go call Devyn before it gets too late," she said, four trees into the task. It was barely four thirty in the afternoon—hardly late—but I had no desire to force her to stay for the grunt work. I was happy enough that she'd grown to enjoy my lifelong hobby.

As soon as Maddie left, Linda leaned her beehive hairdo toward my shoulder and whispered, "What about that murder, huh? Do you want to hear some gossip about the woman they arrested?"

It hadn't occurred to me that Linda would have any inside information on this case. She worked as a nurse at the Mary Todd nursing home, an unlikely place to have run into Zoe or Brad. I wished she hadn't used the word *gossip*. It gave my curiosity an air of sordidness. However, I wasn't so put out that I'd pass on her scoop.

"You have some insight?" I asked.

She laughed. "Insight, yeah, that's what it is. Well, anyway, Ms. Howard was a substitute teacher at the high school last year and Jason had her for English."

I remembered Skip's mentioning that Zoe's finger-

prints were on file with the Lincoln Point school district. I
was retired from the district by then and had never run into
her there.

"I guess it took her a little while to get back to her tech
editing career when she first moved from Chicago," I said.

"Maybe that's why she wasn't the best teacher, you
know? Jason said Ms. Howard was called to the principal's
office more than he was that term, and you know how often
Jason was there."

Though Linda had brought it up, I wouldn't dare comment on Jason's problems in school, especially since he'd
turned it around lately, even making the honor roll in the
last term. Linda had the appropriately worded bumper
sticker on her car, the kind that couldn't be read in total unless you were at a very long red light.

More interesting were Zoe's delinquency issues. "You
don't say." I stated this hoping Linda *would* say more about
Ms. Howard.

Linda was ready, appearing to relish her upper hand in
the FYI department. "She yelled at the kids constantly,
used questionable language, and got fired. Do you know
why they had to let her go?"

I didn't know she got fired. Another thing June forgot to
mention.

If I wanted information, I had to accommodate Linda by
playing her game. "Do tell."

"She threw an eraser at one student and whacked another on the side of his head," Linda said, not losing a beat
in her "tree-planting" chore. "And, no, Jason was not one
of them."

While Linda was reporting, she had multitasked. She'd
glued down two perfect rows of trees in the corner of the
box, placing them diagonally to give the appearance of
added depth. I was relegated to handing her the trees, one
at a time. I loved when Linda took over my project. Everything was straighter, neater, more cleverly arranged than if

I had done it. A heavy woman with relatively thick fingers, Linda was still able to manipulate tiny objects better than most of the women in our crafters circle.

I thought I'd better add my tidbit to the conversation before Linda embarrassed herself. "Did you know that Ms. Howard is June Chinn's best friend?"

"Oops. Sorry."

"There's nothing to be sorry about, but if she stops by, you might want to change the subject."

Linda ran her thumb and index finger along her lips and indicated that was it for the gossip.

Zoe had a temper and had lashed out in class. That was Linda's big news. It could mean nothing. Or everything.

Chapter 7

I noticed Maddie hang up the phone from her call to Devyn and go directly toward her room. Needing some time to herself, I supposed, as Devyn on the other end of the line probably also did. I'd met Devyn on my trips to Los Angeles. She was as sweet as Maddie, with long strawberry-blond curls and a generous sprinkling of freckles across her nose. She seemed as devoted to Maddie as Maddie was to her. But how long could two eleven-year-olds stay in touch? They would change in more ways than either of them would believe right now. I still had a few friends in the Bronx, but I'd been an adult when I left and the relationships were already mature.

I worried that in my happiness at having my son and his family close to me, I'd neglected to notice how the move might hurt my granddaughter. When Maddie came back to the ex-laundry area, I hugged her more tightly than usual. If she wondered why, she didn't ask.

She did ask, "How come Mrs. Reed left already?"

"She just stopped by to chat."

Maddie looked at the Lincoln-Douglas scene. "Wow, she did a lot of work, too."

"How do you know I didn't do that?"

She gave me a sheepish look. "Uh . . ."

Even my granddaughter recognized who was the better crafter.

We got to work on the fabric, one of my favorite parts of making a scene. Even small pieces of cloth brought a dollhouse or a miniature room to life, giving it dimension, texture, folds, and shadows. Maddie cut out long banners from flag-pattern fabric, being careful to have some red, white, and blue on every rectangle. We hung banners from the trees, much like those in Mary Lou's painting. Though Linda would call it cheating, we used long party toothpicks with flags on the end as flagpoles scattered through the area.

Maddie wanted to add some people, but I've never liked adding dolls to a scene. One tiny doll that was lifelike enough to make the scene work was very expensive, on the order of hundreds of dollars. And the less expensive ones had "fake woman" or "toy man" written all over them. It was possible to photograph a miniature scene in such a way that a viewer wouldn't be able to tell it wasn't life-size unless there were a ruler or a coin or some way to show scale. But add a plastic person with hollow, staring eyes, stiff limbs, and shiny plastic hair, and you could tell at a glance that the room wasn't "real."

I told Maddie as much of this as she could stand before giving up.

"Okay, okay, no people," she said.

"But we can make it look like people have been here. We can add clothing, for example."

"Like someone left his jacket behind." (Maddie was a quick study.)

"Or his top hat, or a cane."

"And notes from the speech."

We got a start on all of the above and set the items aside to be added later.

We still had a stage to build. Ordinarily, I would have built that first, but I wanted to take advantage of Linda's skills with vegetation and also give Maddie some fun things to make before pulling out the dull popsicle sticks and wood pieces for the platform.

We put together a four-by-seven platform relatively quickly and stained the wood. Once it was dry (Maddie hated the part where crafters sometimes had to wait a day between steps), we'd place it so that it was surrounded by trees. The stage would be raised three inches from the "ground."

"That's three feet, right?" I reminded Maddie, keeping her honest with respect to scale.

"Do you think the men could climb up that high?" she asked.

"Lincoln probably could, but Douglas was pretty short. Maybe there are stairs around the back, hidden by the trees."

"And we don't have to put them there. We can just say they're there."

I smiled. My granddaughter had grasped another wonderful thing about miniatures.

At dinner, Richard told us about a ten-year-old boy needing surgery for skiffy.

"That's SCFE, slipped capital femoral epiphysis," he explained, a structural defect of the hip that occurs in some children.

By dessert we'd heard about a baby born with clubfoot, another with acute torticollis, and preteens with three different kinds of spinal deformities. Richard rarely shared this kind of detail from his work life. It seemed obvious that he was trying to give a not-so-subtle message to his daughter: there are kids out there with real problems, much worse off than you are, with just a bout of homesickness that would be less than a dim memory in a few years.

Maddie ate her tarragon chicken without much comment during her father's presentation. I'm not sure that trick ever worked when Richard was eleven, either.

Out of the blue, it seemed, Maddie had a story to tell. "You want to hear something really gross?" Maddie asked.

"I wasn't telling you gross things," Richard said. "I just want you to know what some kids have to deal with."

Unlike her parents, I knew what was coming.

"I had to deal with a dead raccoon today."

"That's very sad," Mary Lou said. "Where did you see it?"

Maddie's eyes teared up. "Grandma can tell you. May I be excused?"

Maddie left and I told the story, with as little drama as possible.

"Is Maddie in some kind of danger here?" Richard asked, hearing between the lines.

"It won't hurt her to see a few unpleasant things. It was just a prank," Mary Lou said.

"What does Skip think?" Richard asked.

"That it was a prank," I said. "But he sent the knife to the lab. You know Skip, erring on the side of caution."

I was glad neither of them asked what I thought.

Mary Lou pulled me aside in the living room while Richard and Maddie took their turn at cleaning up the dishes.

"I put in an hour today at the Rutledge Center, working on my painting."

"Are you making good progress?"

"As much as possible with all the talk about the murder. Everyone is caught up in it."

"Of course." I didn't want to seem too eager.

"That Nan Browne is still talking about how her daughter should have gotten one of the commissions for a painting. Evidently she went so far as to ask the debate committee if

Diana could replace Brad, since he's . . . you know . . . gone.
But I guess someone already claimed that spot."

"Really?"

"It's not completely decided, but everyone thinks Ed
Villard will get the commission. He's an old guy—"

"I met him."

"Oops. I didn't mean old old." Mary Lou tried not to
smile.

"Don't worry," I said. "I know what you mean."

"Well, yeah, there's old, and then there's just too old to
be at this stage in his career."

I patted her arm. "I get it."

"Good, because we don't think of you as old, Mom." She
patted my arm the way adult children do to their parents.
She lowered her voice even further. "And also, I thought
you might like to know that the crime-scene tape is down."

I didn't know what surprised me more—that the tape
was down, that Mary Lou thought I should know, or that
she thought she needed to whisper all this information to
me.

I gave her a questioning look. She gave me a nudge.
"You know, Mom, in case you wanted to look into things."

I appreciated my daughter-in-law more every day, even
if she did consider the prime of life "old."

I sat in my atrium with a cup of tea long after my family
had gone to bed. A murder in Lincoln Point had affected
someone close to me and I had a hard time letting go of the
idea that I could help.

Ordinarily I would engage in one of my sessions of
"let's get focused" (out loud, to myself), but a houseful of
people was cramping my style. Or I would call Beverly, but
she was out of range, emotionally, if not technically. I fell
back on another technique and scribbled some notes. I
wrote down key points, hoping that would suffice as a sen-
sory way to organize my thoughts.

First topic heading: Mary Lou.

I knew Mary Lou kept her eye on community problems and was always willing to volunteer or to take a stand for a cause she thought was worthy. She worked at the polls on voting days and put in a few hours a week at a women's shelter in Los Angeles. She'd already sought out a similar facility in Palo Alto for when she moved there. The last time I visited Southern California, she was organizing a fund-raiser to save a children's breakfast program at a school in a poor neighborhood.

But I'd never known her to get involved in police work.

"You could look into things" played back in my mind. Was it the proximity of her cousin Skip in her life these last weeks that brought on this interest? Was my curious nature spilling over now that we lived together? I'd have to find a time to sit alone with her and see what, if anything, she meant by her comment.

Next: June Chinn. Promises aside, I wanted to help her. The sooner the fate of her friend was settled, one way or another, the sooner she'd be able to move on. And the sooner she and Skip could get back to their relationship. Unless it was too late for that. June had turned her back on him twice in twenty-four hours. It wasn't like Skip to stick with a girlfriend once things got unpleasant in any way. I was surprised June had a second chance when he approached her at Willie's. I wasn't sure about a third.

The incident in June's driveway nagged at me. Maybe I'd made too quick a leap from the knifed raccoon to Zoe Howard. What if the message had been for June herself? For now, I had to follow Skip's lead and consider it unrelated either to June or to Zoe's plight. After all, even if someone wanted to make a point or to get under Zoe's skin, she was already in jail, and it was hard to ask for more than that if they wanted to intimidate her.

There was also the remote possibility that June had killed the raccoon. She often got upset when they knocked the top off her trash container and upset everything in it

that was neatly packaged. She'd be especially angry when
they attacked her cats, but it was still all but impossible to
imagine her plunging a knife into an animal, even one as
undesirable as a raccoon.

Next on my list was Zoe Howard herself. I regretted that
my only recollection of her was not a pleasant one—out of
control at her friend's wedding. I thought of Linda's scoop,
but a young woman with a temper wasn't necessarily a
murderer. And though I'd never thrown anything at my students, I understood how a classroom full of high school
students could stretch the limits of a teacher's patience and
equanimity. Especially those of a substitute teacher, always
considered an easy target.

Skip had said Zoe and her deceased boyfriend had been
seen or heard fighting. Well, if that were the inevitable
prelude to murder, we were all in trouble.

I'd met only a few people who worked with Brad Goodman in the Rutledge Center. Ryan the security guard. Ed
the painter. Stephanie the . . . what? I'd have to find out.
None seemed to have murderous looks in their eyes. Nan
Browne, whom I hadn't seen in a while, came to mind also.
But as far as I knew, a mother's love and desire for her
daughter's success weren't on anyone's list of top five reasons for murder.

Except for that case years ago in Texas, I remembered,
where a mother killed her daughter's cheerleading competitor. Or was it the competitor's mother whom she killed?
And didn't she hire a hit man to do it? Why did I care about
the details of these gruesome stories? Nothing like that
would ever happen in Lincoln Point, anyway.

I surprised myself by putting Brad Goodman, the unfortunate victim, last on the list. I hoped there were many
family members and friends who put him first. I was sorry
I knew so little about him—that he was an artist from
Chicago with an ex-wife named Rhonda and a girlfriend
named Zoe and, thanks to Maddie's sleuthing, a prizewin-
ner at art shows in Santa Fe. I felt my mourning of him was

very abstract, the way I would mourn any victim of violent crime. If I were serious about trying to help June and Zoe, I'd have to make an effort to get to know the man Brad had been. Was he pushy, as June had said, to the point of making someone angry enough to kill him, or was he a random victim?

I asked myself what procedure detective Skip Gowen would advise to gather more intelligence. I heard him in my mind, telling me to distance myself from any involvement in his case, except to comfort June. No doubt about that. And as for doing his own job, he'd have to look at more evidence, more suspects than I had knowledge of. The police didn't have the luxury of armchair detectives who limited their investigation to a few obvious participants in a victim's life.

It wasn't out of the question that one of my students, whom I blithely greeted as I'd walked through the workshop area, or a competitor in Santa Fe, New Mexico, had a grudge against Brad Goodman that was serious enough for murder. Neither was it impossible that the killer was a stranger to Brad, a robber or an escaped mental patient. The panoply of people in Brad's life stretched at least from Chicago to Santa Fe to Lincoln Point. My notepaper wasn't long enough, nor my brain keen enough, to include all these possibilities.

I decided that my list of names was useless. I scratched out the names and made a list of what I could do this week instead.

First, visit the Rutledge Center, scene of the crime. The fact was that I had legitimate reasons to revisit the building. I needed some ideas to finish off the debate room box. Though I wasn't making an exact copy of the set, I wanted it to be complementary to the mural that would grace the foyer of city hall and the individual paintings.

I could certainly visit Zoe in jail and hear her story firsthand. Just as a concerned Lincoln Point citizen, of course.

I'd also find some mother-in-law-to-daughter-in-law

time with Mary Lou this week so I could get her take as an almost insider to the Rutledge Center.

A busy couple of days coming up. I conveniently left Skip out of my plans. Every time he sneaked in, in my mind, I saw a look of disapproval on his face.

Thursday morning's schedule called for Richard to drive Maddie to school and me to pick her up. Mary Lou had been picked up by a gallery colleague before anyone was up, thoughtfully leaving a fresh pot of coffee on the counter and our favorite mugs lined up.

"What are you going to do today, Grandma?" Maddie asked. I heard a wistful tone, as if anything I had planned— even a trip to the post office or the dry cleaners—would be more fun than what she had to look forward to at the Angelican Hills school in Palo Alto.

I put an extra cookie in her already bulging lunch bag. The latest family joke was that Mary Lou would prepare Maddie's lunch the night before, with a healthy sandwich, fruit, carrot sticks, and celery. In the morning, I'd unzip the bag and add sugar-based treats. This morning I also tucked a little ceramic heart into the corner, to bring a smile to her face.

"I'm going to the library," I said. "I need to review the new study guides for tutoring Mrs. Pino."

She drained her juice glass. "That's it?"

"I might add an item or two to the debate scene, if you don't mind."

"You can glue down the stage."

"Okay, then, that's it. I'll pick you up at three and we'll go for a snack," I said.

Richard snapped his briefcase shut. "If you two weren't both so skinny I'd have to put a stop to this daily heavy snacking routine. Ice cream twice a day is a little over the top."

I heard a little good-natured envy in his voice. Richard wasn't overweight, but he did have to watch his calories, to keep it that way.

"Not ice cream today, Dad. Mrs. Norman at the bookstore told me there's a popcorn shop downtown, in that new row of stores in back of Springfield Boulevard. Grandma and I are going to try it out today."

"A whole shop of popcorn? How many different kinds can you have?"

"Twenty-three," Maddie said, shoving her lunch bag into one of the many compartments of her backpack. "Chocolate drizzle, cheddar cheese, cinnamon, caramel, strawberry, cherry, apple—"

"Okay, I get it," said her father.

". . . bubble gum, cookie dough . . ." Maddie laughed through several more flavors until her father tickled her speechless as we walked together out to the driveway.

Maddie buckled herself into the backseat of the family SUV. One sacrifice that Richard made to bond with his daughter was to abandon his two-seater sports car on days when he drove Maddie to school. She was down to only once a day with her request that she be able to ride in the front seat of any vehicle. While she technically met the requirements for California child seat belt standards, Maddie's parents (and I) thought the mechanism in Richard's car didn't shield her properly.

"We have hot cars, meant for hot chicks," Skip said once, inadvertently in front of Maddie. The comment brought a blush to Skip's face, a smile to Mary Lou's and Maddie's, and a deep frown to Richard's. I'd laughed out loud.

Maddie made one more attempt to interrogate me from the backseat as I leaned in to the SUV to kiss her good-bye. "Are you sure you're just going to the library?"

"Where else would I go?"

Both she and her father gave me disbelieving looks.

As they pulled away, a miniature cloud of guilt settled over me. Why hadn't I told them my plans? Maybe because I felt I was the one who was going to have the most fun today. And they seemed to know it.

Chapter 8

So that I couldn't be called a liar, I spent about ten minutes on the room box, adding a few small rocks to the sandpaper "gravel" in the debate scene, and gluing down the stage, as promised. I knew Maddie would enjoy making posters and littering the ground with miniature trash, so I resisted those touches. Maddie would be delighted to do the research to see just what kind of trash they had in 1858 (a better topic than looking up obituaries of murder victims). I told her I was fairly sure it was too early for cigarette butts or metal soda cans.

As I dressed for my trip downtown I felt alternately like a spy, an undercover cop, and a sneak. When did I become less than honest with my family? When they started making it difficult for me to help a friend, I answered myself. I had to see Mary Lou soon, to bolster my resolve.

I chose neutral colors, plentiful in my wardrobe, for my outing—casual brown slacks, a gold-toned shell, and a long brown coat sweater. I felt ready for visits to a television studio and a jail. I hoped I didn't forget to stop at the library for the only errand I'd owned up to.

My first stop was Rutledge Center where I arrived around nine o'clock. Mary Lou was right; there was no sign of crime-scene tape, and in fact there was normal activity at all the doors, mostly older people going into classrooms. I had a longing to take a class myself and made a note to pick up a catalog.

It made sense that the debate stage sets were being built and painted in the warehouse part of the complex, where I'd been yesterday afternoon, then would be transported somehow to the civic center auditorium. In times gone by the debate reenactment had been held outdoors, as most of the originals were, but one February rain in Lincoln Point destroyed that tradition and it had been held indoors for the last several years.

I knew it was unlikely that the Channel 29 studio itself was being used as a workroom. If my only purpose was to see the set, therefore, I had no reason to go into the east side studio entrance, where the crime-scene tape had been. But the Rutledge Center was a complicated setup, with its various walkways and interconnected parking lots, so it wasn't surprising that I got lost and ended up entering the building on the east side. (A big *wink, wink* here.)

I was surprised (no wink here) that the door from the parking lot led right into a small waiting room for the television studio. It was empty this morning, except for its furnishings—a few mismatched chairs, a television set that was old even by my standards, and a rickety metal wagon with a coffeepot and condiments.

I looked around for a clipboard or some way to sign in and saw nothing of the kind. A window on the side wall opened onto an area that looked to my untrained eye like a control room. There was one woman at a row of desks that ran parallel to a bank of monitors and control panels. She had her back to me and to the electronics. I tapped on the glass, but she didn't hear me. I noticed she was plugged into something, with long white wires hanging from her ears, her head bobbing from side to side. The iPod generation.

There was one door off the waiting room, with a hand-lettered sign that said STUDIO—NO FOOD OR DRINK. It did not say "no entry." I tried the knob, pushed on the door, and nearly fell into the studio itself, a room draped in black on three walls. I recognized the fourth wall as the set for the morning news program. Enormous lights, not on now, hung from the ceiling; three serious-looking cameras were stationed on the floor like one-eyed sentries.

I figured this was the general area where Brad Goodman's body had been found. Why else would the crime-scene tape have been around only this entry into the complex? I saw no evidence of a crime, however. The shelves full of vases and dried flower arrangements that made up the set looked shabbier than they did on my television screen, but otherwise nothing looked disturbed in any way.

I picked up a book from one of several stools located against the back drapes. I recognized the author as one who was recently interviewed on *Chapter One*, the channel's book-review program.

For a moment I was lost on page seventy-two, where the book fell open in my hands. I read that whatever my age, I had the power to change my life, to live my dreams, no matter what disappointments I'd already experienced. Good to know. My mind drifted to dreams of my youth.

I closed the book and walked toward the back wall of drapes. What did I hope to see? A drop of blood would be nice (when did I start thinking this way?) or, better yet, something left by the killer. But there was no sign of blood, nothing toppled or broken. Silly of me to expect that, I realized. Clearly, I had no training for useful investigation.

I parted the black curtains and entered a pitch-dark area. Is this how Skip went about his business? I doubted it. But I couldn't very well go around interviewing suspects or

checking phone records and rap sheets. I heard a thud and
stopped short, my breath catching. A wave of fear came
over me. I was in what was essentially a blacked-out room,
alone, at a murder scene, when I should have been home
painting miniature park benches for my Lincoln-Douglas
room box.

I needed light. I ran my hands up and down the walls,
which had an almost sticky texture, unpleasant to the touch.
I finally found what felt like a switch plate on the third try.
I flipped the switch. A set of klieg lights flashed on, blind-
ing me momentarily. I heard scrambling and saw two shadows, one fleeing away from me, the other coming toward
me. I held my breath.

"Excuse me? This is a restricted area." A woman's
voice, decidedly unhappy. It looked for all the world as if
I'd interrupted a tryst in the folds of the curtains.

A woman in a flowered skirt with a handkerchief hem-
line stepped from the shadows. Fortyish Nan Browne, hostess of several Channel 29 programs. She looked very put
together, all buttons in place. I looked for signs of messed-
up lipstick, but saw none. Either she was very quick, or I
was wrong about the compromising position I'd caught
her in.

I felt my face flush with guilt—that I was in the studio,
that I'd exposed her to the light, that I wasn't dressed as
nicely as she was.

"I . . . I'm Geraldine Porter." I was sure my stutter
sounded loud and boorish. My craft-show beaded necklace
paled in comparison to the delicate brooch on Nan's black
blouse. "We've met. Not that you'd remember. You've interviewed me a couple of times, once on that feature about
the library literacy program. It was taped in the Old Glory
Hotel downtown."

Ms. Browne hadn't said anything during my pitiful
rambling. Her arms were folded across her chest, her face
extremely pale.

"And you're in the studio now because . . . ?"

Because I want to investigate the murder of a young man I never met. Because I thought I might see something that trained policemen and policewomen missed. Because I promised a neighbor . . .

What I said was, "The door was open. No one stopped me." This was worse than when Skip had occasion to cross-examine me in a similar way. At least I knew he'd eventually buckle under when he saw a plate of my ginger cookies.

"You're supposed to knock on the window and tell them why you're here."

"I did."

"And . . . ?"

"Nobody answered." Enough of this. I stood straighter. I had every right to be here. "I'm doing a miniature scene for the civic center for next Tuesday and I wanted to take a look around at the stage sets. I need to see what the set designers and artists have come up with for the backdrop for the debate."

Not a strand of Ms. Browne's very blond hair moved. She never cracked a smile. Quite different from her "happy talk" news anchoring. "You're in the wrong part of the building," she said.

"I see that. Can you direct me to the correct part of the building?"

She put her hand on my elbow as if she were a bouncer and I'd crashed a party at an exclusive club, and led me through the curtains and through the door back to the waiting room. She refolded her arms.

"The entrance you want is on the north side."

I knew that. "Which way is that?" I asked, not wanting to make it easy for her.

She extended her arm northward and pointed, never taking her eyes off me.

"Thanks," I muttered.

I let out long yoga breaths as I walked to my car. I was annoyed that I'd let myself be intimidated and feel guilty when I hadn't breached security or done anything wrong. Why hadn't I taken the opportunity to make a snide remark about her daughter's not being good enough to earn a commission? And to suggest that she may have copied the actions of that mother in Texas?

As it was, for all my fright and tension, I'd learned nothing about Brad's unfortunate demise or Zoe's alleged hand in it. It certainly didn't pay to be good.

Unlike yesterday's nasty weather, today's was bright and sunny, and I enjoyed a walk around to the north side. I climbed the few steps to the building and entered the enormous work area. There were no black drapes here, but large, open, warehouse-type windows. The workbenches were sparsely populated, with only three or four artists at work, and there was no meeting at the watercooler. As kids we'd always referred to "bankers' hours" to mean short workdays; I wondered what artists' hours were.

My new flats clicked on the hard floor; the sound echoed through the hall. I started down the first row between worktables looking for a project that might be associated with the debate reenactment. I fingered a tapestry-in-progress that seemed meant instead for a medieval scene, with unicorns and swords. I moved on to a wooden stringed musical instrument under construction. There would be music, I knew, at the celebration, and this might be a period piece. I reached out to pluck a string, imagining soft chamber music.

Pling.

The sound needed tuning.

"You're back."

This sound was a woman's voice, deep and resonant, which caused me to inadvertently pluck a second string with more force than I'd intended. Something a bit off from middle C rang through the hall.

It was a creepy, jumpy day at the Rutledge Center.

But this time I turned to see a friendly face. The tall,

slender Stephanie Cameron—who apparently noticed my hand clutching my chest.

"Didn't mean to scare you."

"It's not you," I said, relaxing my shoulders. I turned the next short breath into a smile. "These projects are wonderful. Are you an artist, too, Stephanie?"

"No, I'm everything else. I produce the shows, manage the TV scheduling"—she swept her arm in a large arc—"and oversee this area. Among other things. It's a small operation with no rigid job duties. It's pretty loose around here."

I felt the need to tell Stephanie about my encounter with Nan Browne in the studio wing, ending with, "I was surprised I could just walk in."

"Yeah, half the time there's no one at the window and the door into the TV studio from the waiting room doesn't even have a lock, I don't think. And all the artists have keys to this side. They work such odd hours."

It occurred to me that I didn't know who had discovered Brad Goodman's body. I mentally chided Skip—wouldn't you think my nephew could keep me informed even when I didn't ask the right questions?

I asked Stephanie now, putting it as delicately as I could. "Oh, dear, was it one of the artists who found . . . ?"

"Nuh-uh. And it's a good thing, because most of them are so young, they might've fainted or something. It was one of the Channel 29 cameramen. He was very upset because he had his five-year-old daughter with him. He came in around nine on Monday morning, thinking he could show her around before anyone came in to work."

"That must have been awful." But still I hoped to learn what became of LPPD's questioning of him.

"It makes me a little nervous, I'll tell you. I came to work around eight this morning and the building was already open. But everything was okay, so I figured probably Ryan did it."

"The security guard?"

"The security *force*, actually. But he wasn't exactly sitting on the door, so . . ." She pointed to me with both hands.

"So I could walk right in," I said. "It sounds risky, but I suppose since there are no big stars walking around, the center is not a huge attraction for thieves or the paparazzi."

"True enough. No big stars around here." Stephanie pulled at her long, streaked hair.

Oops. "I didn't mean to imply—"

"No worries. We don't have delusions of grandeur. Just a few artists who've won national awards."

"I understand Brad Goodman took some awards in Santa Fe." Thanks to my granddaughter, I sounded more knowledgeable than I was.

"There's that," Stephanie said. "Not to speak ill of the dead, but a lot of people question his tactics. Anyway, we also have a local TV studio with an audience of seventy thousand households, with a total of a quarter of a million people."

"That many?" There I went again. "I didn't mean to imply—"

Stephanie gave a hearty laugh and poked my shoulder. "I'm just giving you a hard time. Why are you here, by the way?"

I told Stephanie today's mission.

"No prob. I'm also the tour guide. What would you like to see?"

The painting that was slashed. "Oh, just anything that's related to the Lincoln-Douglas debate next week."

Stephanie led me around the work spaces, noting that not many of the artists came in much before ten. "Then they work into the night," she said, making a sign that from Maddie would mean "they're nuts."

A thought flashed across my mind. "Then there were a lot of witnesses to the vandalism of the paintings the other night?"

Stephanie banged her forehead with the palm of her

hand. "Wouldn't you know it. No one was around that night. There was a meeting of all the muralists and all the artists doing one-of-a-kinds over at the civic center to look over the venue, check measurements, that kind of thing. Funny coincidence, huh?"

Either that or someone knew the schedule. For some reason, I didn't want to share that thought with Stephanie.

We checked out the woodworking projects (including the instrument I'd already pluck-tested) and sections of the background mural, which was being done in pieces by different artists, Stephanie explained, including Ed Villard, the man I'd met. The artists had chosen to set the debate in a formal room with wood paneling and portraits on the wall. The look would be similar to that of a rotunda in a government building, an easier scene to paint than outdoors in a town square, I imagined.

I learned why Mary Lou's painting would be displayed outside the auditorium where my room box would also be placed.

"Hers is an outdoor scene, so it wouldn't look right to have an outdoor scene of the debate, which is where it originally was, hanging indoors, which is how we're presenting the reenacted debate."

I thought I understood, but I must have looked confused.

"It would be like a mixed metaphor," Stephanie said.

I let it go at that. Except to recall that the fifth debate in 1858 was scheduled to be held in a park but moved to a shelter on the campus of nearby Knox College when it started to rain. According to one source, that is. You never could be sure about history, Ken always said. It wasn't even clear how many had attended the debate. Reports ranged between fifteen and thirty thousand. It was hard to imagine the sight, with that many people descending on the small town by train, horseback, wagon, and on foot.

We passed a wall of paintings where one portrait stood out in front of several that were stacked against the wall. "Buchanan," I said, admiring the rich colors of his chair, in contrast to the deep black of Buchanan's tuxedo jacket.

Probably Lincoln Point residents were the only Californians who'd immediately recognize the man who was president during Lincoln's time in Congress. This rendering in oil gave the fifteenth president a more formal look than I usually saw, and also a more pleasant countenance. His jacket was unrumpled, his white shirt neat, and his bow tie carefully arranged. He had a smile on his long, thick face and looked like he'd just combed back his unruly hair and slicked down his bushy eyebrows.

"It's a shame Brad didn't get to finish the painting," Stephanie said. At first glance it looked finished to me, but Stephanie pointed out some areas where the paint was not evenly applied and the chair Buchanan was sitting on needed work on the bottom. She sighed. "But at least it didn't get slashed."

At last, an opportunity to talk about the crime scene. "This is Brad's work?" I asked. "I thought all his paintings were destroyed."

"Brad had this and a few other canvases in another part of the building where he thought it was less damp."

"But yesterday you said several paintings were slashed."

"Yeah, the irony is that only one of Brad's paintings was out here; the rest were in the back. So most of the paintings that got slashed weren't even his."

"Irony. Yeah, irony."

From behind me—a voice much deeper than Stephanie's. I was startled, but I didn't jump this time, maybe because I wasn't alone. The voice belonged to Ed Villard, who was accompanied by Ryan Colson, the security guard, out of uniform, his stubbled head shining under the workshop lights.

"Ed lost a couple of paintings that night," Ryan said, his tone expressing sympathy.

"I'm sorry, Ed. I'm sure each one represents a great many hours."

"Indeed. I didn't want to carry on about it when I met you yesterday, Mrs. Porter, especially with your cute little granddaughter all ears and so smart."

Nothing won me over more quickly than a compliment to my granddaughter. Now I was truly sorry about Ed's loss.

"Were your paintings part of the debate set?" I asked him.

"Ed's just a muralist for the Lincoln-Douglas project," Stephanie said.

Ed glared at her. Apparently that was a demeaning remark, though I had great appreciation for murals myself. "I had a number of other projects I'd been working on. For the spring festival, for example," he said.

"Oh, yeah, right," Stephanie said.

"Did any of your paintings survive, Ed?" I asked. In other words, can we talk some more about the crime?

Ed shook his head. "None that I'd been working on in this place." This time his glare was for Ryan Colson. "Maybe if we'd had a guard who didn't wish he were destined for Broadway . . ."

Ryan looked like he wanted to swing at Ed, but Stephanie intervened. "We're loaded with talent in this building, Gerry. Ryan here is an actor in his real life. The next time you see him, he might be Stephen Douglas. He's made the cut at all the stages for the auditions."

Ryan, easily diverted, moved his feet in an exaggerated shuffle. "Aw, shucks," he said.

"As I said, maybe if we'd had a guard." Ed wasn't about to let it drop.

And neither was I. "Why would anyone want to cut up your paintings, Ed?"

"Zoe must have thought they were all Brad's paintings because of the one in front," he said.

"Ed's probably right," Stephanie said. She pulled out from the middle of the stack a large clipboard with a sketch on it. "Brad had this pencil drawing safe in the back room, but the final painting of it was right here in front of the stack." She spread her long arms out. "So Zoe just started slashing whatever was in this whole row."

I looked up at the corner behind me, expecting to see a camera.

Stephanie picked up on this semi-reflexive action. "The police took the camera and VCR."

"Are there any other cameras?"

"Here and there," Ryan said. "You're not supposed to know exactly where."

I tightened my lips and nodded, accepting the terms of security.

I turned to study Brad Goodman's sketch more closely. A young woman in an elaborate, many-layered, white Victorian dress, a quizzical look on her face. No one I recognized.

"It's supposed to be Harriet Lane, but I don't think it looks anything like her," Ed said.

Harriet Lane, the nominal First Lady. I was aware that Buchanan, a bachelor, had adopted his niece when she was a young girl after both her parents had died. She was in her twenties when she made her debut as White House hostess.

Harriet was reputed to have been an attractive young woman with soft features, tall, poised, generous, and cheerful. She wore her ashen hair as most women of those days, parted in the middle and pulled back in a style that was half bun and half braids. But Brad's interpretation of Harriet made her look like a very modern woman, with sharp features and a sensual expression. Someone I might see at a power lunch on one of my infrequent trips to a San Francisco restaurant.

"So we're left with just this sketch for Harriet Lane," Stephanie said. "It was supposed to be part of the stage set with Buchanan on one side of the podium and Harriet on the other." She sucked in her breath. "Poor Brad."

"Did you know him well?" I asked the group.

"He was a newcomer," Ed said, with a shake of his head. "No one had laid eyes on him until he arrived with both a Buchanan and a Harriet Lane commission in hand a couple of months ago."

"I think they figured it would be better on the stage if the same artist did both portraits."

Ed grunted. If he said anything besides muttering sounds, I couldn't make out what.

"Brad had only been coming here for a few weeks. But he'd lived in town awhile and he was, like, still a colleague, you know?" Stephanie said.

"Right, newcomer or not, we knew him and he was killed right here on home turf," Ryan said.

At the last phrase, Stephanie and Ryan looked around the hall, at their turf.

"We're trying to decide whether to put up this sketch on the stage where the painting would have been," Stephanie said. "Like, to honor Brad, or something."

"I think it would be macabre," Ed said.

"You mean creepy?" Ryan asked.

"Uh, what are museums full of, guys?" Stephanie asked. "Pictures by dead artists."

I heard an involuntary gasp from my mouth. All three looked at me.

"She's not as cold as she sounds," Ryan said. He turned to her. "Or are you?" His tone was semi-serious.

"What are the alternatives to using the sketch?" I asked, to defuse the situation. I realized that the stressful atmosphere probably had as much to do with the idea of a murder being committed on their home ground as with the loss of the newcomer Brad Goodman in their lives.

"Ed thinks he can do a painting himself, in a week." She punched him playfully, her trademark gesture apparently. "He thinks he's as good as Brad Goodman. But I knew

Brad Goodman, and he's no Brad Goodman." She laughed
at her not-very-original jab.

Ed was not amused. "We'll see," he said, then turned
and walked away. There was a lot of that going on in the
young crowd these days, but Ed was older than June and
her peers by about twenty years.

"Sorry, man," Stephanie called after him, but he didn't
reply.

Stephanie looked embarrassed. "That wasn't very cool
of me, was it? It's just that Ed thinks he's a genius. He says
he's related to Edouard Vuillard and that he was destined to
be an artist. I think he actually believes that."

"That's why his name seemed familiar," I said. "From
Art History 101."

"Yeah, Vuillard was a Nabi, Ed says, and then proceeds
to give us a lecture on what that is. We get a little tired of
his pontificating. He also has a lot of money and lords it
over everyone with his top-of-the-line art supplies. But
still, I shouldn't have been so crass. Ed's been trying to get
his work in a city-sponsored event for years and always
gets rejected. I hope they let him put his painting up this
time. I can't believe I made fun of him that way. Sometimes I get a little too wise, you know?"

I patted her shoulder. "I guess we're all a little skittish
today," I said.

A clatter of metal and what seemed to be a stampede of
footsteps broke the hollow silence of the hall.

I turned to the large door A.

"It's the television crew. They're taping us again today,"
Stephanie said. "I lost track of time. I'd better get everyone
together." She took a walkie-talkie from her belt and spoke
into it. "Calling all hands. Channel 29 is here. If you want
to be famous, come to the north wing."

Sure enough, a group of people and equipment was approaching where we stood. What sounded like a crew big
enough to cover a presidential inauguration was really only
five people, with Nan Browne in the lead.

"Would you mind if I hang around for this?" I asked Stephanie.

"Knock yourself out," she said. "That tall, good-looking black guy right behind Nan—he's the producer. I have to go schmooze. Last time he came close to asking me to go out for a drink." Stephanie rushed to greet the man who would make everyone a celebrity and possibly improve her social life.

I tried to make myself invisible (if not knocked out) as the television staff set up two cameras and a bevy of lights around one section of the work area. The focus was on a panel that I guessed was part of the debate mural.

I watched from the sidelines, partially hidden by the stack of paintings I'd been looking at with Stephanie and Ed. Both the unnamed producer and Nan pointed and shouted orders and the crew scrambled to follow them. I stood almost motionless through microphone testing and last-minute makeup applications on Nan's face and that of one of the young female artists.

Out of nowhere it seemed, three rows of folding chairs appeared in front of the worktable that held the mural panel. Young people with paint-decorated clothing sauntered in and took seats. I wondered why Mary Lou hadn't gotten a notice about the taping until I realized these were probably the muralists only. One man with a gray beard stood out—Ed Villard sat on an end seat at the front.

When Stephanie was free of logistics duty, she motioned to me to come out of the shadows and join her in the back row. "This is supposed to feature a—quote—representative muralist," she whispered, "who just happens to be Nan's daughter, Diana." She pointed to the young woman wearing a paper collar, her face and eyes receiving attention from a makeup person.

A special monitor had been set up and placed far above the floor so we could all see what the cameras were picking up. Now and then the audience was panned (not as far back as Stephanie and me, I was happy to see), but most of the airtime went to Nan Browne's interview of Diana Browne.

It went in part, like this:

"How does it feel to be part of a citywide event?" (Really neat.)

"Did you do any research to get in the spirit of the painting?" (I watched *Cold Mountain*.)

"Where do you see your career going after this?" (This is, like, such a great opportunity.)

"Do you have any advice for young artists?" (Yeah, work hard and, you know, stick with it.)

Except for the shared name and identical blond hues, a viewer would have no clue of the nepotism at work at Channel 29.

After five minutes, on the third or fourth question, Ed Villard lumbered up out of his chair, making a great deal of noise as he pushed it back. He exited right, muttering. I expected he'd be edited out of the final version of the show.

The taping was over in twenty minutes, which included one or two close-ups of Diana's mural panel and another of herself, her blond hair flipped out accordingly. The equipment was collected, folded, or wrapped up as appropriate and put into large carrying cases with great efficiency.

As soon as Stephanie left me to help with the chairs and to chat with the handsome young producer, I zipped to the back of the hall, near the door. I took a notepad and pen from my purse and positioned myself to intercept Nan.

"What an informative interview," I said. (Was that schmoozing?) "But I'm surprised you didn't mention how one of the artists was murdered right in your studio. Wouldn't that be big news for your audience?"

Nan looked at me as if I were a piece of lint that had fallen on her immaculate brown twill jacket. It took her a minute to recognize me as the interloper of this morning.

"You again," she said. Then her face brightened as she noticed my notepad. "Are you a reporter? You should have said so. I thought you were just curious."

"About the murder?" I asked, my pen at the ready.

"Today's taping is not for our news program, which is very limited, as you know. We stress features over current news since it's so difficult to compete with the Internet or even a daily newspaper."

"I see" was all I needed to say to get her to keep talking.

"What you saw today is for a documentary feature on this year's Lincoln-Douglas debate from the point of view of public art. Our purpose is to highlight the talented men and women who have come together to serve the community in a special way."

"Was the murder victim, artist Brad Goodman, one of the people you highlighted earlier for the documentary?"

"Mr. Goodman was a very talented artist who wasn't shy about sharing his skills." I made a note: *Nan thinks Brad pushy?* "Of course our hearts go out to his family and loved ones."

"Did you know the victim well?" I asked, reporter style.

"Not at all. I only know of him now because of his unfortunate demise."

"Were you able to help the police at all when they came to the crime scene at your studio?"

Nan frowned, but her desire for good press seemed to win out. "We're doing everything we can to maintain and improve security at the facility. That's all for now." She pulled a card from a pocket on the outside of her briefcase. "Here's my card. Please feel free to call me if you need anything else."

I knew it wouldn't be too long before Nan Browne found out I wasn't a reporter. I wondered how quickly I could acquire press credentials.

From Stephanie's big smile as she went about her cleanup business, I sensed that her flirting worked.

"I got a date," I heard her tell a muralist.

So did I, in a way.

Chapter 9

The Lincoln Point jail was in the basement of the police department building, at the east end of the civic center complex. I'd been to the facility only once before today and didn't look forward to this visit any more than I had the last one.

To prepare for the dank, clammy hallways under the old building, I treated myself to a double latte and a brownie at the coffee shop on the corner of Hanks and Springfield, across the street from the Rutledge Center. It was ten o'clock, legitimate break time for a working woman.

The day was perfect for walking. If I were ambitious, I'd have walked the mile or so down Springfield Boulevard to the jail. But fortunately today, as nearly every other day, I had an excuse not to. This morning it was my shoes, dressy flats that were a little uncomfortable around the instep. Another time it would be a tight deadline or a case of the sniffles. Anything could keep me from exercise.

Quite the opposite with my hobby. Very seldom did anything keep me from working on a miniature scene or a dollhouse project. I once got up from a sickbed in the middle of the night to glue a tiny lamp onto a desk. I'd awakened with the fear that a breeze from the open window would blow it away and I'd never find it.

I retrieved my car from the television studio side of the complex and now I drove down Springfield toward the civic center, another complex of buildings, but far different from the Rutledge Center complex. This one comprised stately white buildings that had "government" written all over them. As I approached the set of buildings, one of which was the police department, it was hard to ignore Skip's voice in my head. It seemed strange to be this close to his office and not stop in, but I didn't want him to discourage me from visiting Zoe.

An unusually large number of men milled around city hall, the building in the center of the complex. Tryouts for the roles of Lincoln and Douglas, I guessed. The tradition every year was to try to keep the winners a secret from all but the actors themselves. Thus, when the actors entered the stage on the night of the performance, the oohs and aahs of the audience would be all the more passionate and genuine expressions of excitement.

Mingled with the actors-to-be were a few more informal entertainers, many of whom were fixtures in town. One old man had been fiddling at the northwest corner of the city hall lot for years, his battered instrument case at his feet, ready for donations. An older woman, supposedly an artist at one time, worked her talent in chalk on the sidewalk, drawing nature scenes of rivers, mountains, flowers, and trees. Every evening the maintenance crew would wash down her masterpiece, and the next day she'd be there again, with her scraps of colored chalk.

I looked for Ryan Colson in the crowd as I made my way slowly around the circle, but all the short Stephen Douglas candidates were overpowered by the tall would-be Abraham Lincolns. I'd wanted to ask my nagging question, but not in the presence of Stephanie or Ed: was Ryan on duty the night Zoe did her damage? Had he seen her in person as opposed to on video? I hoped the opportunity would present itself before too long.

I parked facing away from the buildings and entered the police station by a door that led directly from the street level to the basement. Maddie wouldn't have let me do this—she loved climbing the majestic front steps up to the office level. One more reason I was glad she was in school right now. The police station, the oldest building in town, dated back to days when public buildings were models of architecture and design. Most of us laypeople loved the structure, but my architect husband had called it Neo-Renaissance, which to him meant "nothing special."

"It's not Greek and it's not Roman," Ken would say. "It's Lincoln Point."

His profession was the one area in which he could be a snob.

On the downside of "old and classic" was the fact that the building was falling apart and nowhere was that more apparent than in the basement.

I looked past the peeling paint and littered corners in the lower foyer (Ken would have called it a mudroom) and was relieved and delighted to see a friendly face. Drew Blackstone, a student of mine in the nineties, was on duty.

"Hey, Mrs. Porter," Drew said in the cheeriest, most non-threatening voice I'd heard all day. A large man, he lumbered up from a chair behind a desk that was as battered as the walls, the floor, and the ceiling of his workstation. I admired that he could be so jovial in these surroundings. This couldn't have been a plum assignment and I hoped it was rotated through the department.

"Nice to see you, Drew," I said, thinking what a lucky break that I wouldn't need to go through a tortuous ID procedure and a long story about why I wanted to visit a prisoner. The bad news was that he might mention the occasion to Skip.

"What brings you down to these depths? Doing penance?" Drew threw his head back and laughed. "Remember when you taught us parts of *The Divine Comedy*? Well, I think this is, like, a circle of hell."

"I'm so glad you remember."

"I remember a lot from your class. I was thinking of you the other night when I was reading to my kid. You know you always told us to start early when we were parents and all. And little Davey, he loves books."

It was always gratifying to hear that I'd influenced my students for the good, though I knew there were just as many whose memories of Mrs. Porter were not so positive.

I felt I owed Drew another few minutes of chat and inquired after his wife, also a former student (sadly, Amy lost her mother last month). We covered the weather (we sure needed that rain yesterday), the upcoming debate reenactment (not Drew's cup of tea, thanks anyway), and the new popcorn store in town (twenty-three flavors, I was able to inform him) before I finally said, "I was wondering if I could see Zoe Howard?"

"Oh, yeah? You know her? Did you have her in class?"

"No, she's from Chicago."

"Right, no homegrown murderers in Lincoln Point, huh? Well, let me call back and see if she's finished with her facial and pedicure." My confusion must have shown. Drew followed up with, "Sorry. Jailhouse humor. We're not always, uh, sensitive."

To say the least. There was a lot of that going around. "Are there specific visiting hours?"

"Not really. But even if there were, I'd let you in anytime, Mrs. Porter. Let me call back and see what's what."

After a minute or so of phone talk that was filled with police jargon, Drew hung up. He removed his cap, scratched his head, and opened a large logbook. "I think Miss Howard still has a visitor." He ran his finger down a column of names. Was the Lincoln Point jail that busy, or did the logbook go back a few years? "Yup. Here it is. Visitor's still there. George came on while I was on break, so I wasn't sure."

I wondered about the protocol of asking who was visiting Zoe. Should I take further advantage of a former student who thought well of me?

No need to decide since, at that moment, the door to the hallway, where the cells and visiting rooms were located, opened and closed again with two loud clangs. Out walked a young woman in an expensive-looking suit. Zoe's lawyer I guessed. She had a sharp chin, among her other striking features. She wore her pale blond hair pulled back, and looked vaguely familiar. There weren't that many lawyers in Lincoln Point, and I spent enough time around the civic center, between the library and the police station, that I probably saw this woman among the general law enforcement population. She gave Drew a charming smile, me a disdainful look (was it my outfit?), collected her briefcase, and signed out without a word.

Drew scratched his head again. "Well, I guess Miss Howard is free now."

"How do you know that was her visitor?"

He gave me a broad smile. "Come on, Mrs. Porter. How many prisoners do you think we have back there?"

I didn't have the slightest idea and said so.

"We got one drunk who's out like a light. That's it, plus Miss Howard. There'll be more DUIs over the weekend if you want to come back and visit them."

"More jailhouse humor, Drew?"

He blushed. "You can go back. Lois will take you to Miss Howard and she'll be right there if you need her." Drew put his hand to his mouth for the next remark, as if he were sharing a secret in a crowded room. "The prisoner is a cutup, you know."

Was this corroboration of Linda's gossip (could you corroborate gossip?) or a bad pun to describe the slasher in his jail?

"Oh?" I asked.

"The cute, young Miss Howard has a temper. She gets angry, you don't know what she's going to toss at you—her shoes, her dinner plate—I was lucky I just got a pillow in my face when I told her she couldn't have her laptop."

I had second thoughts as I deposited my purse on the shelf behind Drew (student-to-teacher privilege went only so far). I was now unarmed against an apparently all-too-possible assault by the prisoner.

One quick search of my person and one metal detector later I was walking down a dark, smelly hallway, wondering why I had given up my sunny morning to visit someone who might throw her chair at me.

I heard the prisoner before I saw her. Her voice pierced the damp walls of the corridor that led to the visiting area.

The nearest I could come to the exact words being shouted was, "That was her! That was her! Why doesn't anyone believe me?" Then, "She's the one, not me. Don't let her get away." These exclamations were punctuated with sounds of crashing, banging, and grunting. Except that Officer Lois was large and armed, I'd have turned back.

Officer Lois Rosen, whose thick face belied her sweet name, put her arm across my chest, hindering me from further travel down the hallway. I didn't resist. We stood there for what seemed a life sentence until the clamor stopped.

We continued our journey and by the time my escort and I reached the small visiting room, Zoe had calmed down. I wondered if she'd had help from pharmaceuticals.

Zoe's face, paler even than TV star Nan Browne's, showed no signs of the temper tantrum that had assaulted my ears from a distance. She sat with her head in her hands at a small table. Officer Lois, who'd said nothing on our trip down the hallway, directed me to a chair opposite Zoe. She then took up a spot in a corner and folded her arms across her chest. I knew *I* would be discouraged from an outburst

in the presence of such a force, and hoped Zoe would be
also.

When she saw me, Zoe burst into tears, using the too-
long sleeves of her green prison garb to absorb them.

"June said you'd come," she wailed. She stood to reach
out to me but the long arm of Officer Lois intervened. I
could tell that Zoe wanted to throw herself into my arms, a
measure of her desperateness, since we hardly knew each
other. I wished I could accommodate her.

"I see any funny business, I'm over here quicker than
you can say 'gas chamber,'" Office Lois said.

I looked for a smile on the tall, unattractive police officer's face, but saw none. Too old to have been my student
(which was saying a lot), Lois looked like she'd come with
the building. I felt very sorry for Zoe.

Unless, of course, she really was a murderer and/or was
planning to whack me on the head as she'd done to at least
one of her students.

With Officer Lois back against the wall, Zoe took deep
breaths, her only visible struggle now adjusting the neck of
her shirt, which was several sizes too big for her. "This is
so horrible, Geraldine," she said. "I didn't do anything."

I couldn't bear to hit her immediately with "they have
you on tape doing plenty." "What do you think happened,
Zoe?"

"Someone killed Brad—I just know it was his ex-wife—
and they're blaming me because we've been fighting lately."

"Were the fights over his ex-wife?"

She nodded. "You know what? I hope they tape these visits because that woman, the one who just left here, threatened me." Zoe's voice rose with every word, causing Officer
Lois to make slow movements toward us. Zoe looked in the
corners of the room as if she were trying to spot a bug or a
camera. "If I do get out on bail, she might really kill me."

I must have heard wrong. The woman who just left? Was
that what Zoe had been shouting about as I approached?
"Your lawyer wants to kill you?" I asked, remembering the

woman with the pointy chin who had given me the cold shoulder as she signed out.

"My lawyer? No, she *claimed* to be my lawyer because she knew I'd never have agreed to see her. That last visitor was Rhonda Edgerton—she still calls herself Rhonda Goodman."

So much for my educated guess about running into a Lincoln Point lawyer whom I'd seen around the civic center. "That was Brad's ex-wife? I thought she was in Chicago?"

"Well, she's not." Zoe's voice rose a notch. "She was right here in the Lincoln Point lockup a minute ago and she threatened me outright, like, 'I'll kill you for what you did to my husband.' I'm almost scared to leave here." She buried her head in her hands for a moment, then jerked it up. "As if I could."

"Wasn't there an officer in the room at the time?"

"Yeah, but not this Amazon. And Rhonda kept a smile on her face the whole time she was whispering these threats to me. She's a real piece of work. She writes letters and leaves messages on Brad's phone saying, 'From your loving wife, Rhonda.' She calls *me* and tells me to leave her husband alone. She won't take any money from selling the house they owned in Chicago because that would be ac-knowledging the divorce and she says they're still married in the eyes of God. Brad had to get a special court paper, like some kind of a waiver for when people won't sign what they're supposed to."

"And Brad is sympathetic toward her? Is that what you fought about?"

"Uh-huh. He was sympathetic toward her, and that's why we fought."

Too easy. I used my lie-detector training (that is, my ex-perience searching the eyes of teenagers for twenty-seven years) and decided there was more to it.

I offered Zoe a much-needed tissue, then glanced over my shoulder, half expecting the one-woman SWAT team to come down on us, but Officer Lois kept a silent vigil.

It was time for a test. "June says you were with her all night."

"Uh-huh."

"If I remember correctly, you and June had some project you were doing together for work that night. Updating some software manual?"

"That's right. We were doing a software project."

I was sorry to hear this. Zoe flunked my test. I took a long breath and said good-bye to her alibi. While June had rehearsed "watching a bunch of *Sex and the City* reruns," she'd neglected to train Zoe to stick to the story. I supposed it said something that Zoe wasn't so hardened a criminal that she knew how to keep an alibi straight.

"Zoe, there are video surveillance tapes that show you in the building, destroying paintings. Didn't the police tell you that?"

She sank back in the hard metal chair. I barely heard her "yes." Then, "They're doctored. They can do anything these days." She banged on the table. I flinched, not too noticeably, I hoped. "Hey, *I* can do anything if you give me a tape and some decent software."

I didn't doubt that, but I did doubt that's what had happened here.

"Think for a minute, Zoe. I'd like to help you, but I can't if you don't tell me the truth."

I could hardly believe my ears. Where did I get the nerve to imply that I would be able to do something for her, if only she didn't lie to me? Was I a cop now? Apparently I thought so, because I then used a trick I learned from Skip, from one of his many dinner-table anecdotes about interview techniques.

"I am telling you the truth."

I stood up and straightened my coat sweater, preparing to leave. "Okay, then, I guess we don't have anything more to talk about."

Zoe looked panicked. "Wait, wait. Don't go, Geraldine." She got up, nearly tripping over the hems of her ugly green pants. Officer Lois was on her in a flash, pushed her back down onto the chair, and returned to her corner, looking confident that she'd made her point.

I hoped Zoe didn't notice the look of amazement on my face (the mark of an amateur) that my little device worked.

"Yes?" My sternest "are-you-ready-to-tell-the-truth?" yes. A yes that had taken down many a freshman at Abraham Lincoln High School.

"I was mad, okay. And I wanted to talk some sense into him. So I went to the work area but he wasn't there. I swear. Why would I cut up his paintings? Why would I kill Brad? I loved him and I wanted him back."

"Back?"

"I just felt he was slipping away from me."

"What made you think that?"

"Nothing. Just a feeling."

I doubted it, but I took my seat again. Officer Lois coughed as I reached across to take Zoe's hands. I pulled back, just in case.

"Tell me what happened that night."

"I went to the building, okay? I'd gotten yet another phone call from Rhonda that afternoon telling me to back off or she'd make sure I never stole anyone else's husband. I wanted to have it out with Brad. He needed to take a stand and tell her to stop or she never would. He wasn't answering his cell, so I drove over."

Zoe wet her lips. I wished I could at least get her a bottled water, but I was sure that wasn't allowed. Neither Drew nor Officer Lois had told me how long I'd be able to stay and I wanted to make the most of the time, so I filled in while she worked her jaw. "So you went to Rutledge Center to confront him?"

Zoe nodded. "I figured he was working late as usual and had shut off his cell. But I couldn't get in through the door to the artists' work area, so I drove around and finally saw the janitor come out the door to the TV studio. He propped the door open, so I sneaked in while he was emptying the trash."

"So you walked inside the complex from the television studio to the work area? I didn't think they were connected."

She hesitated, then went on. "Yeah, they are if you know your way around. Brad wasn't there, though. He wasn't anywhere in the center that I could see, so I left."

"You just turned around and left."

"Yeah, I swear."

"And what time was this?"

"About ten o'clock. I think."

I couldn't blame Zoe for her halting speech. Not only had she confessed to breaking and entering, but the small visiting room was suffocating. The walls seemed to oscillate, an optical illusion spawned by the lack of any decoration to break up their grayness. And Officer Lois seemed to grow fatter, until she became like a party balloon cop.

I gave Zoe a minute. I needed one myself, as I worked on the timeline and spatial relations in the artists' work area. If Zoe wandered around the area looking for Brad but didn't go near where the paintings were stacked, she wouldn't have been caught on camera at ten o'clock. "You didn't see his paintings and you didn't slash them."

"No, I swear. Sure, I was miffed, but I didn't do anything about it, Gerry. I'm not that kind of person."

There were rumors to the contrary, but I didn't mention them.

"How do you account for the video that shows you cutting up Brad's paintings?"

"I don't know. They won't even let me see it. Isn't that illegal?"

"Probably they'll let you see it once you have a lawyer."

Zoe's head was on the table by now. I didn't think it was a great idea for her to have her skin make contact with the ugly stains, but that was the least of her worries.

I put my hand on her head, Officer Lois notwithstanding. "It's okay," I said, clueless about what that meant.

She looked at me, eyes teary and pleading. "I didn't kill

him, Geraldine. I never laid eyes on him that night. And now he's gone and the last time I saw him, we fought."

I was sure it was a terrible state, to have an argument with a loved one be your last encounter. But I had an uneasy feeling about a couple of things Zoe said. I couldn't put my finger on exactly what, but I felt sure she was still holding back. On the whole, though, I did believe she wasn't a murderer.

In a way I wished I didn't believe her. Then I could tell June I'd kept my promise. I'd explain how I'd visited Zoe and that I'd be around if June wanted me to bake cookies for her friend, but that would be it. Instead, I felt compelled to help Zoe get out of this dismal place. I also felt helpless to accomplish it.

"I'm sorry I was so hard on you," I said.

"It's okay. That was nothing compared to my last visitor. Isn't there anything you can do, Geraldine?"

I can bake cookies. "Don't worry, Zoe. I'll do everything I can to keep you safe."

By the time I left the room I could see that Zoe's spirits were lifted.

Mine, on the other hand, had sunk.

I had a favor to ask Drew Blackstone to whom, I was sure, I'd given a high grade for his Dante paper.

"I was wondering if you could tell me the name of Zoe Howard's last visitor?" I asked him as he retrieved my purse from a rusty metal rack behind him.

I wasn't surprised that a head scratch preceded his answer. "Why not, Mrs. Porter? It's not a state secret or anything." Drew turned the logbook so I could read it. Maybe he thought he was keeping the letter of the law. This way, no one could accuse him of telling me out loud who the visitor was.

I read the elaborate signature: Rita E. Gold.

"Do you look at IDs of visitors?" I asked Drew.

"Yup. 'Course, not if I know them for sure, like you. Something wrong, Mrs. Porter?"

"No, just curious. I thought I recognized her from the high school, but the name is different. I guess my eyes are failing."

"I don't think you would have had her in class. The lady showed me an Arizona license. I remember because it had those pretty red mesas in the background. I wish California had something special like that, don't you?"

"I sure do." Probably Drew was thinking of something different from what I had in mind: a row of San Francisco "Painted Lady" dollhouses, representing its Victorian houses.

I came back to Rita Gold. So much for Zoe's screaming that Rhonda had visited her. I knew it wasn't impossible to get fake IDs, but why would Rhonda bother? She wasn't wanted for a crime and she had every right to visit California.

"Anything else, Mrs. Porter?"

"Not right now, Drew." I turned the book back to face him and gave him a wide smile and a nod. A verbal "thank you" would have been acknowledging that he might have broken a rule for his old teacher.

Not five minutes later, on the way to my car, I realized why the nonlawyer, Rita E. Gold, looked familiar.

I retraced my steps and walked back toward the complex of buildings. The parking lot still had many Lincolns and Douglases, headed to or away from city hall, which stood at the center of Civic Drive. As I walked back toward the police building, I heard evidence of their rehearsing.

From a would-be Stephen Douglas, under his breath: "That I am not now nor ever have been in favor of bringing about in any way the social and political equality of the white and black races." I had a new understanding of the plight of actors who had to deliver an opinion with great passion, whether they believed it or not, even if they might find that sentiment odious in their real-life personas.

A Lincoln candidate had a better deal. A tall young man passed me, seeming unaware of my presence, delivering his lines to an imaginary audience: "I believe the entire records of the world, from the date of the Declaration of Independence up to within three years ago, may be searched in vain for one single affirmation, from one single man, that the negro was not included in the Declaration of Independence."

Much better.

This time I entered the police department by the front steps and headed for Skip's cubicle, toward the back of the great room. I tried to keep Rita E. Gold's face at the front of my mind.

I could only hope that my nephew the cop would be as obliging as my former student the cop.

Chapter 10

I caught Skip in a typical pose, with his feet up on his desk, eating a thick sandwich.

"Hey, Aunt Gerry. What a surprise," he said. Before I could respond, he added, in a deeper voice, "Not."

A couple of years ago I might have been confused by this grammatical construction, but I'd gotten good at interpreting the shorthand of the next generation. "Can't a loving aunt stop by and visit her nephew with no ulterior motive?"

"Not," Skip repeated. A multipurpose word. He brought his chair forward and brushed crumbs off his lap.

I took a seat in his extra chair. "Nice weather," I said. Not that anyone could tell in the windowless cubicle.

"I figure you're here either to check up on how June and I are doing, or you want some inside info on the Goodman case so you can spring his girlfriend."

What could I say? My nephew wasn't the youngest homicide detective in Lincoln Point because he was a dullard. "Let's get to it, then, starting with how are you and June doing? I see you still have her photos on your walls."

"Walls" in this sense meant the fabric partitions between Skip's cubicle and surrounding ones. I'd seen pictures of what the interior of the building looked like when it was first built. This first floor was one great hall with a marble floor, ornate paneled walls, and rows of heavy oak furniture. The décor had been compromised by the need to accommodate a modicum of privacy for the members of today's much larger police force. With my miniaturist's eye, I imagined someone lifting the roof off the building and inserting a grid of panels like the kind that separated glasses or mugs in a packing box, except that these were orange-and-blue nappy fabric instead of white cardboard. At least, that's how I would do it, if I were constructing a model.

I noticed a new photo of June and Skip on his bulletin board, both in hiking clothes, on their recent weekend trip to Lake Tahoe. I was thankful for small favors—at least neither of them had slashed the image. Trying to live up to my protest that I was here merely for a visit, I reached over to finger a black bow tie hanging from a pushpin and gave Skip a questioning, interested look.

"From the Mary Todd Ball in December?" I asked.

"Guess I don't clean that board up as often as I should."

Since we were reviewing Skip's world, I pointed to a postcard next to the tie, with a picture of a line of hula dancers. "We can't say your mom doesn't keep in touch," I said.

"I'll bet it's Nick's idea to send these daily cards."

"What makes you say that?" I asked. From what I knew of Nick, he was very friendly and considerate, but he didn't strike me as this much of a touchy-feely kind of guy.

"He's going overboard trying to prove everything is the same as far as the family goes. He's very concerned about being seen as 'taking Beverly away from us,' as he puts it."

"Who gave him that notion?"

Skip grinned. "I might have mentioned how close we all are, especially since my dad died seventeen years ago. I

might have added how great my uncle Ken was, kind of
taking me in when I needed a dad. How neither of them
could ever be replaced. That kind of thing."

"Subtle," I said.

I wanted to ask if he'd given June or his legion of past
girlfriends the same message about our tight-knit, apparently exclusive family circle, but I filed the question away
for another time. There was also the issue of how Skip had
tried to get Nick and me together over many months before
it became obvious that Nick and Beverly had been eyeing
each other. Was I dispensable in the family, available for
"taking away"? (I knew better.)

"I'm just glad your mom is enjoying herself," I said.

"I know. She deserves it." He put his feet back up on his
desk. "Say, I have a meeting at twelve thirty. So, we could
stall with this chatter for a few more minutes, and then
you'd get no time to tell me what you really came here for.
Or you could come out with it."

"Where are all the slashed paintings?" I asked.

"In the police evidence room. Next?"

"Can I see them? Just one of them, really."

"How come you didn't ask Drew Blackstone?"

Busted. Too bad for me, the Lincoln Point Police Department was a miniature world in itself.

Skip really did have a twelve thirty meeting. He obliged
me more quickly than I thought he would, sending me
down to the evidence room with (this time) an attractive
female officer, Laura Fischer. I recognized her as one of
Maddie's fans, or one who played up to my granddaughter
when she visited, in order to impress my nephew.

Officer ("Please call me Laura, Aunt Geraldine") Fischer led me down a stairway to the basement. I worried
that we'd be walking down the odiferous hallway to the
jail, but we took the opposite direction at the bottom of the
stairs. This hallway, only slightly better smelling, dead-

ended at a half door with a wide wooden ledge. Barely visible behind the door, a uniformed officer about my age was napping on a jailhouse-style chair.

"It's a boring job," Laura whispered to me. She tapped on the ledge, and the officer sprang to action. Lucky for us he didn't reach for his weapon.

"I wasn't asleep," he said, smoothing down his white hair. He gave us a pleasant grin, as if he'd been waiting patiently through his whole shift for our visit. The evidence room stretched behind him, larger than an average furniture store, and not the crafts kind with miniature living room and bedroom sets.

Laura introduced me to Frank Ramos and we kibitzed for a few minutes, with Laura twirling her longish brown hair the whole time. If Frank weren't old enough to be her father, I'd have thought she was flirting. Their chatter was about an "important" football game, not Lincoln Point's most recent murder as I wished for, but I felt I had to allow them a holiday from shoptalk.

"Do you need something from here, Laura?" Frank asked, looking at me. I figured it wasn't often that an officer took a civilian to the ledge with a request. Did he think Laura simply wanted to introduce us? I was a little surprised that Skip hadn't called Frank with a "Geraldine Alert" using the rapid communications system that seemed to exist within the building.

"We need to see that cut-up painting from the Rutledge Center 187," she said. It didn't say much for the crime stats of our neighborhoods that I knew that code: 187 meant homicide.

"That's a pretty big item, you know." Officer Ramos opened his arms and stretched them as far as they would reach. "You're not signing it out, are you?"

Laura shook her head. "No, no, we're"—she looked at me—"what are we doing with it, Geraldine?"

"I just need to look at it," I said. I reached into my purse and pulled out a notepad and pen, hoping to look less like a

Lincoln Point busybody. Taking on the persona of a reporter had worked with Nan Browne; maybe it would make
a difference here. I had to walk a thin line, however, lest I
act like the unwelcome kind of media representative. The
dollhouse drawing on my notepad should take care of that
image problem, I mused.

The three of us walked back through the aisles of
evidence. The vast room was laid out like a neat garage
with non-matching storage boxes. A variety of racks, some
wooden, some metal, held cardboard cartons, plastic containers, and paper bags, many with neon-orange labels.
The area was very cold, but still I held my breath, lest I
breathe in something not quite dead. I shuddered to think
what that might be. I tried not to study the packages and labels too closely. Did one of them say RACCOON, CHINN
RESIDENCE? I turned off the image in my mind.

We reached the back of the room, where oversize pieces
littered the area. I counted no fewer than six mattresses,
four dismembered straight-back chairs, and assorted lamps
and unidentifiable, but clearly broken, large objects.

Against the back wall was part of a sink, leaning on one
of its pipes. Officer Ramos responded to my strange look.
"That was a case where there was trace evidence in the
sink." He leaned over and pointed to a brown stain on the
porcelain. (I didn't get as close as he did.) "We couldn't get
a good wet sample for analysis, so we just took the sink."

"The things you miss when your home has never been a
crime scene, huh?" Laura said.

Brad Goodman's painting, with several others the police thought exhibited Zoe's handiwork, was just beyond
the sink. I stopped a few feet away, already zeroing in on
something familiar about the oil. Having seen her only
once, I still had no trouble identifying the woman in the
painting. The deep gashes that sliced across her face, neck,
and bare shoulders couldn't hide the features, so well drawn
and articulated. The woman was not any soft, sedate Harriet Lane I'd ever seen, but a sharply defined, flirtatious Rita

E. Gold. It couldn't be a coincidence. Even the initials fit: Rhonda Edgerton Goodman. It made sense that when she changed her name, she'd keep the same initials.

Harriet was Rita, who was most likely Rhonda.

Consciously or not, Brad had produced a flattering painting of his ex-wife and planned to display it to the town of Lincoln Point.

What kind of boyfriend (hadn't June said they were "in love"?) was Brad Goodman that he'd keep the image of his ex-wife alive in his paintings? Whether the resemblance was deliberate or not, this would have made it clear to Zoe that he wasn't "over" Rhonda by any standards.

It seemed to me that if Zoe had seen this, she might have reacted more strongly than being "miffed" as she'd called it. The slashed face and upper body of Harriet Lane looked like more than a random act of vandalism. Without a great leap, it could be interpreted as a message to her boyfriend that Zoe recognized the face he'd painted. Once started, she might have continued slashing what she thought were others of his paintings. And maybe the ripped-up paintings were only the beginning of the message.

I didn't like being misled. First by Zoe's false alibi, and now by a possible motive for her destroying this painting in particular.

The one thing Zoe didn't lie about, apparently, was that her visitor, Arizona license notwithstanding, had been Rhonda Goodman.

In deference to the signs in the basement of the police building, I'd had my cell phone off. I sat in Willie's now at nearly one thirty, well past my lunchtime, and turned the phone on. Four new messages. I knew the first two would be from Richard and Mary Lou, reminding me to pick up Maddie. As if I could forget.

I smiled as I heard each parent in turn pretend to have called me for another reason and then end with "Maddie will be so glad to see you this afternoon at three" (Mary Lou) and "Tell Maddie I love her when you pick her up at three" (Richard).

The next two calls were from crafter friends. First, Susie, our southern belle, confirming that our Friday-night meeting was cancelled because of the Lincoln-Douglas deadline. We'd each chosen to make different scenes to be raffled off and worked on them together in the initial idea stages. But now it was a matter of final placement and serious gluing, a phase we preferred to work on alone.

"I figured out how to make a working mini television set," she said.

That was good news. I'd call her back before our next crafts meeting and get the scoop. I allowed myself a reprieve from deadly motives and deceitful suspects and took a mental trip back to the last miniature show I'd been to with Susie in nearby San Jose.

We'd been fascinated by a large room box with a video. Lighted rooms were a common sight and I had my share of them around the house, but I'd never seen a movie in miniature. The crafter had built a futuristic art deco setup (if that wasn't an oxymoron) with black furniture and chrome and brass ornamentation. The floor beneath the coffee table was disco-lighted and against the back wall was a "working" television screen.

Not that I was a fan of elaborate television sets or anything high tech. I remembered the days when you could plug in one piece of equipment, like a record player, and be set to go. Now it seemed to take more and more separate components to hear a single song, and it was increasingly difficult to hide all the parts of the system in my attractive walnut cabinet. But the sheer creativity and craftsmanship of this miniature room box had impressed both Susie and me. We weren't sure how the crafter had done it and Susie had volunteered to research it and help anyone in the group who wanted to try it. I wanted to put an old (working!) black-and-white television set in my Bronx apartment model.

The fourth and last call was from Karen Striker, our crafts club president (it was her turn to serve), excited about an invitation to do a demonstration for some organization or other on Friday afternoon.

I called her back, knowing she'd need an answer as soon as possible. "It's really short notice," I said. "I haven't finished my Lincoln-Douglas box for Tuesday."

"I know it's an impossible deadline, but it seemed like a good opportunity, so I thought I'd ask."

I was usually very cooperative when it came to teaching crafts classes and sharing techniques with anyone who'd listen. But I couldn't imagine fitting in another project in the next twenty-four hours. When Lourdes delivered my toasted poppy seed bagel, I remembered yet another commitment—that I'd promised her an extra session soon to help her with an essay.

"It's a really busy time, Karen."

"Yeah, that's what everyone else is saying, too. I've already tried Mabel, Betty, and Gail. I guess it's really about the murder this week, and I can't say I blame you all. I'd do it myself, although Don says I should stay away from there until they're sure they have the killer. But anyway, I'm going out of town in the morning for the long weekend, so I can't make it."

Karen wasn't making much sense. "Are you talking about the murder of the young artist, Brad Goodman?" I asked.

"Uh-huh. It's awful, isn't it? Of course, I didn't know him, but it's scary when something like that happens, and right there in our own local television studio. I can see why no one wants to do a show there very soon. I guess I'll have to call the Channel 29 lady back and tell her we can't accommodate her."

"The Channel 29 lady?"

"Yeah, Nan Browne, you know, at the TV station at Rutledge Center. She's the one who called at the eleventh hour to ask me for a crafter for tomorrow."

A chance to visit the crime scene, the studio I'd been

ushered out of so recently had fallen into my lap. "You know, Karen, I just realized I *can* rearrange some things. Tell Ms. Browne I'd be happy to do it."

"You sure?"

"Quite."

"Well, okay, then. I'll call and tell her, and let you take it from there. I'm happy to be out of the loop."

"No problem," I told Karen.

"Thanks, Gerry. You're a lifesaver."

I hoped so.

Karen had explained the setup. The program for Friday at one o'clock was to have been a live musical segment by the local violin teacher and she'd had to cancel. Channel 29 needed a fifteen-minute "educational" slot filled. I wondered if Karen knew what had changed my mind. From her enumeration of our friends' rejections, it seemed most people knew the studio had been a crime scene. If so, it was by word of mouth. I doubted Brad's murder had been given much coverage in the major San Jose newspapers, and the *Lincolnite,* our local weekly, had switched to Friday publication. For those of us who didn't use the Internet in our daily lives, that meant a lag in our awareness of current events.

Karen suggested I do a demonstration of crafting a simple item or two. Again, no problem. I had a number of things I could create using materials I had at home. In fact, I could make several items on the spot with the loose supplies in my purse. I took out a notebook and listed a few possibilities. An evening purse with a chain strap (from a broken necklace). A soda fountain chair (with a bottle cap for the seat and thick wire for its twisted legs). A quilt or an article of clothing (from fabric scraps).

Whenever I engaged in such brainstorming, the last idea was usually the most complex and telling. This time I pictured a miniature crime scene—a toppled table, scattered

books, a spilled wineglass, a broken lamp, the chalk out-
line of a victim.

How insensitive, I mused, but not without a smile. I
scratched "crime scene" off the list, and added "lady's van-
ity with perfume bottles."

A young waitress I didn't know arrived to refill my coffee mug and to ask if everything was all right. Grateful as
I was for the attention, I wished she hadn't interrupted
my concentration. I hated to leave the make-believe life of
miniatures, where the decisions were easy—one-inch-scale
or half-scale? Paint or varnish?

In the real world I was wrestling with choices with
higher stakes—tell Skip about the resemblance between
Brad Goodman's portrait of Harriet Lane and his own ex-
wife, Rhonda Edgerton, or not? I felt I'd be betraying Zoe,
and therefore June, if I did, and possibly obstructing justice
if I didn't.

I looked around the restaurant at all the New York City
photos, stalling, thinking of the good old days in the Bronx
with Ken. (Never mind how we barely scraped by while he
was in graduate school.) My gaze landed on a formal photograph of the NYPD's finest, with row after row of policemen in the uniform of days gone by. The men (only) were
lined up on the steps of New York City Hall. They all
seemed to be giving me knowing, accusing looks.

I punched in Skip's number.

"Have you had your dessert yet?" I asked him.

"No, and I had to rush my lunch, so I'm starving."

"How does eating quickly make you less full? Never
mind. I'm at Willie's. Do you want to join me?"

"Can you come down here instead? It will be quicker. I
have to be at a budget briefing at city hall in an hour and
I'm still putting the last numbers on the chart."

"Where shall I meet you?"

"There's a cafeteria in the basement of city hall. What's
this about, Aunt Gerry?"

"There's a cafeteria down there?"

"Okay, you learned that technique from me. I'll wait. The cafeteria's not exactly listed in the best of the Bay Area restaurant guide, but we can get a snack."

"I'll be right there."

I had the young waitress, "Sunny," wrap the rest of my bagel and give me three chocolate chip and three peanut butter cookies to go. If my nephew wanted a snack, it was going to be classier than the city hall cafeteria could offer.

Chapter 11

Once more I found myself among debate hopefuls in the civic center. I heard a tall would-be Abraham Lincoln.

"Now, I confess myself as belonging to that class in the country who contemplate slavery as a moral, social, and political evil, having due regard . . . having due regard . . . due regard"—he snapped his fingers—"darn."

Oops, more work needed. A short Douglas candidate, who needed one arm to hold up his padded belly, did better.

"Does Mr. Lincoln wish to push these things to the point of personal difficulties here? I commenced this contest by treating him courteously and kindly . . . Mrs. Porter?"

Old as I was, I hadn't been at Galesburg, Illinois, that rainy October day in 1858. I turned and saw Ryan Colson, dressed in a tuxedo made of soft black fabric. He was probably the same height as Douglas, but not as broad-chested as Douglas appeared in photographs, and clearly needed help keeping his fake paunch in place.

"Are you trying out, too?" he asked, finally letting a small pillow fall free from under his cummerbund.

I laughed at the sight and at the thought of my taking the stage anytime soon. "Hardly."

"You know, there are a few women applying. Really. My wife gave it some thought and almost signed up for an audition. She'd have been stiff competition for me." He gave a wry laugh. "That's kind of her goal in life."

"Well, that's how they did it in the early days of theater. I mean, not husbands and wives competing, but men and women playing opposite gender roles."

"You don't say?"

Ryan's inattention to his high school Shakespeare class was showing. "Of course, it was mostly men playing all the roles, male and female."

"Wouldn't you know. Well, I do believe an actor is an actor and good actors can play either gender." Ryan straightened his silky black cummerbund and patted his now flat stomach. He tucked the pillow under his arm. "I don't even need this prop. Stephen Douglas was much less fit than I am, but that doesn't mean I can't take on his persona."

"I'm sure that's true."

"By the way, have there been any breakthroughs in that murder investigation? I know your granddaughter's first cousin once-removed"—he laughed at his wit—"is a homicide detective."

The question sounded strange coming from a man in faux nineteenth-century formal wear, an antique watch hanging from his vest pocket. Ryan had put his hand inside his jacket, Napoleon style, and I thought I detected a wig with graying sideburns. Apparently some props were needed even for accomplished actors.

"I'm not privy to the inner workings of LPPD, I'm afraid. But I'm sure they're doing all they can."

"Yeah, I'm still a little on edge, you know. I mean, I could have been in the studio when Goodman bought it. I mean, when the poor guy, you know . . ."

At last. "Were you working that night?"

"I, uh . . ." Ryan seemed caught off guard by what should have been a simple question.

I felt an arm around my shoulder. "Hey, Aunt Gerry."

Of all the times for my nephew to interrupt a conversation. "Skip. You probably know Ryan. He was about to tell me—"

But it was the moment Ryan needed. He all but sang out, "Gotta go," and headed for the steps to the city hall, top hat and pillow in hand.

"I changed my mind about the cafeteria," Skip said. "It can be disgusting this late in the day when all they have is leftovers. The place reeks of mustard and old French fries."

Though he wasn't aware of it, I forgave him for coming between me and another piece of the crime-scene puzzle. "I brought Willie's cookies," I said, holding up the bag.

"Better than anything they'd ever have in the cafeteria. Let's take a seat on one of the benches out here. You won't be too cold, will you?"

I assured him I wouldn't be uncomfortable, sparing him my speech about how when you've lived through more than twenty Bronx winters, nothing in Lincoln Point, California, could compare.

Skip pulled a chocolate chip cookie out of the bag and bit into it.

"Let's have it. You visited Zoe, you went to the evidence room. Now what? You want a badge?" His words sounded less harsh through a mouthful of chocolate chips.

"I . . . uh . . . figured something out. You may already know this, but I had to tell you."

I described my visit to Zoe, giving him the gist of our conversation, and then the painting, ostensibly of Harriet Lane, but really of Rhonda Edgerton Goodman. I told him how Rhonda, aka Rita, had brushed by me in front of Drew Blackstone's station in the jail.

"Interesting," Skip said, pulling the word from column A: words to use while thinking things through. It was a signal to those who knew him well that what you'd told him was new to him, an idea or fact he hadn't heard before.

I prodded. "I guess that makes Zoe look worse?"

"Did Zoe know Rhonda before today?"

"I imagine so. She told me Rhonda was the visitor just before me and that Rhonda threatened her life."

"And you saw Rhonda Edgerton today?"

Was he missing my point? "Yes. This morning. In the jail. She signed in as Rita E. Gold, but I'm nearly one hundred percent sure it was Rhonda."

"Do you happen to know where she's staying?"

"No, I—"

"Okay, then."

I knew better than to ask, "Okay what?" I took another tack. "Is the department convinced Zoe is guilty, by the way?"

Skip looked at me. "These cookies are great"—he started on his second, this time peanut butter—"I guess they're worth telling you at least as much as we'll be releasing to the press."

"Thanks a lot."

"We're not positive." He turned serious. "We never are, you know, no matter what we tell you. It's not that (a) Zoe gave a credible confession, or (b) that a reliable witness saw her do it."

"What about the security tape?"

"It shows her back in the work area. And in fact, that's just what it shows, her *back* is on the video. And Brad's body was found in the television studio, not the work area. So . . ."

The television studio, where I was going to be tomorrow afternoon. No need to bother my busy nephew with that boring detail.

"And the knife?"

"The one in the studio next to the body? There's a problem getting an exact match between that knife and the wound."

"What kind of problem?"

"A statistical problem. We like a higher probability than they're able to give us, but the lab is working on it. By the way, do you know that your friend Zoe still denies that she slashed the paintings?"

"My friend?"

"Last I heard she's saying it was all some kind of conspiracy. Like someone dressed up as her and did it."

"Could that have happened?"

"Only if the person has the same overall appearance and wears the same very unique jacket."

"Is 'very unique' more unique than 'unique'?" I asked.

"Huh? Oh, is this one of those distraction-by-grammar techniques?"

"Sorry. What about the jacket?"

"It's black leather with a big Z in rhinestones on the back. Pretty unique . . . I mean, unique."

It wasn't looking good for Zoe. I wished I'd known about the jacket before I visited Zoe. As it was, I gave Skip even more reason to think her guilty.

I thought of my promise to June. Some help I'd been.

As if he'd tuned into her name in my mind, Skip said, "June wants to break up. I talked her into waiting a few days at least, when things are more calm."

"You saw her?"

He smiled and shook his head. "TM."

"I beg your pardon?"

"Text messaging. By cell phone. That's how we do it these days. My buddy, Randy, proposed to his girlfriend by TM."

"How romantic. But let me tell you what I think—June is not going to be calm until her friend is out of jail and you apologize for arresting her."

Skip's breath came out in a low whistle. "Like that's going to happen."

I thought about what Beverly and I had talked about

often, through all of Skip's busy dating life. Neither of us
had ever asked him, however. Now seemed the time.

"Do you love her, Skip?"

"I do. It's the first time I've felt this way. Well, except
for when I was nine."

"Mrs. Johnson."

We both laughed at the memory of Skip's crush on his
history teacher.

"I keep thinking if I solve this case and it turns out that
Zoe is innocent, June will be happy with me. But that can't
be the basis of our relationship."

"No, it can't."

"Do you think you can talk to her?"

Considering that his mother was three thousand miles
away, I owed my nephew a surrogate. "I can try."

"That's all I'm asking."

A passing stray cat reminded me of a loose end. "Have
you heard anything about the knife? I mean the raccoon
murder weapon?"

"Nothing yet. Things don't happen as fast as they do on
television cop shows, you know. The other day I took a box
of evidence on another case to the lab and they looked at
me as if I was crazy. 'No way can we go through all that,'
the main tech told me. 'You're going to have to choose
what you want most.' Can you imagine? I have to pick and
choose among pieces of evidence they'll analyze. That's
how backed up they are."

I was sorry I'd reminded him of his favorite and very
important issue—the sorry state of real crime laboratories,
with understaffing and underfunding. "I didn't think—"

Skip looked at his watch and jumped up. "Oops, I better
get to my next meeting. It's ten to three."

My heart skipped. Ten to three? Not possible. I checked
my watch. Ten to three. I checked the tower clock behind
us. The enormous Roman numerals showed the same, or
close enough. Ten to three.

I'd forgotten to pick up Maddie.

* * *

At three o'clock, when I should have been sitting in my car across from Maddie's school, I was stuck in traffic on the Bayshore Freeway.

I had the school telephone number in my purse. I hadn't wanted to take the time to dig out my little phone book before jumping into my car and heading north. Now crawling along 101, I felt it was safe enough to look up the number and call on my cell phone. Their answering machine kicked in. "You have reached the Angelican Hills school. Our office hours . . ." I clicked off.

I couldn't believe the time had gotten away from me like this. How could I have forgotten about Maddie? It served me right for laughing at her parents' constant reminders. I wasn't laughing now. The thought of Maddie, stranded, made me sick with worry. I hoped the school would take care of her until I got there. I was dismayed that I didn't know the school policy on children who were abandoned.

Here was a vote for getting Maddie her own cell phone. She'd joked about it the last time she asked her parents for one. "What if you forget to pick me up?" she'd argued.

I called the school again and I heard, "You have reached . . ."

I groaned. My poor granddaughter . . .

When a black SUV cut me off for the second time, I leaned on my horn. Didn't he and everyone else know that my granddaughter was standing out in the cold, waiting for me? I should have had a police escort, not people getting in my way. I imagined predators lying in wait for the last child on the sidewalk. Every child abduction case that I'd read about or seen on television flashed before me. I recalled reading a novel where a teenage girl was hauled away in a van while waiting outside school for a delinquent parent. I blocked those images, swung around, and cut off a green minivan.

I growled when I realized I missed the traffic report on the radio. Maybe I should take an earlier exit and wind through the streets? I dialed the school again and hung up again when I got the recorded message.

I checked the clock on my dashboard. Three twenty and I was at least three exits away, traveling in fifteen-mile-an-hour spurts. I gripped the steering wheel as if it were about to fly off, then banged it, a better release than banging my head.

When the calming tones of "As Time Goes By" rang on the seat next to me, I thought it was the radio. I hadn't had this new cell phone tune very long and wasn't used to it. Add to that my frantic state and it's a wonder I recovered in time to take the call.

I clicked the phone on. In the few seconds it took me to say a weak "hello," I imagined a call from a Palo Alto emergency room, a call from the police, and a call from monsters who were holding my precious Maddie for ransom.

"Grandma? Where are you?" Maddie. Annoyed, but not hysterical or wounded, was my quick judgment.

I allowed myself a breath. "Are you okay, sweetheart? Are you at school? Is someone with you?" Someone responsible, I meant.

"Yeah, I'm in the counselor's office." My heart slowed, but it was still a long way from a normal rate. "This is where they take kids who don't have cell phones when their parents are late picking them up."

I laughed in spite of the situation. I was glad to see she wasn't so overwrought that she was off her stride.

"I'll be there in a few minutes, sweetheart. I'm stuck in traffic, but I'm getting close to your exit. I'm so sorry, Maddie."

"Were you investigating? Is that why you're late?"

Investigating (in all its inflections), case, solve—these had become my granddaughter's favorite words of late.

"I think there must have been an accident on 101."

"You got all caught up in helping June's friend get out of jail and forgot me, huh?"

"What do you know about that?"

"I know June's upset because Uncle Skip put her friend in jail, and now you're snooping around."

"Can you stay in the school until I get there?"

"Yeah, I'll be in here with all the other kids—"

"Who don't have cell phones. I get it."

"So can I have one?"

She had to know I'd have agreed to deliver the moon to her at that point. "We can bring it up again to your parents."

The traffic was loosening up ahead. I made my move to the right lane. I hated doing it one-handed, but the speedometer was creeping up to only twenty-five, so I didn't feel unsafe. And just about every other driver I could see had a cell phone to his ear, so we'd all be punching for help at once if we did bump into each other.

"And you'll take my side?"

I smiled and grew envious of the energy of an eleven-year-old negotiator. "We'll talk about it when I see you. I'm exiting now."

I hung up and took the longest breath of the day.

Chapter 12

Maddie was standing in the school driveway with three other cell-phone-deprived children and one adult, or near adult, in her midtwenties, I guessed. Maddie gave me her wild, two-handed wave with her long, skinny arms and bounded down to the curb. I'd never been so happy to see her. "It's my grandma," she called back to the adult.

She threw her backpack onto the backseat and jumped into the front passenger seat. Still taking advantage of the situation, I saw. At the edge of the requirements for backseat safety, Maddie had decided today was a good day to cross over the line. Maybe she thought her survival of being stood up earned her the right. In any case, this was her day to get all she could from the system that was keeping her behind.

I let her stay up front. I straightened the hood of her sweatshirt behind her neck so she'd be more comfortable and patted her head. She really was safe in my car.

"How was your day?" I asked, relieved that a boring, half hour wait was likely the most dramatic thing that had happened to her.

She shrugged her shoulders. I had to say, it was easier to communicate with Maddie sitting up front than trying to manipulate the rearview mirror to catch her expressions. "Okay."

"You get off early tomorrow, right?" This Friday preceded a long weekend and the school districts added an extra afternoon.

"Yeah. Are you going to pick me up on time?"

"I promise."

It wasn't like Maddie to be grouchy. I knew part of the reason was that she felt very isolated here at her new school. I wanted to ask if she was close to making a friend, but I didn't want to nag. Maddie had entered Angelican Hills school in Palo Alto in January, halfway through sixth grade, the highest grade in the school. Groups and bonds had been forming for more than five years without her. When we'd all talked about this before the move, we figured Maddie would be fine for half a year. Then, in September, she'd enter junior high where many grammar schools came together and she'd be starting fresh like everyone else. No one had anticipated that this half year would be so tough on her.

"Did you pass in your science report?"

"Yeah, yeah."

"When is the science fair? I'd like to come even though I can't be a judge. You already know so much more science than I do."

"It's okay. They have plenty of judges. Can we go for ice cream instead of popcorn like we planned?"

"Of course."

"Then what?"

"What do you mean?"

"Can we investigate? Maybe I can figure out why someone killed that artist."

I could almost taste my desire to know how much Maddie had absorbed of the details surrounding Brad Goodman's murder. We'd all tiptoed around the situation, straining our inventory of euphemisms, but short of standing over her shoulder twenty-four/seven, we had no control over what she could find out online.

"How come you're so interested in him?" I asked her.

"I'm getting a head start for when I become a police-woman."

I snuck a look at her. A wide grin told me she was kidding.

Sort of.

We were both so full of Sadie's enormous sundaes, we plopped on the living room chairs, shed our outer layers of clothing, and laughed at our overindulgence.

"I really didn't need that extra whipped cream," I said.

"I did," Maddie said, rubbing her stomach and giggling.

She didn't giggle nearly enough these days. If all it took was fifty cents extra at Sadie's, I was happy.

Beverly's daily postcards also brought smiles. Today Maddie got her own card, with a map of the islands. "Save this for a geography project," was the message. My card had a close-up of the official patch of the Maui Police Department, with three amorphous shapes that probably represented the islands of Maui County. The message: "Nick says show this patch to Skip when he catches you investigating. Ha ha."

I tucked my card away. Not a good one to leave around. It occurred to me that Beverly didn't know about Brad Goodman's murder and its repercussions through our family. Skip and I had agreed not to bother his mother and Nick while they were on this trip and I felt sure he'd kept his part of that arrangement also.

As for me, I missed talking everything over with Beverly, who was clearheaded and logical. If she were with me now, what would I ask her? I mused. What made a good motive for murder? would be one question I'd have liked to toss around with her. We all knew that betrayal in love was high on the list. But I had no right to assume that only Zoe and Rhonda fit this profile. Brad might have had a liaison with someone else. Stephanie? Even Ryan was a possibility. What about advancement in a career as a motive? I asked myself, in lieu of Beverly. That would apply to any of the artists who moved up a notch when Brad Goodman was out of the picture.

I hoped Beverly was lying on the beach on one of the Hawaiian Islands. It would be a shame if no one in the family was able to relax at this moment.

Maddie and I had planned to work on the Lincoln-Douglas set, which badly needed some color, in the form of mini posters, flags, and balloons. But I had only a few hours to get a demonstration ready for Channel 29, so that had to take precedence. At Sadie's, I'd told Maddie about the project while we both struggled to scrape every sticky glob of chocolate sauce from our dishes.

I'd decided on a project that was apropos of the season: a top hat and cane. Maddie liked the idea and seemed eager to help. We changed into old sweats—mine had enough paint on them to redecorate a standard dollhouse—and went to the currently unused fourth bedroom, the one closest to the front door.

It took a while to prepare a work space since I'd stuffed all the overflow crafts supplies into this room while my house was in its highly populated state.

"Are you going to teach me how to put the hat together, Grandma?" Maddie asked.

"Sure. Do you want me to teach you before I do it on television?"

"Well, I was thinking . . ." Deep frown lines crossed her forehead. Heavy thinking.

"What is it?"

"Have you ever been on TV before?"

"A few times, but never in the studio. The station covered

a miniatures fair once and they interviewed me at the Old Glory Hotel downtown. And another time I was on during Library Week talking about the Lincoln Point literacy program. And, oh, our book club was on talking about our novel of the month."

Maddie seemed more attentive than she normally would be when I rattled on with a longer answer than required. "I've *never* been on TV," she said. "Do they ever have kids on?"

"I don't know. I suppose they've had kids at one time or another. I don't watch that channel very often." (I hoped I wouldn't let that little fact slip out in front of Nan Browne tomorrow.)

"Well, I've *never* been on TV."

It didn't take a brick to wake me up, but close to it, before it dawned on me. "Would you like to be on TV yourself tomorrow afternoon? We could do the demonstration together."

Her eyes lit up. "Really, really?"

I'd read that public speaking was the third most dreaded thing for most people, after death and taxes. I'd never been afflicted that way since I'd loved teaching for as long as I could remember. I was glad Maddie didn't have that fear to worry about, either.

"I don't see why not. I probably should call the people in charge and be sure, however. Shall I see if it's okay with them?"

She was off the couch and rubbing her hands together, as if getting them ready for some serious work. "Yes, yes. We can rehearse and I promise to practice over and over."

I needed to call Nan anyway to confirm that I'd be our club's representative tomorrow. Club president Karen Striker had said she'd take care of that, but ordinarily I still would have called the station myself immediately. My meeting with Skip and then near miss on picking up Maddie had distracted me from doing that.

But there had been something else. I realized I was in-

timidated by Nan Browne—maybe because she'd been pre-
siding over a crime scene I was interested in. And because
once I showed up as a miniaturist, it would blow my cover
as a reporter. Apparently she'd forgotten all our previous in-
terviews. Not that I'd claimed to be a reporter, I reminded
myself. She'd assumed it and I hadn't corrected her. It was
what some groups called mental reservation (acceptable)
and others called a sin of omission (unacceptable).

To bolster my resolve, I tried instead to picture her in
the arms of an illicit lover. Not many people could make as
much of a fleeting shadow as an English teacher.

She picked up on the third ring.
"Channel 29, Nan Browne." The friendly voice of a television talk show host. After seeing the operation yesterday, I wasn't surprised that she answered her own phone.

"This is Geraldine Porter, Ms. Browne. I met you yesterday—"

"I remember. Karen told me you could do the demo, but,
you know, you don't really have to. We have some inter-
views in the can that we can run. It's just a twelve-minute
slot, by the time you add the promos."

"It's no trouble at all. I have everything ready." Or, I
would have by showtime.

"Maybe some other time. We're really all set for tomorrow."

How rude that she hadn't called to tell me. She must
have known I'd prepare for the show unless directed otherwise. Had she planned to usher me out of the studio when I
showed up with all my props?

I didn't mind so much being disrespected and bumped
as unnecessary to Channel 29's programming, but I wasn't
going to give up so easily with Maddie's pleasure at stake.
If I believed in such phenomena, I'd say I had a premoni-
tion about this possibility because I'd sent Maddie off to
find narrow black ribbon in one of my five ribbon drawers

while I called. That was an approximately ten-minute diversion out of earshot of the phone.

I felt my fingers tighten around the telephone receiver. "Ms. Browne, I have an eleven-year-old granddaughter who is extremely excited about being my assistant on this program. As we speak, she's gathering supplies and thinking about her presentation. Now, unless you want to give the next generation a very bad impression of the media, you'll let us keep our scheduled appearance in the Channel 29 lineup."

A long pause. Apparently, I had amazed Ms. Browne, not to mention myself, with that allocution. My rereading of the Lincoln-Douglas debates and its stern, pompous language, was taking its toll.

I heard a pronounced cluck, then, "Okay. But you'll have to be here by eleven for a one o'clock show."

I hadn't counted on "afternoon" meaning anything before two or three. Maddie had school until noon tomorrow. I wasn't sure it was a great idea to keep Maddie out of classes for something as frivolous as making a mini hat and cane in a television studio. I had a good sense of how her parents would vote. (Richard: no, school is more important than entertainment. Mary Lou: yes, this is all part of her education. She'll probably learn more at Channel 29 than she will sitting in class all morning.)

I didn't mind being the tiebreaker. It had been a pretty general pattern since Maddie was born. I supposed I should side with my son during one of these votes (real or imagined) but not today.

"See you at eleven," I told Ms. Browne.

"Don't wear a busy print," she said, as if she was used to seeing me in flowered housedresses.

"Thanks for the tip," I said, hoping some of the irritation I felt had seeped into my voice.

Before settling down to work, we had a few phone calls to make. Maddie had a list of people that included her best friend, Devyn, and her second best friend (her term), Melana, in Los Angeles, plus Linda's son, Jason. I hoped against hope that there were some Palo Alto youth on her list.

While she took care of her potential fans, I called Mary Lou on my cell phone to prepare her for the conversation we were sure to have at dinner (was this what lobbyists did?).

"Great," Mary Lou said. "I don't see the big deal for her to miss one morning of school before a holiday weekend. It's all part of her education. She'll probably learn more in the field anyway."

I smiled. "Richard was so smart to find and keep you."

"Huh? Oh, I get it. Don't worry about Richard, Mom. We're carpooling home today. I'll have him prepped."

"Did I ever tell you what a great mother you are?"

"All the time. But don't stop, okay? I have a feeling it's going to get a lot harder before it gets easier."

I made a few calls myself to recruit viewers for the show and got positive responses. I hoped there was a way that Nan Browne could check the statistics and see a spike in tomorrow afternoon's viewers.

From my older crafter friends, I heard, "I'll be watching," and from the younger ones, still in the workforce, "I'll TiVo it," or "I'll post to all my lists." The comments didn't all fall along expected lines, however. I was taken off guard when our oldest member, eighty-something master bead worker, Mabel Quinlan, asked, "Will it be on YouTube?"

I should have expected what I got from Skip: "There's no blood left at the scene, you know."

"I have a badge from the Maui PD," I said and hung up.

By five thirty we'd finished our calls and, thanks to multi-tasking, had gathered supplies for the hat. Maddie had finished clearing a small table in the crafts room for us to work on. The idea was to have at least one practice run before we sat down to eat.

It was Mary Lou's turn to get dinner, which meant that at least eight different boxes of food from San Francisco's Chinatown would be arriving in about an hour. Maddie would hold her nose and forego it all to eat leftover pizza.

Maddie had dug out enough black paper and fabric so that we could afford to cut out one set of pieces to make the hat at home for practice, and still have enough to be able to cut out the pattern in real time on camera tomorrow.

We made measurements to determine how big the hat should be. Maddie was certainly better at math than I'd been at her age, so she did the calculations easily, except for a haberdashery question.

"Lincoln was over six feet tall and Douglas was under five feet, so whose hat shall we make?"

"Let's just make an average-size top hat, say about eight or nine inches in real life."

Maddie moved her lips around as if she were using her mouth as a calculator. "Nine inches would be easier. Then it's just three-quarters of an inch for the main part of the hat."

"Maybe a little longer if we want to do a stovepipe hat. That's what Lincoln usually wore, and it's a little taller and floppier than a formal top hat."

"Cool."

We cut a rectangle about an inch on one side and two inches on the long side. Maddie made a cylinder by gluing the long ends of the rectangle so the diameter of the circle formed was about a half inch. We were on our way, with just the top piece, the brim, and the ribbon binding to add. Maddie completed the project while I looked on.

I wondered if she needed me at all, except to drive her to the studio.

"Where's Lincoln's real hat?" she asked.

"I'm sure he had a number of them. But the one he was

wearing when he was assassinated is in the Smithsonian, a museum in Washington, D.C."

"We should go see it sometime. The cane is going to be easy. Can we do something harder?"

"Let's time this project first. We have only ten minutes for the whole show."

"You said twelve."

"Well, twelve, but they might put extra promos on or cut us off for some breaking news." We both chuckled at that. "In any case, I think you'll be surprised at how quickly ten or even twelve minutes will go by."

And even more surprised at how the years go by. I wondered if Maddie knew why I interrupted these proceedings to give her a long hug.

Chapter 13

I'd called June at work earlier, planning to invite her to dinner. I knew she had more pressing things on her mind than Maddie's television debut, but I needed to keep her grounded. She wasn't in her office at the time. I left a message but wasn't surprised when I didn't get a call back. I enlisted Maddie to go and knock on June's door to see if she was interested in American Chinese food, but no answer there, either.

"Where has June been?" Maddie asked. "Is she mad at us?"

"What makes you think that?"

She hesitated. "She didn't thank us for cleaning up her trash."

"She may not even know we did that."

"Right, right."

"Is there something else?"

"Nuh-uh."

But I suspected there was. With Maddie there was always

the chance that she picked up much more than we would like.

Her parents' arrival with bags of food cut off further discussion for now.

Homecoming time in the evening was almost as mad a scramble as breakfast in my newly busy home. Now at six thirty, everyone was talking at once, eager to share the best and the worst of the day, carrying snacks to the bedroom so they could nosh while changing their clothes, too hungry to wait for dinner. Maddie nearly bit her lip waiting to take her turn and talk about her upcoming television appearance.

Arms and elbows bumped during our table-setting tasks. As we opened each box, another delicious aroma filled the room: jumbo shrimp, kung pao chicken, hot and sour soup, fried wonton, fried rice, pork egg foo young (for Richard only), and two vegetable dishes.

Much talk and eating later, I needed one more shrimp and jabbed my fork (Mary Lou was the only one who used chopsticks) into one of the last pink chunks. After a few bites, "As Time Goes By" sounded from the kitchen counter, where my cell phone was charging. I was glad for the excuse not to participate in the usual debate about dessert whenever Mary Lou brought home Chinese take-out.

"Why don't the Chinese eat dessert?" Maddie would always ask.

"They do eat dessert," Richard said tonight. "They have green tea ice cream; they have sponge cake with coconut icing . . ."

I smiled in her direction while I unplugged my cell and answered.

"Hey, Aunt Gerry," Skip said. "If you're home, don't say my name, okay?"

"Okay."

"It's not that I don't love my cousins, but things were simpler when you lived alone."

I put one finger in my ear to drown out the noise from

the dining room. An advantage for me was that no one cared who was on the phone right now. Maddie had commandeered the floor, talking with excited gestures, describing her hat tricks for the umpteenth time. I knew her parents were happy for anything that got her spirits up, and I heard no negative comments from Richard about missing school for entertainment.

"What would you like?" I asked Skip.

"Meet me outside."

"Now?" I whispered.

"Yeah, I'm just turning onto your street. Say you have to take out the garbage or something."

It had been a long time since I'd gotten an SOS call from Skip. The last one I could remember was when he was almost twelve, right after his father died. He'd broken his nose falling from a fence in his own backyard. He'd called me because he thought his mother would be mad at him for ruining her flowerbed and getting blood on her roses. That's when Beverly realized the depression that had set in while she was mourning her husband was taking too much of a toll on her son. She made an impressive turnaround after that.

My guess was that Skip wanted to talk about his relationship with June, and with his mother three thousand miles away in Hawaii, I was the best he had.

Maddie had been allowed to break a dinner rule and have "stuff" at the table. At the moment she was demonstrating how to roll a rectangle into a cylinder. I walked as casually as I could from the kitchen through the atrium, making it look like I was headed for one of the bathrooms. I was out the door without having to make up a story about the garbage.

Skip looked as despondent as I'd ever seen him. He was in his work clothes, except for the tie that he'd thrown onto the backseat.

"Sorry to do this to you, Aunt Gerry. Is everyone wondering why you left?"

I reminded him that Maddie was going to be on television tomorrow and explained how details of that event commanded more attention than anything I might be doing.

"Who knows when they'll miss me," I said. "I'm all yours."

"Thanks." He reached to the back floor of the car and pulled up a briefcase. "This is kind of informal, but I want you to look at some photos." He slipped a folder out of the briefcase, opened it, and handed it to me.

I squinted, then reached up and turned on the dome light, which helped a little. I looked at a set of six photographs, all of women in their late twenties or early thirties, all blondes. "A photo array? Like a lineup?"

"This is not official. We already have Drew's ID, but it never hurts to have a backup. My car's not the best environment, I know, but see what you can manage. I want you to look at these photos and tell me if you recognize any of these women."

We sat in his very plush sports car, turned to each other as much as possible with an enormous gearshift in the way. Skip drank from a large plastic soft-drink cup that had been sitting in a holder. It was a mild night; in many other parts of the country, where February still meant ice and snow, it could be called a spring evening.

I tapped the middle photograph in the top row. All the women had fairly thin faces, but this one's pointy chin was unmistakable. And she had an attitude that was apparent even in the grainy photograph. "Her," I said. "I recognize her."

"From where?"

"She was coming out of the door to the jail, walking into the foyer this morning." Was that just this morning?

"Okay, that's it. Thanks."

"What's this all about? I know this must be Rhonda Edgerton, or Goodman, as she still believes, because Zoe told me she had just left the visiting area."

"We don't always take the word of a defendant, but it's nothing you have to worry about."

"Skip, I'm missing my dinner here." Not quite true, but there was that one shrimp impaled on the end of my fork.

"You have a point." He shifted in his seat, replacing the folder in his briefcase. "The Chicago PD is looking for her, just to question her as they always would an ex, and they have no record of her taking a trip in recent history. No flights, no trains, no buses."

"Maybe she drove?"

He took a long breath. "Maybe. But also no hotels or motels, no credit card activity, and no relatives in the area."

"She must be using that alias for everything, then. Did you look up Rita Gold?" He gave me his what-do-you-think expression. I answered his nonverbal accusation. "How do I know if you had time to do that? I just told you this afternoon."

"If Rita E. Gold is indeed Rhonda—"

"Three people said she was," I reminded him.

"If Rita is Rhonda, clearly that's not the only alias she's using. But it's nothing you need to bother about, Aunt Gerry. It's under control."

"It doesn't seem so. Do I get a question, by the way?"

"Shoot."

"Did you ever question . . . excuse me, I mean, when you questioned the cameraman who found Brad's body, did you learn anything?"

"What makes you ask?"

"I just like to have my file complete."

Skip grunted. "I'll bet you do. The poor guy is on extended leave, just trying to deal with the trauma to his little girl. He wasn't much use to us as far as having seen or heard anything before he arrived."

"Thanks."

"My turn again, okay? There's something else. I didn't bring you out here just to look at a photo array."

At last, the real reason for the emergency meeting. "June?"

He nodded, slowly, as if the topic had been on his mind a long time. "I think it's my job. I don't see how I can have a normal life."

"With June or with anyone, Skip?"

"It's always going to be a problem. I'm never going to be able to guarantee that I won't be investigating one of her sorority sisters or a dear aunt, let alone that I can be home for dinner every night."

"I think June knows about the dinner part already. And you're not always going to be arresting her best friend."

"No, but it could be just a speeding ticket for someone in her book club and that might set her off."

"You don't give out speeding tickets." Why was I being so literal? I knew what he was trying to say. "Sorry to be so difficult, Skip. If you can forget about your job for a minute, do you think you want to be with June for the rest of your life?"

He started, nearly spilling his drink, then laughed. I realized the phrase was daunting for someone so young. "Do I love her? Yes. Do I want to marry her? Well . . . more than I have anyone else, if that means anything."

"Have you told her that in a way that she understands? You don't have to answer me, but answer that for yourself."

"I see what you're getting at. If she doesn't know where she stands in general, that might be why she's reacting this way. I mean, I know it's more complicated than that, with Zoe in jail and all, but I think I know what I need to tell her."

"What can I do for you, Skip?"

"Just talk to her, kind of pave the way? I'm sure she's come to you for help proving Zoe is innocent. Maybe you could just, you know, feel her out about me."

Was this sixth grade, where Tiffany would ask Courtney to find out from Derek if Josh liked her? I noticed he hadn't warned me off the case, which he usually did.

"I'll do what I can." I ruffled his red hair, just as I did often to Maddie's. If he was going to act eleven years old, I was going to have the benefit of it.

"Look who was knocking on the door when I walked by the entryway," I said. Mary Lou gave me a suspicious look, Richard waved "hey, man" to his younger cousin, and Maddie jumped up with "Uncle Skip, Uncle Skip."

Fooling two out of three—not bad for having been out of the house for ten or fifteen minutes.

Skip got himself a plate and dug deep into the boxes of food, using chopsticks. June's influence, we all knew.

Maddie was sharing research she'd done on the Channel 29 website. She read from the pages she'd printed out.

" 'Lincoln Point and the Lincoln Point Park District are proud of its community-oriented shows, including news, sports, lifestyle, and education.' Which one are we, Grandma?"

Richard cleared his throat. Mary Lou jumped in. "I'd say part lifestyle, since you're promoting a wonderful, fun hobby, and part education, because you're educating people." She turned to Richard and gave his arm a nudge. "Who knows, sweetie, this might kick-start a career for our daughter in show biz. Then we can be the wonderful, supportive parents who get thanked at the Oscars."

"Terrific," Richard said. His look said, "Spare me."

"Wow," Skip said, around a mouthful of egg foo young. "What are you going to wear? One of those glitzy designer gowns?" (Who said he wasn't a sensitive guy?)

"More likely a tie-dyed caftan and peace symbol," Richard said. He gave his wife a playful look.

"This might be something you can talk about or write about in school," Mary Lou said, swiveling back to face Maddie. "You still have show-and-tell, right?"

"We don't call it that anymore," Maddie said.

"No busy prints," I said, in case Skip's wardrobe question was for me. This cross talking was almost worse than breakfast.

"Maybe you should wear that little lavender smock you have," Mary Lou said to Maddie.

"It's way too small. And we're not painting, Mom, we're crafting. What do you think, Grandma? What are you going to wear?"

I hadn't given it much thought beyond wearing my NAME pin (and no flowered housedress). I'd been a member of the National Association of Miniature Enthusiasts since it started in the 1970s and loved its little member pin, in the shape of a house.

"I read somewhere that Lincoln used to put papers, like, his lawyer documents in his hat sometimes, because his office was so messy," Skip said, surprising me again with the breadth of his interests. "Maybe you could do that with the little hat you're making."

"What are you doing reading history?" Richard asked, dipping his napkin in water to clean a spot on the table-cloth. He'd made a mess trying to emulate Skip and Mary Lou using chopsticks for the last of the egg foo young.

"Something plain," I said, getting around to Maddie's question. "We want people to be looking at the hat and the materials, not us."

"Too bad," she said.

Uh-oh. Were we encouraging a career in entertainment? I consoled myself with the thought that, for the time being, she'd forgotten about police work.

Maddie agreed that it would be a good idea to take along the Lincoln-Douglas room box, even though it wasn't finished. It would be nice to show the television viewing audience where the top hat and cane would fit into the scene (on a folding chair that was yet to be made). We had a couple of hours in the morning to add some touches.

One positive thing about Maddie's day off from school—

I wouldn't be leaving her stranded as I did yesterday. The memory of it was enough for me to give her extended hugs throughout the morning.

I looked out the window to check for June's car. It wasn't in the driveway. Either she'd already left for work or she hadn't come home. I missed her and decided I'd make more of an effort to find her and make sure she was all right. As far as I knew, she had no knowledge of the unpleasant message left in her trash. I wasn't sure whether that was good (she didn't need anything to make her more upset) or bad (but did she need to be warned?).

Maddie had continued to ask questions about June. I knew she was worried. I wished I could keep this and all unpleasantness forever out of her world. Although that wasn't possible, I was certainly stalling as long as I could.

Maddie and I spent about an hour after Richard and Mary Lou left making tiny rally posters, some with VOTE FOR LINCOLN, others with VOTE FOR DOUGLAS, and mounting them on long toothpicks. We stuck them in the "dirt" around the stage, along with flag toothpicks that came ready-made from a party store. I wished I'd used different flowers for the vegetation around the stage. It was too late to change now, however. Miniaturists were never completely happy with their creations, but, for better or worse, there was nothing more permanent than a good glue job.

We'd come to the fun part of building a scene—we looked through countless drawers and boxes that held tiny random objects to see if we could use anything for the debate scene.

A wooden box had potential for a podium, but it would take some creative woodworking. We put that in the pile of "maybes" for weekend work. Maddie found a button that was in the shape of a saxophone.

"There must have been a welcoming band," she said. "And someone left their instrument." Maddie told me about rallies she'd attended with her mother where there was music. (Some of the gatherings were beyond her re-

membering, I knew, since Maddie had been strapped to her
mother's back.)

"We can use bells also," I said. "People at these events
used to ring them to cheer their candidate. There were also
parades and picnics on the day of the debates back then,
but we don't do that anymore."

"Too bad." I knew my granddaughter was a parade-and-
picnic kind of girl. "There was a lot of trash around at our
rallies," she said.

"We can sprinkle trash on the ground," I said.

"And water bottles."

"I don't think so."

"How about stapling flyers to the poles?"

"We'll have to check to see when staples were invented,
but I know for sure that scanners and copy machines were
not around in 1858."

"I guess we're lucky to be here now."

I hugged her. "We certainly are."

We showed up at the Channel 29 studio ten minutes
early, in our best unbusy clothes. Maddie had settled on her
brown corduroy pants and a pale yellow long-sleeved
T-shirt with no logo (hard to find in her wardrobe of sports
apparel). It had taken an emergency run of my washer and
dryer to get her ready. She allowed me the rare opportunity
to throw her sneakers in the wash, also.

I looked presentable in my dry-clean-only pants and
tweed jacket, in colors complementary to Maddie's outfit.

This time there was a sentry, a young African-American
woman, at the window between the waiting room and the
control room. Maybe they had security only when they
were expecting someone. I thought that would defeat the
purpose, but it wouldn't be the first example of poor management I'd encountered at the Rutledge Center.

"I'll tell Ms. Browne you're here," the woman said. Her
intricately braided hair was covered with tiny, colorful hair

clips, no more than half an inch long. I'd seen them in bags in the cosmetics section of the market and wondered what I could use them for in a miniature scene. Now I noticed that the part that clipped onto the woman's hair looked like the jaws of a dump truck. And some of them were yellow. Hmmm.

We waited about twenty minutes, reading year-old magazines and reviewing our shtick a few more times. When I called a halt to reiterations, saying I thought we were ready, Maddie rehearsed by herself, mouthing the words and using hand gestures to mimic the crafting of the hat.

When Nan Browne appeared, Maddie jumped off her chair, wide-eyed. I thought she was going to salute. Or bow down. As far as I knew, Maddie had never seen Nan on television, but even hearsay star power was strong, it seemed.

"Come on back," Nan said, her tone resigned.

"Good morning," I said in a cheery voice.

She leaned into me, nearly knocking me off balance. "I don't appreciate being lied to," she said to me.

"I didn't lie—"

"Misled," she said. "You deliberately misled me. Once I got back here I thought I remembered who you were and made a few calls to confirm. You're just a—"

"This is my granddaughter, Maddie," I said, bringing Maddie between us. "We're looking forward to—"

"Yes, well, hi, Manny—"

"Maddie," I said, since the real Maddie was too starstruck to care if Nan said her name correctly.

Nan sighed, but didn't repeat her greeting to Maddie. "We'll have to get set up. Let's see your stuff."

I never minded when Beverly or Richard or Skip referred to my supplies and raw materials as "stuff," but coming from the put-out Nan Browne, it sounded offensive. If it weren't for Maddie (and, yes, the potential of seeing a clue to Brad's murder in the studio), I might have walked out.

Instead I chose another way to annoy Ms. Browne.

"How's your daughter doing?" I asked. "Did your interview with her put her out front in the running to replace Brad Goodman?"

Nan gave me a look that would have melted the lens cap (if they had such things) on the studio camera. "She's doing just fine, thank you."

"I was sorry to hear she didn't get the commission for one of the debate portraits." I amazed myself at how far I was willing to push this.

"Nothing has been decided yet. Now, if you intend to go on the show this afternoon, we have prep to do," Nan said.

I took her statement, combined with her look, as part threat, part ultimatum and buttoned my lip as we entered the studio.

The same black drapes hung in folds, with an extra day or so of dust on them, and the same lights, but no fleeing male this time. I wondered if the police still drew chalk outlines to indicate the location and position of victims, or if there were now some laser light that scanned the area. I looked for a molecule of chalk. Better than that would be to uncover a clue to the identity of a killer. In the last twenty-four hours, I'd done exactly nothing to keep my promises to June (wherever she was) and to Zoe (still in jail as far as I knew).

Unless you count wondering, which I'd done a lot of. Was Ryan Colson on duty the night Brad was killed? Had the police questioned him? Why couldn't the police track Rhonda Edgerton/Goodman? She'd been in the basement of their very building yesterday morning. Zoe had a temper, but was it out of control to the point of murder? Why would June risk her own freedom by lying about Zoe's whereabouts?

The sound of Nan Browne clapping only added to the questions of the day. Had she been a kindergarten teacher? She was ready to get down to business, using two hands to show us the set. Had she also been a point model at a car show?

I was ready for business also. I saw a small table in the

corner near the door to the waiting room. I motioned to Maddie to help me move it across the room, in front of the large Channel 29 logo that would be the backdrop of our video. Maddie yanked at her end but was unable to move the table.

"Wait, this leg is caught on the curtain or something," she said. She knelt down to release the leg. "Yuck, yuck."

Uh-oh. Not another dead animal. Or worse. The phrase "dead human" came to me and my breath caught. I dropped my side of the table and nudged Maddie aside. "I'll get it," I said.

"Oh, it's just a cloth," she said, extracting a piece of black fabric before I could reach it. "But it's all sticky." She smelled it. "I think it's coffee."

I snatched the black silky fabric from her hands. Maddie was right. Coffee, not blood. I let out my breath.

I held out the black fabric and examined its shape. A cummerbund. It had been a while since I'd seen one out of the context of a man's waist. This one looked handmade and was dusty from being in a corner of the room that the janitor seemed to think off-limits for his broom.

"It's the tuxedo thing," Maddie said, spreading her hands across her own tiny waist. "Maybe it's from Abraham Lincoln when he was here on a show."

"I'll take that," said Nan Browne, who had a habit of startling me with her surprise interruptions and quick retorts. I thought she'd left the room.

What I perceived as a blush on her face fueled my imagination. I pictured a would-be Lincoln or Douglas losing parts of his tuxedo yesterday around the time I entered the studio unannounced.

"People leave things here all the time," Nan said, rolling up the cummerbund and tossing it in a wastebasket.

"Sure," I said, giving her a knowing look, more to annoy her than anything.

Nan cleared her throat, but didn't acknowledge my insinuation. She pointed to the table Maddie and I had been

about to move to center stage. "I didn't know you were going to need a table. It's an old wreck. The top is all marked
up and we don't have a cloth for it."

"We do," I said. I produced from my tote a pale blue
cloth, neatly pressed and chosen for maximum contrast with
our black top-hat fabric, but not too bright for television.

She sighed. Her face had returned to normal color; her
mood had remained the same throughout our interaction.

I had a sudden thought and a question for Nan, one that
was not as disquieting as my others. "Is it possible to go
from this studio to the work area where the artists are,
without going outside or needing a separate key?"

"No, why?"

"Just wondering. Someone recently told me that this
studio was connected to the north side artists' area and you
could walk through if you took a certain route."

Nan shook her head. "Not possible. Believe me, I wish
it were."

The blush was back on Nan's face, and another claim of
Zoe Howard moved to the "false" column.

Why would Zoe lie about how she got into the building?
If you break into a building, does it matter how? I'd have to
ask Skip.

Once Maddie's television debut went down in ratings
history, I'd have to get back to visit Lincoln Point's only
prisoner.

**With quite a bit of finger-snapping on the part of Nan
Browne**, such that I pitied the young producer and the even
younger cameraman, we all got through the segment. Nan
had flubbed the introduction on the first rehearsal ("and her
granddaughter, Marty . . ."), but the show itself proceeded
without a flaw.

I followed Maddie as she skipped and twirled out to the
waiting area when we'd finished. And nearly bumped into
our new friend, Stephanie Cameron.

"I saw you on the monitor out here," Stephanie said to Maddie. "You were terrific! Wow!"

I gave her a grateful smile. I knew the praise would mean a lot more than mine to Maddie. There was something about the approval of strangers . . .

"Don't forget to get a copy on DVD to show all your friends at school," Stephanie said.

"We can get ourselves on DVD?" Maddie asked, in a high-pitched voice reminiscent of her toddler years. "Can we get it, Grandma? Huh? Huh?"

Stephanie turned to me. "You have to pay fifteen or twenty bucks, but it's worth it."

No question.

"I'm looking for Ryan," Stephanie said to me. "Did you see him in there?"

I shook my head. "Does he work in this part of the complex, too?"

Stephanie threw her head back. "Ha! You might say that." She crossed her middle and index fingers. "He and Nan, you know?"

I didn't know. "Good friends?" I said.

Stephanie winked.

I was sure that Ryan had mentioned a wife when I met him in the civic center. Was Ryan the mysterious shadow? Did it matter?

I wondered what size cummerbund Ryan wore.

Chapter 14

On the way home, Maddie's chatter was peppered with terms like "wide shot," "zoom in," and "post- (pos-) production." She held on to the DVD as if it were a treasure. Or an audition to solicit greater exposure, I mused. I was pleased to see her so happy and hoped she'd garner a lot of mileage out of the experience to make some new friends at Angelican Hills.

My cell phone rang and Maddie answered. "Uncle Skip! We were just on TV," she said, wiggling her legs on the front seat, now her established perch. She turned to me. "He saw us. He saw us."

"Great, great," I said.

By the time Maddie finished basking in her uncle's praise and handed me the phone, Skip was ready for more important matters.

"Remember the . . . uh . . . message left in June's trash?"

"Yes, I remember." I tried to keep my voice steady, as if Maddie's Uncle Skip had asked if I remembered how to make birthday cakes.

"There's nothing to report, really, but I wanted you to know there were no fingerprints on the knife, and nothing unusual."

"Wasn't that unusual enough?" *To put raisins in a birthday cake,* in case Maddie asked.

"Have you seen June?" he asked. "I can't find her."

Now where had I heard that tone before? I wanted to ask him if he and his girlfriend were playing some sort of unfunny game of hide-and-seek, with me at the center, as "it."

"Did you call all her numbers?" I asked my homicide detective nephew, realizing too late that I made the question sound like a brilliant idea on my part.

Skip spared me the obvious, waiting a few seconds before speaking. "I thought she might have gotten in touch with you."

"Not since Wednesday at Willie's." *When you barged in on our meeting.* "Do you want me to call her? Maybe she's screening her calls and will talk only to females." My poor attempt at humor brought another pause.

"Could you? Call her?"

"Of course. I'll let you know what happens."

I hung up, not optimistic about my chances, female or not, of reaching June. Her last words to us as she roared out of Willie's came back to me. "Apparently, I have to do this on my own."

"I know where she is," I said half aloud. Maddie was plugged into her iPod and didn't hear me. Otherwise, I was sure I'd have had some explaining to do.

Saturday was booked—an all-girls day, featuring a miniatures and dollhouse show, one of the biggest of the year, in San Jose.

I had an important phone call to make before we left, however. So far, things were working in my favor. I had the advantage of the time difference between Lincoln Point, California, and Chicago, Illinois, and could make the call at seven o'clock Pacific standard time, before anyone else in my house was up.

I sat at one of my crafts tables, in the bedroom I was using while my family was here. I took a breath, rehearsed my story for the eighth time, and dialed June's parents in Chicago. I'd found their phone number last night, grateful to the gods of listed numbers, and finally thought of a way to ask if June was there without alarming them.

June's birthday was in April. My story was that, although it was early, I wanted to get started on a miniature scene I was making for her. I needed to know what her favorite toys were as a child, what her room looked like, what kind of furniture she had, and so on. I thought it was a brilliant idea.

"What a surprise," said June's mother, Emily Chinn.

"I hope I didn't wake you."

"No, not at all. How is everything there? We still remember the lovely dinner party you had for us on our last visit."

We spent a few minutes discussing how cold Chicago was at this time of year and how next winter Emily and her husband were going to plan a trip to California for February. If only they could predict when the worst of the snow would be.

I was about to launch into my birthday present fable when Emily said, "Oh, you probably called for June."

"Uh . . ." I wasn't prepared for an easy time of it.

"She's still in bed. We were so delighted to see her. I guess she just needed a break from all the stress at work."

"Yes, she's been under a lot of strain. It's nice that you're there for her."

As a base of operations, I wanted to say. For finding Rhonda Edgerton Goodman, was my guess. I wasn't surprised that June hadn't been completely open with her parents. I wondered if they even knew about Zoe's predicament.

"Shall I wake her up?" Emily asked. "Is it something urgent?"

"No, no, just a neighbor-to-neighbor question about

the . . . uh . . . garbage pickup." (How come I thought of that?) "Please tell her I called and she can call me on my cell phone anytime."

"I'll do that. Nice to talk to you."

Then I had a better idea. "Oh, and can you tell her also that the . . . uh . . . consultant she asked me about, Ms. Edgerton, is now here in town?"

"I surely can."

"Good, that might relieve some of her stress."

The call certainly relieved mine.

While Mary Lou and Maddie were dressing for our excursion to San Jose, I made up two roast beef sandwiches and arranged crudités on a tray for Richard. I didn't fool myself into thinking this would keep him from reaching for the potato chips and the cookie jar, but I wanted to leave him some options.

"You spoil him, Mom," Mary Lou said when she saw me at the counter spreading butter and Dijon mustard on dark pumpernickel bread.

"She spoils everyone," Maddie said.

I heard Ken's voice in both of them and knew they were all correct. I wouldn't have wanted it any other way.

At nine in the morning (California time) we left Richard on the couch with his newspapers and remote controls and piled into the dark green Porter SUV, our vehicle of choice for the day.

"The better to carry our purchases," Mary Lou had said.

"They're miniatures, right?" Richard had asked. "How big a trunk do you need?"

I smiled. "It's a miniatures and *dollhouse* show." Enough said.

I had three goals for the day, the first being to enjoy my daughter-in-law and only grandchild. I'd been selfishly relieved when Linda said she couldn't join us because she had to take Jason shopping for a uniform (soccer? basketball? track? I'd pretended to know when Linda talked about it). This was part of their family bonding program, wherein Linda promised to support her sometimes troubled teen if Jason made the effort to join a team and play nice.

My second goal was to find a few minutes alone with Mary Lou to brainstorm with her. I wanted to know if she'd seen or heard anything interesting or useful in the work area of the Rutledge Center these last couple of days. I planned to tell her where June was and have her help me figure out how to approach her when and if she called me back.

Enjoying the show was third on my list, but, as usual, taking delight in my hobby rose to the top when I entered the cavernous exhibit hall.

Front and center was an enormous Victorian home, its exterior painted in layers that were many shades of pink. The wallpaper designs in the bedrooms, parlors, and hallways were flocked, striped, or gilded throughout. The style would have been too flamboyant for Ken, representing the other end of the spectrum from the simple lines and flat roof of our home.

I had the same taste as my late husband's in life-size abodes, but found it exciting to see this example of nineteenth-century rebellion against classic order and symmetry in miniature. The one-inch-to-one-foot-scale house in front of us had an array of tall, steep-pitched roofs, seven gables, a wraparound porch, and lovely gingerbread trim that accented the eaves.

Before the ink was dry on the tiny red dollhouse stamp on my hand, I'd bought a set of embroidered linens with the initial R, as a present for Linda Reed, for a bathroom scene that she was working on (and because I felt guilty feeling glad she wasn't with us); a tiny antique, wooden wagon for my Lincoln-Douglas debate scene; and a half-inch box camera on a tripod for the same scene.

Maddie was still busy on the interior side of the Victorian, counting the number of rooms (twelve), fireplaces (five), and stairways (six).

"No, seven," Maddie corrected herself. "Seven stairways, if you count the one to the basement. Wow, wow."

When Maddie started counting the number of windows, the draperies, and the place settings on the elaborate dining-room table, Mary Lou and I tuned out and leaned into each other like a couple of femmes fatales with a secret mission. Except that the little tote bag holding my purchases had pink lettering with "Minis 4 All," detracting from the covert look.

"Anything new at Rutledge Center?" I asked Mary Lou.

"Nothing substantial. But I'm so curious. I'm alert for any scrap of gossip. Is that bad?"

"I hope not."

"Everyone's trying to get back to normal. We have a guy who says he's going to come up with a replacement Harriet Lane."

"Ed Villard?"

Mary Lou grinned. "You do get around, Mom. Yeah, Ed thinks he's an artist by birthright. He even wears the same mustache and beard as the famous Vuillard. What's funny is that I loved the real Edouard Vuillard." Mary Lou spelled it for me and placed him for me as a Postimpressionist. "When I was in college, I had a print of *Annette Roussel with a Broken Chair*. Then I saw the original when it was on tour in Washington, D.C., and realized it's kind of a sad painting. This little girl kneeling on the floor . . . what could I have been thinking?"

"Our tastes change over the years, don't they? What do you think about our present-day Ed as an artist? I know Stephanie doesn't have a very high opinion of his work."

"She's not exactly a critic, but in this case she's right. He's tried every year, I heard, to have a showpiece, like Brad's Buchanan and Harriet portraits, but he's mediocre and gets relegated to the mural. It doesn't help that a lot of the younger artists make fun of him, saying he's not much better than the homeless lady who draws in chalk in front of city hall."

"That's pretty brutal."

"Uh-huh. Probably because he doesn't have what they think of as a true artist's vision. He's trying too hard to be someone else."

"The"—I drew quotation marks in the air—"real Vuillard?"

"Exactly. I understand he lives with his mother just as the real one did until her death. He's supposedly quite wealthy, so he's not after riches, just fame. Ed's good for some of the younger artists, though. From what I gather, he's mentored a lot of them. And he's more practical and down-to-business. Even about this murder, he's almost blasé about it."

"That fits with what I observed in our brief encounters."

"It helps to have someone who's grounded. Some of the mural workers won't even come to the studio since the murder, and the rest are looking over their shoulders every minute and jumping if someone drops a brush."

I remembered Stephanie's concern when she took custody of Mary Lou's painting from me, but it hadn't sunk in that my daughter-in-law might be in danger. "Do you really think there's a chance that someone is after the local artists?"

"We're all a little concerned, you know. I understand that you want to clear June's friend, but I have to admit it feels better thinking that she did it—I mean Zoe, not June—because then it's personal and not some serial killer who's after all Lincoln Point artists."

"Oh," I said, groaning inside. Just what I needed, something else to worry about. It was always unnerving when a violent crime occurred in our little town, but the fact that this might be related to someone in my family made it harder to bear. I was embarrassed that I hadn't given more thought to that possibility. Once again I felt admiration for

Skip and police detectives everywhere. They didn't have
the luxury of forming an opinion with very little to go on,
ignoring countless equally plausible theories.

Mary Lou poked me in the arm. "Hey, Mom? I don't
want to worry you, or Richard, with that crazy idea," she
said.

Too late. I mentally tacked another concern onto my list,
but casually moved on to the next booth where a crafter was
working on a Shaker-style rocker. Just what I needed to
calm my nerves. The simplicity of the Shaker furniture,
quilts, and home accessories were in stark contrast to the
ornate chairs and yards of cloth draped throughout the Victorian next door. In many ways, I knew, reproducing an authentic, silky-wood Shaker kitchen was more difficult than
filling in every corner with a knickknack or artifact.

"Why would anyone want to kill Lincoln Point artists?"
I asked, unable to let go of the idea.

"It wouldn't be the first time artists have been a target.
More than once in L.A. galleries there have been
incidents—though, granted, not murder. Like one time
someone painted a nude all over with black paint, symbolically clothing the naked lady, I guess. And another time
someone ruined a painting that was almost ready for sub-
mission for an exhibit. The artist came in one morning and
found his sky had been painted over with ugly clouds and
obscene graffiti. And guess what? Another artist in the
group who'd been rejected just happened to have something ready for the exhibit. No one could ever prove he'd
done it, but . . ."

"Wow," I said, borrowing a term from Maddie. I had
certainly read of similar incidents but was unaware that my
daughter-in-law had been close to any of the scenes or that
they would be commonplace. "I wouldn't have thought
artists would be so competitive—to the extent of being
nasty."

"We're no different from anyone else who thinks the

only way to get ahead is to trample on the person in front of us."

Food for thought. Mary Lou's comment reminded me of something related to Brad's murder, but before I could connect the dots, Maddie came by, begging for spending money. She'd spotted the refreshment stand.

"Can I get some popcorn?"

Mary Lou and I vied for who could get to her wallet first. It's a wonder Maddie didn't notice how eager we both were to get her out of earshot.

"Does anyone at the Rutledge Center have an opinion about who killed Brad?"

Mary Lou shook her head. "I'm afraid we're all too busy thinking, 'what if it had been me working late?' Remember, some of the paintings that were slashed belonged to other people than Brad. Not mine, thank God, because mine are all over your dining room." Mary Lou chuckled. A moment of nervous relief. "We're all trying to convince ourselves that that part was a mistake, that Zoe—I mean, whoever—thought they were all Brad's paintings."

I felt like Mary Lou's comments set me, and the case, back to the beginning. I wondered if the police had considered this aspect—that Brad was simply in the wrong place at the wrong time, dying, in a sense, because he was a conscientious artist working late, not because he was Zoe's boyfriend or Rhonda's ex-husband. This would mean that Zoe slashed Brad's painting (if I trusted the accuracy of the video) and some random killer came along soon after and killed him.

Ask Skip, I told myself, suppressing a shiver. How would he ever do his job without me? I mused.

While we were still two adults unaccompanied by a minor, we stopped to admire the miniature brothel that was one of the highlights every year. The small window-like opening to the room box was suitably high so only adults would be at eye level. Mary Lou had never seen it. She looked in and started to laugh, as we all did the first time we saw the very red room, with clothes (red lingerie included) scattered everywhere, and the bare, upper torso of a doll sitting on the bed, discreetly facing away from the viewing window.

"This scene reminds me of another little tidbit of gossip," Mary Lou said. "Completely unrelated to Brad's murder."

"Oh?"

"Ryan Colson, the guard, and Nan Browne, the TV studio talent," she said, raising her eyebrows and using the same universal crossed-finger gesture that Stephanie Cameron had used.

"I knew that," I said, disappointing both of us.

"I should have known you'd pick up on that, but did you know she's roaring mad at him at the moment?"

"Since when?" I asked, remembering the man-in-the-shadows incident just a few days ago and the suggestive cummerbund.

"This was just yesterday. All we heard was, 'How could you have done that? I can't believe you thought that was a good idea,' et cetera, et cetera. We joked that Nan was accusing Ryan of sleeping with his wife." Mary Lou covered her mouth. "I guess that's not very nice, but there it is. I think there was also something like, 'I'll be visiting you in prison.' "

It was hard to come up with a motive for Ryan to kill Brad, so what was it that he shouldn't have done? That might land him in prison, no less?

Maddie descended on us, putting a stop to thoughts and talk of crime. "Look, look. It's chocolate cinnamon popcorn," she said, offering us a chance to dig into her bag. We passed.

I'd saved one vendor's booth for last, knowing Mary Lou would love it and would want to linger. This year a fine-arts crafter I'd met at shows over the years had reproduced Vermeer's *A Girl Reading a Letter by an Open Window*. The scene was in the standard full- (one inch equals one foot) scale, in a portrait setup, about ten inches tall.

I could tell Mary Lou found it as breathtaking as I did. The crafter had managed to orient the box so that it caught the beams of a convention center floodlight through its stained-glass window. The rich red curtain hanging at an angle over the window, the woman/doll with a pensive look on her face, the tapestry bedspread, and the washed-out green curtain—all were positioned in a way that duplicated the shadows in the original Vermeer painting.

I'd always thought it curious that artists named their paintings with such pedantic titles, like Cézanne's *Apples, Peaches, Pears, and Grapes,* or Renoir's lovely *A Girl with a Watering Can,* which I'd seen so many times. And even Mary Lou's favorite of Vuillard, *Annette Roussel with a Broken Chair*. It was as if all their creativity went into the art itself, with nothing left over for an interesting title.

I mentioned this to Mary Lou.

"Uh-oh. Good point, Mom," she said. "I'm calling my newest—besides the current Lincoln-Douglas I'm working on—*California Hills in the Sunset*. Is that really bad?"

"Don't worry about it. I'm guilty of the same thing, in spite of my background in literature."

I thought of recent titles I'd given to my miniature scenes: *A Reading Corner* and *Christmas Dinner for Twelve*. I'd been calling my latest scene *The Lincoln-Douglas Debate in Galesburg, Illinois, 1858*. Then and there, I renamed my scene, *Debating the Morality of Slavery*. It would do until I had time to give it more thought.

We searched for Maddie and spotted her in front of a miniature aquarium with moving fish. That would keep her attention for a while. I only hoped she wouldn't decide we should try to build one.

I told Mary Lou about my call to June's parents in Chicago. "I think she's gone there to find Brad's ex-wife, and the irony is that she's here in town."

"Isn't Skip looking for June?"

"Yes, but I don't want to tell Skip right away. I feel like I'd be betraying her."

"Aren't you sort of betraying Skip if you don't?"

I groaned. "Thanks for that reminder. But I suppose you're right. I'm hoping she'll call me back and I can get her home soon."

"And then what?"

I hadn't thought that far ahead.

Chapter 15

When we arrived home, Richard was in the same posi-tion on the couch in front of the television set.

"I've been here, just like this, all day," he said, but smells from the oven—pot roast and potatoes—said otherwise. He'd offered to get dinner since we'd be gone until dark. I wondered if he'd jumped back onto the couch as he heard the car pull up, just so he could say his one-liner.

There was no postcard from Beverly and Nick today. Instead there was a case of pineapples, with a note: "To be used with or without rum." Richard had dragged the case through the foyer and parked it in front of the glass door between the atrium and the living room.

We explained to Maddie that there was a popular cocktail with rum and pineapple juice.

"Rum? Yuck, yuck. That would ruin the pineapple."

I agreed and hoped she'd hold that thought for many years.

                        *   *   *

We took our places at the table, eager to dig into tender
beef and tasty vegetables drenched in juice.

Bzzz, bzzz.

If I didn't know better, I'd have assumed that lifting my
fork for the first bite of roasted carrot was a mystical cue
for the doorbell to ring.

All the grown-ups sighed heavily. Maddie jumped up.

"I'll get it. I'll get it. Maybe it's Uncle Skip or June."

The three of us dug in and had at least one forkful of
food down before we heard Maddie's screams.

We tripped over each other getting to the door and inter-
cepted Maddie on her way back from the doorway. I held
her close and drew her back toward the living room while
Richard and Mary Lou checked the cause of her alarm.

"What the . . . ?" Richard asked.

"Is that a pineapple?" Mary Lou asked.

It didn't sound like much of an emergency, but I sat with
Maddie anyway.

"It was like the raccoon, Grandma," Maddie said, already calmer. "Except it was a pineapple." Then, to my relief, she giggled—a nervous giggle, but better than tears. "I
didn't mean to scream but I thought it was alive. I mean, an
alive thing, but dead now."

"Don't touch it anymore," Richard said.

It was all I could do not to march to the door to find out
for myself what was going on. Maddie had a firm hold on
my arm and waist, however, so I tried to be patient.

"It's just a pineapple," Mary Lou said.

"We should call Skip."

Skip? Uh-oh. Another police matter? After what
seemed like an hour, Richard and Mary Lou came back
empty-handed, except that Richard had his cell phone
out.

"Not exactly an emergency," he said into his phone. "But
we could use your advice at this point." A pause. "Dinner?

Pot roast." He clicked the phone shut and addressed us. "Skip will be right over."

For some reason no one returned to the dinner table. The roast and luscious vegetables went the way of my shrimp marinara earlier in the week. Linda Reed, who believed in such things, would have said we had bad cooking karma lately.

I left Maddie with her parents and hurried to the front door.

"Don't touch it," Richard said.

"Oh, for heaven's sake," Mary Lou said, amused. Maddie leaned against her on the couch, all smiles now.

Had the incident with the raccoon hardened my granddaughter against nasty (why else call Skip?) sights? If so, was I happy about that or not?

I opened the door and gasped in spite of myself and in spite of Mary Lou's and Maddie's chuckling. A squashed pineapple sat on the welcome mat, its translucent juice running along the cracks in the concrete.

A knife pierced its thick, scaly skin.

I almost screamed myself.

"Did you notice that one pineapple was missing from the crate?" Skip asked Richard, barely containing a smile.

Richard shrugged, the least amused of all of us Porters. "No, I didn't count them. I could see through the openings on the top what it was. And I was getting dinner ready." (This came out with a defensive ring.) "The crate was crushed all over, just like you see it. I assumed the box got mashed during shipping."

"Do you know what time it was delivered?"

"Not a clue. I was—"

"He was getting dinner ready," Mary Lou said.

All any of us knew was that at some point, while the crate was sitting on our doorstep, a pineapple had been stolen, and returned later with a knife through its heart.

"What could this mean?" Richard asked.

"Maybe someone is going door-to-door on our street and leaving mementos," Mary Lou said.

"Some sick someone," Richard said.

"And maybe next week Charlie and Isabel Curry on the other side"—she pointed in the direction of our neighbors— "will have an unsolicited present," Mary Lou continued.

I hadn't noticed Maddie's absence from the living room until she returned from a visit to the stabbed pineapple, now on a paper bag in our foyer, waiting for Skip to cart it away.

"It's from Willie's," Maddie said.

"Huh?" could be heard all around.

"The knife. Come and look at it."

We huddled around the slain pineapple in the close quarters of my foyer, as if we were peering into an open grave—bodies bent, frown lines on our foreheads, pursed lips, hands behind our backs.

Maddie pointed to the knife, still sticking out of the pineapple. "It's the same as the other knife. The one in the . . . you know. I saw this little design"—she came within an inch of touching the handle of the knife— "they're circles. It's from Willie's. I guess the circles are supposed to be bagels or something."

Skip leaned in closer. "Sweet," he said. "I think you're right. The one in the . . . you know . . . is scratched up more than this one is, but I'll bet it's from the same set."

If Maddie's grin were any bigger, it would have fallen off the edges of her face.

My grin, too, was wide. Even in her anguish over the dead raccoon, Maddie had noticed a detail that might help solve the mystery of the slashing of nonhuman subjects. At the very least, she'd saved the police a lot of research.

"You are so smart, Maddie," I said, hugging her from behind.

"My amazing child," Mary Lou said, planting a kiss on her forehead.

"Weird," Richard said.

Even with all of the cross talk going on, near the front of my mind was the fact that I hadn't told Skip where June was. It had been easier not to tell him when he wasn't in my living room. Now he picked Maddie up as high as he could these days. "If I had an extra badge, I'd pin it on you," he said.

"Weird," Richard said again. "Someone from Bagels by Willie is leaving knives stuck in . . . things . . . all over town?"

At times like this, I missed Ken, wondering how he would have reacted. Richard didn't have his sense of humor, but he did have his sense of logic and practicality, both of which I had to only a small degree. I decided that Ken would have run to the kitchen and brought back a huge bowl of ice cream for his super-intelligent granddaughter.

So, that's what I did.

There was one more voice to be heard on the case of the battered pineapple. Linda Reed stopped by to give me some news.

"Two pieces of news," as she put it.

Richard had disappeared and came back now to announce that he'd reheated the pot roast dinner and there was enough for all.

"I was counting on it," Skip said.

"You're so lucky, Gerry. You have someone to cook for you," Linda said.

I passed on the chance to remind her that I took my turn every third night, and that soon I'd be back cooking for myself full time.

I knew that Linda had felt out of it the last few days. She was always eager to help me or to be the first one to give me the latest gossip. I often thought it might have been due to her feeling that she was competing with Beverly for a top position on my nonexistent "best friend" list. Today she was delighted to have the added attention of my whole family.

Once we were settled around the table, napkins on our laps, Richard and I looked at each other. We'd left our forks midair, as if waiting for the doorbell to shatter our plans once again. Then we burst into laughter.

"What's so funny?" Linda asked.

"Never mind," I said. "What's your news, Linda?"

Linda straightened the fleece vest she wore over a sweater, which was in turn over her large bosom. "First, there's this thing going on between Nan Browne over at the TV studio and—"

"And the security guard at the Rutledge Center," Mary Lou said.

In deference to Maddie who was wiping up the juice on her plate with a hunk of bread, no one specified what the "thing going on" was.

"Okay, well, I should have known."

"The question is how did you find out, Linda?" I asked.

"Nan's mother is at the Mary Todd and she's kind of gone over the edge, so she spills family secrets all the time. She said she saw them . . . you know . . . before she got moved to the home a couple of months ago." Linda gave a hearty laugh. "In fact, I wouldn't be surprised if Nan moved her into the home just because she saw them . . . you know."

The presence of a minor certainly brought out a lot of hand waving and "you knows."

"Are you saying that's how long their . . . thing . . . has been going on?" I asked.

"I guess. I actually wasn't sure the old lady was right until you just confirmed it. I figured there was a good chance that old Mrs. Browne was making things up."

I'd had enough experience at the Mary Todd Home, where Linda worked and I taught crafts classes, to know that the (very) senior citizens who lived there were sharper than most of us thought.

"I guess we all know how to keep a secret, huh?" Mary Lou said. "What else can we confirm for you, Linda?"

Linda cut into a potato on her plate. I wondered if this meal were approved by her latest weight-loss program. "This pot roast is terrific, Richard," Linda said. I had a feeling that Piece of News Number Two was juicier than Number One and Linda was taking her time, getting more mileage out of it.

"There's a lot more out there," Richard said. "You can take some home for Jason if you want."

"We're waiting for your news, Mrs. Reed," Maddie said. That's my girl, I thought.

"Okay, this other is really crazy though. You know the new condos next to my house? The ones Zoe Howard lives in?"

We all nodded, mouths full, chewing.

"Well, we had a homeowners neighborhood meeting last night and something weird came up. I almost called you, Gerry, but it was a little late, and then there was Jason's game today."

"And . . . ?" Mary Lou said, expressing the impatience we all felt.

"On the walkway up to one of the condos, there were three grapefruits." Linda paused for effect, but she needn't have bothered.

"And they had knives stuck in them," Maddie said, as if she'd been the first to hit the right button on a game show, while the rest of us were still tongue-tied.

Skip had put our maimed pineapple in his car so there was no way Linda could have known about it.

"I don't believe you people," she said, wide-eyed. "How could you possibly have known that?" She looked at Skip, her expression accusing him of a leak in the police department. "I should have called you last night," she said to me.

"Was the department called in?" Skip asked.

"Oh, you don't know?" Linda responded.

With Linda, it was always questionable whether she was teasing or seriously put out.

"We need you, Linda," I said, trying to appease her. "Tell us the whole story."

She speared a roasted carrot and bit off half. "Okay, the woman who lives there, who's a good friend of Zoe's by the way . . . tripped over them." Linda prepared another forkful of food with some of everything on it—a piece of beef, a chunk of potato, and a slice of carrot, the whole assembly dipped in juice. Done with amazing skill. "The grapefruits. She tripped over the grapefruits and flipped out. She actually called the police, but they didn't make much of it. They almost laughed at her." She gave Skip another accusing look.

"The fruit was left there last night?" Richard asked. I could almost hear his mind working: *We weren't the first. That's probably good.*

Linda nodded. "Her point was, she's Zoe Howard's neighbor to the north, and she thinks it was supposed to be for Zoe, to mimic the stabbing?" She ended in a question. "So now she's worried that if they think that's where Zoe lives, what will they do next?"

"Maybe it was because she's a friend of Zoe's," Mary Lou said.

"That's even worse. But I didn't really know Zoe," Linda said, her case for exemption from threatening gestures going largely unheard.

"Did you hear about any"—Richard lowered his voice—"raccoons that were harmed?"

"Raccoons?" Linda mimicked Richard's low tones. "Nuh-uh."

"Stabbing fruit now? Isn't this a step down from killing a raccoon?" Mary Lou asked. "I thought bad guys escalated their crimes, I mean first assault, then . . . you know, something more serious. This guy is going the other way."

"Where did you learn that?" Skip asked.

"She watches *Law and Order* reruns all day," Richard said.

"You'd better be kidding," Mary Lou said.

"If there's all this slashing going on, and Zoe's in jail, isn't that a point in favor of her not being the painting slasher?" I asked, too weary to generate a more intelligible question.

"I think it's the crazy lady we're always seeing hanging around Willie's," Maddie said, giving voice to what I'd been thinking. She'd cleaned her plate of everything except the carrots. At a more ordinary dinner, her father would have cajoled her to eat them. But this was no ordinary dinner.

Skip's cell phone ring gave us a breather from a conversation that was getting out of hand. I, for one, had a headache, and I imagined I wasn't the only one.

Skip left the table, carrying a piece of bread with him, and leaned on the kitchen counter to take his call.

We ate in silence, our ears on Skip's side of the conversation, but all we got at first were "uh-huhs" and "nuh-uhs."

Then my imagination took over and I thought I heard him say, "June?" It turned out to be "raccoon."

He clicked his phone shut and came back to the table. "Guess what was *not* killed by a knife wound, besides that pineapple and Linda's grapefruits," Skip said.

"Not *my* grapefruits," Linda said.

"The knife hardly penetrated the raccoon's body, because it was already stiff, having died of natural causes."

"How can you tell if a raccoon has a heart attack?" Mary Lou asked.

"What raccoon?" Linda asked.

"The same way you tell if a human has had a heart attack," Dr. Richard said.

"There was a raccoon in the trash in June's driveway," Maddie said.

"They're all over. They love garbage," Linda said.

"I had a buddy in animal control take a look at the raccoon," Skip said. "His opinion was that the raccoon was probably kept as a pet for a while until the people realized that was not a good idea. Then they released it and the animal didn't know how to survive. Something like that."

"See, this wasn't just a raccoon eating garbage. Someone stuck a knife in it and threw it in June's trash can," Maddie explained to Linda.

"Wow," Linda said. She shook her head and made the kind of sound you make when you've lost the upper hand.

"What do you think, Skip?" Richard asked. "Are we in danger here? I'm not so sure we should be laughing at all this. I mean, two pranks in less than a week?"

"Three," Linda said. "Darn, I wish I'd gotten a look at the knife at the condo."

"My professional opinion?" Skip offered. "This is not the work of a killer or of anyone who is going to attack you personally. I'm not saying the cliché is absolutely true, that no criminal backtracks like this from animal to vegetable—"

"Fruit," two people said, but I couldn't be sure which two.

"—so to speak," Skip continued. "And I'm not saying you shouldn't be suspicious of someone you don't know in the neighborhood, but I wouldn't panic."

"I guess you got the pineapple because there just happened to be a crate of them on your doorstep," Linda said.

"Seems that way," Skip said. "And possibly it was the same with the raccoon." (Maddie had opened the door to using the word outright when she told the story to Linda.)

"The person saw a dead raccoon handy and used it? So they carried fruit to do the deed but then used the dead animal instead?" I almost laughed at the image, but truly, I didn't know what to think. If I had to record my feelings, I'd place them somewhere between Mary Lou's cavalier attitude and Richard's full-alert status.

"I wonder why we got grapefruits?" Linda asked.

Now my headache was bad. I rubbed my forehead and got up to get an aspirin from the cupboard. I noticed that

Maddie had left the room before our so-called conversation was over. This was not like her. I walked down the hallway toward her room and heard tub water running in the bathroom we shared. I smelled fake strawberries.

Maddie was taking her second voluntary bath of the week.

What was that saying about an ill wind?

Before he left, Skip drew me outside to the walkway. No one questioned why he needed a minute alone with me.

"Any word from June?"

"Not yet, but—"

"I didn't think so."

"Oh."

He interrupted me, I reasoned. It's not my fault that I'm not telling him where June is. I sincerely hoped she was on a plane to the San Jose airport.

"I have something," he said. "Uniforms picked up a woman for disturbing the peace downtown. In front of the courthouse, no less. She was carrying a sign about 'can't put asunder.' Something from the Bible, against divorce, I guess."

Skip had missed the wedding-going era when we all knew the phrase, "What God has joined together, let no man put asunder." I had to admit I didn't know for sure whether it was biblical or not.

"Rhonda?" I asked, picturing her marching for her cause.

He nodded. I took a moment to admire the way my outside light captured all the different shades of red in his hair. Like his mother's hair, and his uncle Ken's.

"She had a Florida DL on her this time—Rebecca E. Garrity. It has to be the same woman, though she changes her appearance a little and uses a different ID each time."

"Where could Rhonda be getting all these different IDs? And why would she do it?"

"It's not that hard to do. It's not even as hard as identity theft to have fake IDs made up. How old is your driver's license photo, for example?"

"Very," I admitted. I'd been renewing by mail for the last several years. My hair was longer, my face fatter. "I figure the authorities are trained to notice the basics."

"You wish. As to why, who knows what a vindictive ex-wife will do?"

"Do you think Rhonda's the one putting these things on doorsteps?"

"It's entirely possible. She seems nuts enough, but we have no evidence."

"Can you search her hotel room or wherever she's staying?"

"I think they let her go without even putting in for a search warrant. I have a call in to a buddy on that beat to check out the details."

I felt my jaw tighten. "How could that happen? That they would just let her go?" I seemed to have no control over the shrillness of my voice and its accusatory ring.

Skip stayed calm, at least in terms of his tone. "You heard Linda. No one at the station is taking this very seriously. There's a disconnect between the guys on the street and what's going on in the Goodman case."

"LPPD isn't that big, Skip. Don't you talk to each other?"

He raised his eyebrows and gave me a look that said I was close to crossing a line. I took a step back, both physically and symbolically.

"I'm sorry. I know it's not your fault."

"Believe me, I'm working hard on this. I'm trying to get my case together to show that this woman has now been identified as a person of interest in the murder investigation and not just the wild protestor or the dead raccoon and fruit slasher."

He turned to go to his car.

"Is there anything I can do?" A weak gesture, but I needed to offer.

Over his shoulder Skip said, "Yeah, try to keep Maddie away from checking out Willie's silverware."

I laughed, relieved that he wasn't as upset with me as he looked. But I didn't promise anything.

Linda hadn't left yet. Apparently she also needed a word with me before she went home to bed.

"If you need anything, anything at all, Gerry, just ask, okay? I can cozy up to old Mrs. Browne at the home and see if I can pick up anything. Whatever. Just ask."

"I need someone to finish my room box for Tuesday."

She gave me a look.

"Just kidding," I said.

But I wasn't.

Chapter 16

Middle-of-the-night phone calls weren't as rare as they should have been in my home, and they were never welcome. At one in the morning, with Richard and his family safe under my roof, that left only Skip and Beverly at the top of my worry list as I reached for the phone next to my bed.

"Gerry? I know it's late, but I just got in and got your message."

I sat up, pulled the covers up to my neck, and cranked up the heat on my electric blanket from three to five.

"June! Everyone's concerned about you."

"Hello?" from Richard.

I'd unplugged the extension in Maddie's room, but not the one in my usual bedroom from which Richard might be summoned at any hour. I'd picked up on the second ring, but my son had been quicker.

"It's okay, Richard. I have it."

"Who is it? Everything all right?" he whispered, sparing Mary Lou.

June was silent, so it was all up to me. "It's a crafts emergency," I said with a hoarse, sleepy chuckle.

"Right," he said and hung up.

"Is Rhonda really in Lincoln Point?" June asked. "I tried to get hold of Zoe, but of course she can't take calls. It's so frustrating."

"Rhonda's here. She's using several different names, but she visited Zoe."

June groaned. "That's all Zoe needs."

"When are you coming home?"

"Who wants to know?"

"We should talk, June."

"I feel like I'm in Lincoln Point. There's a big celebration going on here in Chicago because it's some number anniversary of the Republican convention when Lincoln was nominated for president."

"Do you need a ride from the airport when you get here?" I asked, to get her on track. I knew the answer was no, since her car had been missing from her driveway since she left. I figured it was now in the airport parking lot.

"I really do want to talk to you, Gerry. I've spent a lot of time going to all of Rhonda's old haunts. I can't tell you how many people I've found who'd be willing to swear that Rhonda told them she wanted to kill Zoe."

"But Zoe wasn't killed."

"That's not the point."

"What about Skip, June?"

"What about him?"

"Have you called him?"

"I've been doing a lot of thinking."

I felt I couldn't go any further if she wasn't forthcoming. I wasn't a matchmaker, or even Skip's mother. If June wanted to confide any more in me, she'd have to take the lead.

June never said what conclusions she'd come to as a result of all her thinking. She said she had "more evidence" that Rhonda killed the man she still thought of as her husband, but every time I asked her to be specific, she lost track of the topic and went off on a track about her and Skip.

We finally hung up, at an impasse as to when or whether June would return, how she would deal with Zoe's guilt or innocence, what she saw as her future with Skip.

There was nothing for me to do but go back to sleep.

Before anyone else was up on Sunday morning, Mary Lou and I sat in my atrium with mugs of coffee and a plate of mini scones, ready to hatch a plan. A Southern California girl who thought February was much too cold here in "the north," Mary Lou had bought a space heater for the area. She sat close to it now, wrapped in an afghan I'd knitted for her when Maddie was born.

We needed to make the most of the day, when Richard and Maddie would be at a reading program at the library and then out to lunch. It was their special father/daughter time together and we couldn't be more grateful. We'd encouraged them also to take in a movie.

"And even if you want dinner out, that's okay," Mary Lou had said.

"I don't think we're fooling them one bit," I said now. "But at least we won't need to make excuses to snoop around for a while," I said.

"Amen," Mary Lou said. "Has June called?"

I briefed Mary Lou on the phone call that had awakened her husband, but apparently not her. "She says she can come up with witnesses and has evidence that Rhonda killed Brad," I told Mary Lou. "I'm not putting much stock in it, however," I said. "She has too much invested in the outcome."

"And we don't?"

"Good point."

* * *

"I suppose you're going to do 'errands' today," Maddie said at breakfast. Her air quotes around *errands* said it all. She couldn't say much more without offending her father and appearing ungrateful for the special day he'd planned for them.

"What kind of errands do you do on a Sunday?" Richard asked. "The banks are closed. Also, the post office and the shops on Springfield don't open until noon."

I wondered if he really were oblivious to our intentions. I searched his face and saw no telltale signs that said he was teasing. His high forehead had frown lines that just meant he was serious about eating his Spanish omelet, one of his wife's specialties.

"They're more like odds and ends," Mary Lou said. "Finishing up little projects. Getting ready for our move. That kind of thing."

"I want to hear everything when we get back," Maddie said. She threw up her hands. "Or . . ."

I leaned over to tickle her. "Or you won't kiss me good night?"

She grinned. "You got that right."

It was a big price to pay.

Once Mary Lou and I were free, our first stop was at the Rutledge Center. Mary Lou would do some legitimate work on her painting and I would assist (carrying her notebook? mixing paint? rinsing brushes? If challenged, I'd think of something).

I'd decided to try to recreate the timeline of the night of Brad's murder. I couldn't help thinking that if I found a way to clear Zoe, all would be well. June would come back from Illinois, the land of Lincoln, and be Skip's wonderful girlfriend and my helpful neighbor, and there would be no more messy animate or inanimate objects left on the doorsteps of our neighborhoods. We could all celebrate Lincoln's birthday on Tuesday and (I didn't like this part) a family farewell party the following week when my dear houseguests would be moving into their new Palo Alto home.

Once Mary Lou was set up, I took off for the east wing.

"I'll cover this end, and see what I can pick up," Mary Lou had said. "Putting in a sky doesn't take too much concentration."

At that moment, she'd sounded like me, or any of my miniaturist friends, known for such statements as, "It will take me about ten minutes to put a new stairway in my house."

Parking close to the television studio was not a problem on Sunday morning, especially now that I knew my way around the maze of chain-link fences and chunky concrete barriers. I sat in my car facing the stairway that had been encircled by crime-scene tape only a few days ago. My intention was to enter the studio (I didn't know how yet) and make my way around to the artists' work area, as Zoe claimed to have done on Monday night.

The single studio window was dark. I tapped my steering wheel. Thinking. My thoughts included a reexamination of my motives and goals for this exercise. Did I have nothing better to do with my time? Wouldn't this morning be better spent organizing my fabric shelves? Visiting older friends, some of whom have lost mobility over the past few years? Giving more time to the library's tutoring program?

I knew there was a next-to-zero chance that the door would be unlocked as it had been the last times I'd been here. But I was here now, and there was no harm in trying to get in. I might even be warmer if I moved around outside than I was sitting in my car. I wished I'd worn a heavier jacket than my unlined corduroy, but by midafternoon, I'd be turning on the air-conditioning in my car. Such was the climate of the Bay Area, where we experienced four seasons a day.

I got out of my car, one of only a half dozen in the huge lot, and headed for the entrance.

On the landing at the top of the short flight of steps, I

pulled at the handle of the dark brown metal door. Nothing budged. I leaned as far as I could to the left, trying to see into the window. I had a narrow view of a desk lamp and a table full of papers. Nothing else. I knocked, knowing it would be fruitless.

Tap, tap. Tap, tap.

"Can I help you?"

I jumped back and grabbed the railing. The deep voice hadn't come from inside, but from behind me, at the bottom of the steps.

Why did those words startle me so much lately? Whether from security guard Ryan Colson, television star Nan Browne, or this young man—the phrase had caught me off guard at times when I knew I was an interloper.

A considerably overweight young man stood still, one hand deep in the pocket of his thick down vest, the other leaning on a large, blue, barrel-shaped container on wheels, with mops and cleaning supplies sticking out from its rim.

"I . . . uh . . . was on Nan Browne's show the other day"—establishing credentials, dropping a name, implying: don't hurt me—"and I think I left my bag in the studio."

"Huh," he said. Believing? Suspicious? I couldn't tell from his you-don't-say tone.

I rethought my lie. I wasn't at all sure I wanted this man—the huge ring of keys on his belt notwithstanding—to let me in. The idea of being alone with him in the black-draped studio wasn't appealing. My cell phone was far away, in a pretty Vera Bradley case in the bowels of my tote (the one I didn't leave in the studio on Friday, wink, wink). What good was emergency equipment if it wasn't handy? I resolved to change that habit, given the chance.

"I'm Mrs. Porter," I said. Tell a potential threat your name, I remembered from somewhere. Make it personal. On the plus side, as I studied his pudgy, friendly face, I was beginning to think of the young man as an ally.

"Dirk," he said.

"I'm surprised you're working on a Sunday, Dirk," I said, looking down on his bulk. He was taller than me by a couple of inches, and I didn't even want to guess by how many pounds.

"Yeah, I go to school, so they let me flex my hours."

"What are you studying?" The teacher in me genuinely cared.

"Computer science at San Jose State."

The more Dirk talked, the better I felt. "Do you work nights, then?"

"No, I take classes at night."

Hmmm.

"How about last Monday night? Were you working then?"

"No, I take classes at night." I detected a slight slowing of his speech, as if to accommodate the dull Mrs. Porter at the top of the steps. "I don't get out of class until ten thirty on Mondays, Wednesdays, and Fridays. Now I'm kind of glad, after . . . you know."

Maddie's not here, I wanted to say. *You can use the word* murder. "Did you know the victim, Brad Goodman?" I asked Dirk.

"Nah, I sweep up over there, too, but you'd be surprised how stuck-up those artists can be. They look right through a janitor."

"Is there another custodian who works nights?"

"Nah, they can barely afford me, and believe me, I'm not a big-budget item."

Like the chilly breeze that swept my scarf up from my chest, there went yet another part of Zoe Howard's story— that she'd snuck into the studio when a janitor propped the door open on Monday night.

"Well, I'm sure you have work to do," I said, still on my perch on the stairway landing.

"Yeah. I know you want to get in and I'm sorry about your bag, but you'll have to wait until tomorrow when the staff comes in. I'm not supposed to let anyone in, especially on this side. They're very fussy, with all the equipment and all."

Not during the day, I thought.

I had another Zoe-lie-detector test for the ponderous young man. "That's okay. My daughter-in-law is working on the other side of the center, in the artists' work area. I can just go in over there and walk back through to the studio."

He shook his head, sending long straight hair across his pudgy forehead. "No way. You can't get through from the studio to the other parts of the complex. Or vice versa."

I smiled, pleased that he didn't say "visa versa." He was a credit to his school.

"No secret way, known only to the in-crowd?" I asked.

"No way." For a moment I thought he was going to repeat his whole response. "I'm really sorry I can't help you, Mrs. Porter, but as little as this job pays, I still can't afford to get in trouble."

"You've already helped me a great deal, Dirk," I said.

Having waved good-bye to Dirk, who waited until I got in my car (lest I break in to retrieve my tote?), I drove around to the north side and parked near the door to the artists' work area. I couldn't wait to tell Mary Lou my latest discovery—that Zoe lied about how she got into the complex on the night of the murder.

My daughter-in-law was one of only a handful of artists at work on this Sunday morning. Not everyone waited until the last minute, it seemed. I interrupted a delicate application of gray paint to an already fluffy cloud to give Mary Lou the lowdown on my chance meeting with Dirk, the computer scientist–cum-janitor.

"I'm feeling a little lighthearted since I now have not only Nan Browne's comment about the lack of connecting portals from the studio to here. I have corroboration from a disinterested professional as well."

"Why would Zoe lie about how she got in?"

"Not only is that a mystery, but consider this. The studio is where Brad's body was found, not this work area. If she never went into the studio, why would she say she did?"

"It doesn't make sense."

I agreed. "Maybe she thinks breaking and entering is a more serious charge than destroying a painting."

"Not to me."

"I knew that."

Mary Lou scratched her head with one end of a brush, the other end being filled (it seemed to me) with paint. I had the feeling it wasn't the first time she'd made this move. "Then how *did* she get in?"

It might have been the adrenaline rush generated by my fear that Mary Lou was going to spill paint on her hair and face, or just a random connection among pieces of the puzzle. Something put my brain in high gear. "I think I know."

I remembered how Ryan Colson had refused to answer the simple question, asked first by Maddie, of whether he'd been on duty the night of Brad's murder.

"I think Ryan Colson let Zoe in," I said. "I don't know why, but I'm convinced he did it."

"Well, all in all, you did better than I did today," Mary Lou said. "I got all involved in my sky and forgot to snoop around."

A true artist. "You're entitled," I told her.

Chapter 17

A half hour later, Mary Lou and I climbed the stairs of city hall, on our way to the community center annex, where the debate would be held. The mural had been completed, and Mary Lou wanted to watch the stage crew set it up.

The air of excitement around city hall was more electric than at Christmas, more exciting than at any sporting event—Abraham Lincoln happenings trumped them all. I noticed even our itinerant fiddler was wearing a top hat today, our resident artist was attempting a Lincoln portrait, a new entertainer, a mime, was decked out in a silver tux. I reached into my purse and pulled out bills for each of them. Their thank-you smiles were warm, their eyes distant. I wished my community service skills included more than tutoring.

I would have thought the auditions for a (short, Democrat) Stephen A. Douglas and a (tall, Republican) Abraham Lincoln would have ended by now, but there were still hopefuls around the front of the building. To our right was a knot of Douglas wannabes in floppy bow ties and Lincoln

hopefuls in stiff bow ties. Some Douglases had ineptly
padded their stomachs, giving them a deformed torso; others looked the part naturally.

Nearing the top step, four men in work clothes carried
an enormous banner reading KNOX COLLEGE FOR LINCOLN,
Knox College being the venue of the Galesburg debate.

More debate snippets swirled around us. By now I felt I
could take up Ryan Colson's challenge and audition for a
role myself (my physical appearance would qualify me as a
Lincoln candidate). "I don't mind admitting that I'll be relieved when we've met for the last time," bellowed a Douglas, and ". . . blowing out the moral lights around us when
he maintains that anyone who wants slaves has a right to
hold them," a Lincoln chimed in.

I wondered how many of the aspiring debaters were
aware that the lines they'd memorized were by no means
guaranteed to be authentic. None of the manuscripts of Lincoln's prepresidential speeches had been preserved—neither
Lincoln nor anyone else thought that to be important. What
we had were transcripts that relied on newspaper accounts
and notes by on-the-scene stenographers.

Not that knowing that would lessen my enjoyment of
the reenactment.

Mary Lou had gone ahead of me. I saw her meet up
with Ed Villard near the top of the steps and watched as
the two of them moved on to the foyer where the mural
would be arriving in pieces. I stayed behind to look out for
one Douglas especially, and saw him a few steps above
me, carrying a plastic bag full of bells for the audience to
use in its simulation of the 1858 rally participants (by all
accounts, they'd been a rowdy crowd, booing as loudly as
they cheered).

I rushed to catch up with Ryan and heard his latest debate excerpt.

"If the people of Kansas had only agreed to become a
slave-holding state—" he said, with a pompous air.

"Ryan Colson," I said, interrupting. "I see you're still in the running."

"Oh, yeah. Great news, Mrs. Porter. I got a callback. This means I'm on the short list." Ryan looped the handles of the plastic bag around his wrist and rubbed his hands together, gearing up for what was probably the last of the auditions.

"That's wonderful. Do you know how many are on the list?"

"Not really, but other years they're down to only two or three finalists by this time." He gave me a thumbs-up. "I'm feeling like I have good karma today."

"Well, I wish you luck." (Was luck necessary if one had karma?) I paused, Columbo-style, I'm embarrassed to say. "By the way, I have a question for you, Ryan, about last Monday night."

Ryan's face fell, becoming thinner than Stephen Douglas's ever was. He looked at his watch. "You know, I'm in a big rush right now. Like I told you, I got a callback."

"Oh, it can wait. I'm just curious about why you let Zoe Howard into the Rutledge Center around the time Brad Goodman was murdered." Now his face was both fallen and pale. "You go on now, though. I'll catch you at another time." I glanced to the left, toward the police station. I couldn't remember ever being this dramatic to make a point.

Ryan moved three or four short steps along the wide tread we stood on, then came back. "Mrs. Porter, I could lose my job," he said in a whisper.

I whispered back. "I'm not trying to get you fired, Ryan. I simply want to know the circumstances under which you abused your position." (Put that way, it did sound like I wanted him fired.)

"Can we meet somewhere later? I promise I'll tell you."

"When?"

"Do you have a cell? Can I call you when the audition is over?"

I gave him my number. His wig seemed lopsided now as

a result of his nervous rubbing of his forehead. I felt bad
that I'd probably thrown him off his Stephen Douglas persona. On the other hand, I had a murder to investigate.

After a little more jostling on the steps, during which I
learned even more about the debate over the conditions
under which Kansas might be admitted to the Union as a
state, I joined the crowd witnessing the setup of the multi-
sectioned mural in the foyer. The elaborate collage had
been done in giant panels depicting highlights of the seven
original debates. Five panels stretched nearly floor to ceiling across each side of the large foyer, joined by a long
narrow panel over the wide doorway in the middle. Each
artist had worked in his or her own style, but the overall effect was one of admirable cohesion and complementarity.
An eclectic project, and worthy of its subject.

Throughout the mural were triangles and other shapes
containing lettered quotes from all the Lincoln-Douglas
debates, from the first one in Ottawa, Illinois, to the sev-
enth and last in Alton, Illinois. Overlapping images represented indoor and outdoor settings and the two senatorial
candidates themselves—Lincoln with his bony, drawn-in
cheeks, Douglas with a knobby dark pompadour at the top
of his round head.

Mary Lou came up to me. "Isn't it magnificent? I wish
I'd been part of it." As we watched a dozen artists erecting
the mural, putting on finishing touches, making small re-
pairs, Mary Lou looked almost wistful. "We used to work
together on murals all the time in college. It can be more
fun than doing your own individual painting."

Ed Villard approached us at that moment, a palette in his
hand. His jeans and loose white shirt looked stiff with paint.
"That's easy for you to say," he muttered, as he walked by.

"What was that all about?" I asked.

"As I mentioned before, Ed's not the happiest artist I've
ever met. But in all fairness, he's the oldest of the group, as

you can see. It's kind of a tradition that young people would be involved in a group effort like this, but that once you're older and established, you'd have your own painting in a show. Either that, or you're Diego Rivera."

As scanty as my knowledge of art history was, even I knew the great muralist and his equally famous wife, Frida Kahlo. "I've seen his mural in San Francisco several times," I said, thinking back to the stimulating trips Ken and I had made to the city.

"The Pan American mural. That's just one of many. He gave the world public art of the most amazing proportions and brilliance. But it seems sad, to wish you were Vuillard or Rivera or anyone else."

I agreed with Mary Lou. I was glad I had no aspirations that were so high I couldn't achieve them.

Mary Lou showed me the spot where her own water-color of the Galesburg debate would be situated—in front of the five panels to the left of the doorway. On the other side would be a watercolor of Galesburg, Illinois, as it was today, a city said to have one of the largest railroad yards in the country.

"Who's doing the watercolor of contemporary Gales-burg?" I asked.

"That's another sore point with Ed. The mayor's daughter, Barbara Roberts, got the commission. She's an art major in San Francisco. It's not a bad painting, but you have to wonder about the objectivity of the committee who chose her. Poor Ed can't catch a break." Mary Lou pointed to the center doors. "Excuse me for a minute, Mom? I need to see that stagehand."

If my calculations were correct, there were four commissioned paintings for this year's reenactment. The two watercolors outside the auditorium were by Mary Lou on one side, and the mayor's daughter on the other. The two oil paintings inside were to have been the Buchanan and Harriet Lane portraits by the late Brad Goodman.

I had a new worry—what if Brad was killed by someone

who wanted to replace him and that someone still didn't
get the commission? Didn't that put Mary Lou and Barbara
Roberts at risk?

I shook my head—no, no. It didn't make sense that
someone would just kill everyone in his way until he was
the only one left to paint.

That was silly.

Wasn't it?

Leave it to me to think of the worst scenario. I went
back to the spurned lover theory, which made me much
more comfortable with respect to the safety of my family.

Some cop I'd make.

I wandered around, catching fragments of artist talk, and
more orations on slave versus free states. I saw Ryan Colson
in the crowd, heading for the community center annex,
where auditions were being held. I wondered if or when he'd
call me and what I would do about it in either case. Skip's
office was a stone's throw from where I stood in the city hall
foyer—one building over in the civic center complex. He
wouldn't necessarily be there on a Sunday, but the proximity
of his workplace made me think I should tell him what I'd
learned from the Rutledge Center janitor about Zoe's story.
I'd call him after I talked to Ryan, I decided.

I took out my cell phone to check for messages. In all
the noise of the foyer, I might not have heard the ring. I
hoped to hear June's voice or Ryan's, but heard only "You
have no new messages," and then, a few seconds later, the
melody of "As Time Goes By."

I saw Mary Lou's ID and clicked my cell phone on to
receive her call.

"That was fast," Mary Lou said, from somewhere in the
crowd. I'd lost track of her petite frame in the throng. "It
only rang once. Are you ready for an early lunch? I'm
through here for now."

"I'll meet you out front. I'm through, too," I said.

* * *

As soon as we were seated in Bagels by Willie, Mary Lou and I picked up our knives and checked out the handles, expecting to see the concentric, if not quite perfect circles Maddie had an eye for. We both laughed at the gesture, then frowned as we saw that the knives were devoid of any design or symbol.

"These are not Willie's usual knives. I think Lincoln PD has been here already," Mary Lou said.

"It looks that way," I said and took the opportunity to ask Lourdes about it when she came to take our order.

"Oh, yeah." (She pronounced it *jah*, something we were working on since Lourdes was determined to lose her charming accent.) "That crazy lady in town? She took some of our knives, I heard. And today the police came by and took all the rest of them. Johnny, our supervisor, he had to go to the discount store and buy new ones."

"Why would they take them all?" Mary Lou addressed this to me. Was I the authority? Oh, dear.

I shrugged, thinking of the many names of Rhonda Goodman. "Maybe for fingerprints, to see if she's been in the shop touching all the knives?"

We all shook our heads at that theory.

I thought of my trip to the evidence room and the sink leaning against the wall. It gave me a clue to the real answer to Mary Lou's question.

"They took them because they can," I said. "The police can take everything *and* the kitchen sink if they think it might matter to their investigation."

"Don't get me started. Don't even try to figure out how the police work," Lourdes said. "I could tell you some stories." From her expression I gathered the stories didn't have happy endings. "Will I see you this afternoon, Mrs. Porter?"

"Yes, of course," I said, though I'd temporarily forgotten our date. "In the library at three."

She went off to get our bagels with a wide smile on her face. If only my high school students had been as thrilled at the prospect of a class with me.

"Here's something," Mary Lou said. **"It's been nagging** at me, but it may be nothing."

I straightened up in my seat. I was ready for any morsel of information or informed opinion. "Let me be the judge."

"While I was in the foyer, I ran into Ed Villard again. He'd just gotten the word that Brad Goodman's Harriet Lane commission is his."

"That's good news. As you said, he can use a break."

"Yes, but get this. He told me he's finished with the painting except for some final touches and the framing."

"And?"

"I don't care how good you are, it's almost impossible to come up with a decent portrait in less than a week."

"He was highly motivated," I said.

She shook her head, a doubtful expression on her face. "Motivated or not, there's a certain amount of time required. Portraits in oil take longer than almost any other medium, especially if you do them in the classical style, as Ed does. It's not a matter of being a fast painter, you have to allow time for one layer to dry before you put the next one on. And then he said he already had sealant on it. That's another whole layer."

"Could he have taken some shortcuts?" I wasn't sure why I was working so hard to defend Ed, except that it was easy to feel sorry for a guy my age who "couldn't catch a break."

"Well, there's van Gogh. He had a different method. He just slapped on one thick layer, but he was impressionistic, not classical, and anyway—"

"Ed Villard is no van Gogh," I said, finishing Mary Lou's sentence. (I hoped we wouldn't have to go through all the major figures in art history with this nugget from political history.) "Did Ed have an explanation about why it didn't take very long to come up with the replacement portrait?"

"I did express surprise when he told me, and he back-tracked. He said the canvas had already been prepped for another portrait and that he happened to have the appropriate palette ready for that project. He didn't say the sealant was on it, but that he was *going to* put the sealant on it . . . but I'm not totally buying it."

We accepted our identical lunch plates from Lourdes—toasted sesame bagel with cream cheese, fruit, and a side of potato salad.

"I have an errand to run this afternoon," I said, once I was fortified with a couple of hundred calories.

"You mean tutoring Lourdes?"

"That, too, but before that, I need to . . . uh, do something else," I said, pretending to be chewing at the same time, to mask my words.

"This is not Maddie you're talking to, Mom. What are you up to?"

"Well, when you put it that way . . . I need to find out more about Brad Goodman. What kind of person he was. What kind of relationship he had with Ed, for example, and with Ryan Colson." I ticked off my questions. "How did he get along with the television crew that was taping the artists, for that matter? Or with Nan Browne? And what about our friendly crazy lady, allegedly Brad's ex-wife? Was she always like that? And Brad's gone, so I can't ask him, so—"

"You're going back to jail."

"I'm afraid so."

As I'd predicted, the afternoon was mild—sixty-five degrees (according to the reading on the bank's electronic billboard). I'd made arrangements with Mary Lou for her to keep the car. I'd call when I was ready and either she or Richard would pick me up.

I walked the few blocks along Springfield Boulevard back to the civic center. I passed Abe's Hardware store, which had been in its location for three generations. In the window was a display featuring a log cabin kit for sale, surrounded by an assortment of tools needed to build it. I slowed down, tempted to buy the kit. But I didn't need another dollhouse and I had business at the Lincoln Point jail. Just like every other grandmother, I mused.

Looking ahead, I could see that the steps were sparsely populated compared to the way they'd been the last few days. It was possible that the latest Lincoln and Douglas had now been chosen. I wondered whether Ryan had made the grade.

My cell phone rang as I passed between the two main entrances of Abraham Lincoln High School, where I'd spent many years expounding on the usefulness of commas and the many joys of literature. Or was it vice versa? I dug out my phone and caught the call.

"Good news, Aunt Gerry. The results on the murder weapon are inconclusive. All the lab can say is that the knife with Zoe's prints is the same kind as the one used to murder Brad. That, plus some very fancy footwork on the part of Zoe's PD, and the judge is allowing bail."

We both gave a relieved sigh. "I'm so glad," I said.

"So, in case you're in touch with June, you can tell her, okay?"

"What makes you think—?"

Skip broke in with a loud "ahem." "It's okay. I know where she is."

"Oh?"

"I have a key to her house, so I put on my civvies . . . my June's boyfriend clothes, not my official on-duty cop clothes . . . and had a look around."

"She just needed to check on Rhonda, Skip. She had no idea Rhonda might be in Lincoln Point." I felt myself rushing to get everything out, to explain June's actions. "Naturally, she figured the woman was still in Chicago."

"Ha," Skip said. "So that's where she is."

I took the phone away from my ear and looked at it. *Busted again.* How many busts this week? I couldn't count.

"You tricked me," I said, with a definite whine in my tone.

"How could I do such a thing, huh? Treat you like a common criminal? Yada yada. You'll get over it."

I shouldn't have been surprised. "We do that all the time," he'd said one evening when his mother and I questioned a tactic we saw on a television crime drama. "Last week we told this guy his friends ratted him out, and we told his friends the same thing. We told another guy we found stolen goods in his house." His response to our strange looks had been, "Come on. It's not exactly water boarding. And of course, we only use it when we're sure the guy's guilty."

"You didn't even go into June's house, did you?" I asked him now.

"I didn't have to. You did the work for me. Thanks."

I hadn't heard Skip's voice so light all week. I let him enjoy the moment.

I took a seat on a bench at the edge of the high school lawn. Its worn green slats were carved up with sets of initials that catalogued romances through the ages.

"What are you going to do about it?" I asked.

"You mean, am I going to charge you with obstruction of justice?"

I sighed. Enough was enough. "What are you going to do about June? Charge her with something, too?"

"Now that you've confirmed her location, I'll take it from here."

It didn't seem fair that Skip got what he wanted out of this conversation, and I got nothing. "Do you know where Zoe is now?"

"She's still in jail. I said she's been granted bail, not that she had *made* bail. She hasn't been able to get the money together. Her PD is working on it."

I was sure there were some very good public defenders,

but I was surprised to hear that a professional woman would not be able to hire her own lawyer. On the other hand, Zoe was still quite young and trying to make it in an area of California where housing costs were nearly double those in Chicago.

I got up from the bench, where JT had loved MF, and continued my walk toward the civic center, still on the phone with Skip.

"Thanks for the information," I said, a little snideness working its way into my voice.

I clicked off before he could get the last word.

Chapter 18

"Working on Sunday?" I sympathized with my former student, now coconspirator, Drew Blackstone, at his post in the basement of the Lincoln Point police building.

"The guys in here don't get weekends off, so neither do I," he said.

I extracted a tin of ginger cookies from my tote (thus proving premeditation). "These are for Amy," I said, putting the tin on top the tote. (I'd reasoned that giving Drew a gift might be considered bribing an officer; giving a gift to his wife who was still mourning the loss of her mother was innocuous.) "Please tell her I'm sorry I didn't know about her mother's passing, and I'm thinking of her."

"She'll like that," Drew said. He took the tin into his beefy hands and put it in a drawer of his gray, government-issue desk, then deposited my empty tote and purse on the shelf behind him. I had my doubts about whether Amy would ever taste a ginger-flavored crumb, especially since I saw Drew's lunchbox (the old-fashioned black metal type) lying open, most of its contents gone. A little after one in the afternoon was probably just the right time for dessert.

I wouldn't want to say that the actions were connected, but a few minutes later I was walking through the metal detector and then down the hallway to the visitors' area, accompanied by Officer Laura Fischer, the nicer of my latest two brushes with policewomen.

I found a much more subdued Zoe Howard in the visiting area this time.

"Thanks for coming, Gerry," she said in a voice I could hardly hear.

I wondered if her lawyer should be present, but figured it was her choice and I shouldn't worry about it.

Officer Laura allowed us a hug. Zoe felt as limp in my arms as the rag dolls I'd made for Maddie when she was a toddler.

"I heard the news," I said. "You got bail." I tried to sound upbeat, but it was hard to be too excited knowing she was still a long way from abandoning her ugly, ill-fitting uniform.

"Yeah, as if." Zoe sniffed. "My brilliant PD, whom I've already fired, got them down to three hundred thou. Do you know what my house is worth? Less than I owe on it. I got one of those miraculous loans and now I really do need a miracle."

I swallowed hard and managed to stifle my desire to comfort her (or put up my own home) at the expense of learning anything useful. I wished I'd heard from Ryan so that I'd know for sure he was the person who let Zoe into the Rutledge Center.

Then I remembered lessons learned from Skip. There were the theoretical lessons, what he'd told us in what he probably considered casual conversation—that the police could be ruthless in interrogations, inflicting not physical, but emotional and psychological pain. And then there was the very practical lesson he'd just given me when he lied and manipulated me into telling him where June was.

If the police could be as cavalier about evidence or eye-witnesses, surely I could get by with something less egregious.

I sat across from Zoe and looked her in the eyes, as if I had all the authority of the Lincoln Point Police Department behind me. "Why did you lie to me about how you got into the building where Brad was working?"

She put her head down. I thought she'd fallen asleep, until I heard her small voice. "I didn't lie."

I let out an exasperated sigh. "Zoe, first, there was no custodian on duty on Monday night. I checked on that. And second, it's impossible to walk straight through from the television studio to the artists' work area as you claimed. I checked that, too. You'd need at least three keys." (I made that last part up, in keeping with my new investigative strategy.)

Zoe ran her fingers through her hair, which was badly in need of a shampoo. I heard a whimper, then a growl. I looked around for something she might throw at me but saw nothing. Except the chair she was sitting on.

But I needn't have worried. When Zoe picked her head up I saw that tears had formed in her eyes.

"I didn't want to get him in trouble."

"Ryan Colson?"

She nodded and sighed, resigned to what I hoped was the last of her lies being uncovered. "Uh-huh."

"How did that come about?"

"I went to the north side of the complex, where I thought Brad was working, and Ryan happened to be outside. He was in a dark corner. With someone." Zoe emphasized "with," and I got the message. "When I pulled up they tried to duck into deeper shadows, but I saw the shiny buttons on his uniform, so I went over to see if he'd let me in. He hemmed and hawed."

"The security for the building doesn't seem that tight."

"Well, I guess they're supposed to be a little more careful at night. The management is afraid someone might . . ."

Zoe paused as we both realized that management's greatest fears had been realized that night.

"Did you know Ryan before then?"

"Not that well. I'd seen him around and knew he was security, but that's all. One thing I did know was that he wasn't supposed to be fooling around with the little honey in the corner."

I had a hard time thinking of Nan Browne as either little or a honey. "Are you saying you threatened to expose his liaison if he didn't let you in?"

"Uh-huh. Stupid, I know. But it worked."

"But everyone knew that he and Nan were . . ." I paused, giving consideration to using the entwined index finger/middle finger gesture that was so popular lately. Instead I finished up with, ". . . an item."

"Right. That's the point. He wasn't with Nan. He was with Nan's daughter."

There was no end to the surprises of the day. "The one who's an artist?"

"Uh-huh. Diana Browne. At least she's closer to Ryan's age. Can you imagine? Getting it on with mother and daughter both? I think he's more afraid of Nan than he is of his wife."

I sat back from my intense listening position. Ryan Colson was busier than I thought. I wondered how he was going to fit in a role as Judge Stephen A. Douglas on Tuesday if he got it.

Something else made sense now, too. Nan Browne had been overheard yelling at Ryan, saying she'd be visiting him in jail. Either she found out he'd breached security by letting Zoe into Rutledge Center or he confessed it to her as pillow talk. What would she yell out if she knew her boyfriend was also her daughter's? I didn't want to be there when she found out.

Or did I?

"Anyway," Zoe continued (since I was speechless), "he just said, 'let's call it even' and that I should make up some other story about how I got in. I guess I should have checked whether my story was even plausible."

We heard the static-laden sound of a walkie-talkie approaching. Officer Laura left her post in the corner of the room and opened the door.

Uh-oh. The intimidating Officer Lois Rosen loomed in the doorway. Had she heard that Officer Laura had been lax, allowing a hug and the occasional hand-patting between me and the prisoner?

Zoe and I stared at the two women, who stood deep in conversation. When they broke apart, the bad cop left and the good cop came over to us.

"You're free to go," she told Zoe.

Zoe jumped up, pushing her chair back. "For real?"

I hoped they weren't sending her, unprotected, into the arms of the bad cop.

"Yup. Your bail's been posted. You can pick up your things back in the east wing."

Officer Laura seemed pleased to be the one to make this announcement. I had the sneaking suspicion that she was still trying to impress me, Skip's aunt. She probably hoped I'd pass the message on to my nephew about how nice she'd been to a woman she thought was my friend. Questionable logic, but I'd seen it before among Skip's fans.

Zoe, in a new spurt of energy, brushed past me to the door.

"Zoe, I still need to talk to you," I said to her back. "I have a lot more questions."

"Some other time."

She was out the door. I couldn't blame her for not wanting to spend one extra minute in the airless basement.

Neither did I.

I had another short but refreshing walk ahead of me, from the police building to the library. I needed air to cleanse me of the feeling of frustration I felt. I'd been

blocked at every turn, it seemed, getting close to information only to have it walk out on me—with June, with Skip,
and now with Zoe as soon as she was free to leave.

I wondered if Zoe realized she wasn't yet off the hook.
She'd been bailed out, not exonerated. I had to find a way
to get answers to my questions about Brad Goodman. And
another interesting question had materialized.

Who had posted Zoe's bail?

I sat on a bench outside the library, too early for my
three o'clock meeting with Lourdes. This bench was free
of carvings, which might have meant that few young lovers
frequented the library on a regular basis. I felt a twinge of
regret that I'd agreed to the two-hour tutoring session. I
wished I had the afternoon clear to pursue the information
I needed. Where was the Geraldine who not long ago
wished she could do more volunteer work to help people
like the town's ad hoc fiddler and sidewalk artist?

Bad tutor! I told myself.

And where would I do more good even if I were free? In
Chicago urging June onto a plane to San Jose? Pounding
the streets of Lincoln Point looking for Rhonda? Taking a
magnifying glass and pipe to the Rutledge Center to look
for clues?

I was better off tutoring.

I still had time for phone calls, however. I called June's
home and cell phones, just in case she'd slipped into town
without notifying me. I had an idea that she might have
been the one who posted Zoe's bail. She'd been away for
all of the latest, nonfatal stabbing incidents and I felt she
should know about them, for her own and Zoe's protection.
I left messages for her.

I came upon Ryan's card in my purse and considered
calling him, but let it go. I had what I needed about his role
in letting Zoe into Rutledge Center. The only thing left was
for me to intimidate him further into talking about what

else he saw the night of the murder, and I could do that anytime.

During a lull in my own dialing (as we used to say), my cell phone rang.

"Hi, Grandma! It's me!"

"I can tell. Are you having a good day with your dad?"

"We're home. Guess what he bought me?"

"A new, frilly dress for parties."

She let out a loud laugh. Maddie probably thought she'd never want that to happen, but I had a feeling it was just a few years away, though maybe not the frilly part.

"Guess again. Be serious, Grandma."

"A new computer game."

"No, no. Guess again."

"I can't imagine."

"Okay, here's a hint. How am I talking to you right now?"

I hesitated. Did Richard buy her a cell phone? I didn't want to bring it up—if I was wrong, it would only start a storm of whining. I stalled just long enough for Maddie to run out of patience.

"I have my own cell phone, Grandma! I have my own cell phone and it's red!"

"That's wonderful, sweetheart. Now instead of picking you up on time, I can finish all my investigating first and just stay in touch by phone."

"Nuts," she said. "You wouldn't do that, would you?"

"Never."

I had to admit, I felt a weight lift at the idea of Maddie's being in constant reach.

Skip was next on my list to call. (But not until I'd called Maddie three times at her new number, "to test it.") Skip's office was just across the great lawn from where I was sitting, but I doubted he was there. I called his cell.

"Hey, Aunt Gerry," he said. I heard traffic noise and pictured him with his new car headset. He was on a campaign for everyone in the family to use one. "I suppose you want to know who posted Zoe's bail. I have no idea. I just heard she was released."

"I know." I didn't feel the need to tell him I was there when she walked out. He probably knew anyway. "I'm concerned for her safety. What if whoever is the real killer is just out there waiting for her?"

"What if she's the real killer?"

"Then I guess we're the ones who need protection."

"You got that right. Anything else I can do for you?"

From his grouchy tone I gathered that June hadn't called him. "Since you're so pleasant and cooperative today—yes, I do have a question for you."

"Sorry. I'm just . . . you know. How can I help you, Aunt Gerry?" Skip used his standard falsetto when he wanted someone to know he was forcing pleasantness. I was pleased there was a touch of humor left in him.

"What became of Rebecca Garrity or whatever was the latest name Rhonda Goodman used? The last I heard, she was pulled in for disturbing the peace and you were going to check on a search warrant for a hotel room."

"Nothing ever came of that. She walked away. She quoted some laws that made it okay for her to be marching out there, and when that didn't fly too high, she pointed out that she was from Florida and the laws there are different and she couldn't have known. No one had time for a nuisance like that, so they let her go since she didn't really hurt anyone."

"As far as we know," I said.

"As far as we know."

I'd already committed a faux pas by implying that the various sections of the LPPD should be more on speaking terms with each other, so I held back now. I wished I could find a circuitous way to point out how likely it was that Rhonda had done all the stabbings, from the paintings, to the raccoon, to the fruit. And, on the way—to Brad Goodman.

I tried another tack. "I'm sure there's a procedure in

place to find her and question her about all the stabbings. The fruit and all."

"Yeah," Skip said.

I seemed to have exhausted my sources and my ability to extract information. All I could do now was return to my normal life and meet Lourdes.

Once I pushed distractions to the back of my mind, I enjoyed working with Lourdes. She was a very willing and conscientious student. The hardships she'd endured as an immigrant had made her more appreciative of the opportunity to learn than most of my teenage students through the years.

I'd collected excerpts from the texts (or alleged texts) of the Lincoln-Douglas debates for Lourdes to use for reading comprehension exercises and for her civics questions.

"It makes me feel part of the festival," she said now, as she read a Lincoln statement. " '. . . There can be no moral right in connection with one man's making a slave of another.' Lincoln was a very smart man," she added. To which I agreed.

Lourdes was able to answer a test set of tricky questions on states' rights and moral law, the essence of the 1858 debates. I was proud that I'd had a small hand in her success.

In response to the library's warning bell—ten minutes till five o'clock closing—we packed our books and papers and headed for the exit.

"Did you hear about the crazy lady this morning, Mrs. Porter?" Lourdes asked.

I stopped short. "What about her?"

"I didn't want to talk about it before because you would think I didn't want to do my lessons. But now it's okay, right?"

Very okay, I thought. "What about the crazy lady?"

"She got attacked. She was in back of our store in the alley. Johnny thinks maybe she was looking for more knives that got accidentally thrown out and someone attacked her. An ambulance came to take her away."

I drew in my breath. "What time was that, Lourdes? Do you remember?"

"It was before I left to come and see you, Mrs. Porter. First I changed my clothes, though, so I think it was about two thirty."

I let out a long sigh. Two thirty. About one hour after Zoe was released.

Chapter 19

We left the library on the dot of five o'clock. Lourdes of-
fered to give me a ride home, but I didn't want to take her
on my next errand—to visit Rhonda in the Lincoln Point
Hospital. Neither did I want to wait very long on the bench
outside in the chill, already dark evening. As soon as Lourdes turned away from me to walk toward the parking lot,
I punched in Mary Lou's cell phone number. I had a reason
for not using my home number.

"I need a ride," I said to her. "Come alone."

Mary Lou chuckled. "What is this, Mom? Are we in the
CIA now?"

"I'll explain when you get here. Can you make up an excuse for not going right back home?"

"Sure. I'll tell my daughter I want to call her on her new
cell from some remote location."

"Smart."

Once we clicked off and I was left in the now-deserted
civic center, I wished I'd taken Lourdes up on her offer. I
crossed my legs and pulled my jacket closer around me. I

looked in vain for signs of life. Where were all the artists and actors? Wasn't there a considerable population of dogs that needed walking? Intrepid joggers or cyclists that should be exercising? Dedicated teachers working late at the high school across the way? (Not even I would have been there on the Sunday evening of a long holiday weekend.)

The city maintained a large expanse of lawn around the three civic center buildings and another lawn on the other side of the semicircular Civic Drive that was the Abraham Lincoln High School campus. I remembered times when I'd enjoyed a quiet, solitary evening walk in this neighborhood, especially after a long day of classes and meetings. Ordinarily a beautiful urban setting, the area now felt like a frightening, shadowy wasteland.

Would I be this nervous if there weren't a murderer loose in Lincoln Point?

I told myself the murderer might right now be in the very hospital I was on my way to visit. I was safe. Except from whoever put her there. Zoe? I pictured the newly released Zoe, in the midst of a temper tantrum, on her way to harm everyone she thought had wronged her.

I sat huddled on the bench, my jacket collar up around my ears, trying to make myself small and invisible until Mary Lou arrived. Though it wasn't late, the overcast February sky and deserted streets contributed to an atmosphere more like the dead of night. I looked behind me, past the enormous city hall, at the back of the police building, and saw a few lighted windows, but they seemed far away and gave little comfort. There were many shadowy walkways, overgrown trees, and dark corners between me and the dim lights of the LPPD.

A flash of light brought my head up. A vehicle came from my left, from Nolin Creek Pines, the housing project where Lourdes lived with her two sons. The lights were high enough to be on a minivan or an SUV. Not Mary Lou's, however. Unless she'd decided to take the longer route via backstreets, she'd be coming straight down Springfield Boulevard, approaching from my right.

Where was she, anyway? Without traffic, it was little more than a five-minute drive from my house. She might have had a hard time leaving Maddie behind or making up a story for why she wouldn't be back with me in a few minutes. She might be changing her clothes, thinking our errand required more than the casual garb she'd worn all day.

She couldn't know how desperate I was to be picked up.

The vehicle on my left had slowed down. An SUV for sure. I strained to see the color. The dark green of the Porter SUV? Impossible to tell. To make matters worse, the vehicle had pulled over between streetlights. On purpose? I felt my heart race. I couldn't determine the driver's gender, let alone intentions.

The vehicle had drawn close to the curb and was rolling along at a very slow pace. Not parking, not driving through. I could think of no other reasons for this maneuver except to grab and mug me or abduct me. I saw now that it was an SUV of a light color. Silver or beige. I wished I knew what kind of car Zoe drove.

I thought of getting up and walking to the right and toward the street. Maybe Mary Lou or some other benevolent motorist would come along just in time. If I walked in the other direction, back toward the projects, I'd be deep in narrow tree-lined pathways and would end up in a neighborhood that was not the best even in the light of day.

In my panicky state, no option seemed good to me, but I chose to move rather than be a sitting target. At one point in its crawl toward me, a sliver of light fell on the SUV's windshield and I saw a hooded driver of undetermined gender.

I looked ahead of me, down Springfield Boulevard. Two vehicles, both SUVs, were lined up behind a red light at the crosswalk in front of the high school on one side and Rosie's bookstore on the other. I grumbled at the inanity of having that traffic light operate whether school was in session or not.

I took a breath. Surely one of the two waiting cars would be a safe harbor. Springfield Boulevard dead-ended at Civic Drive, so the vehicles had to either turn into the parking lot next to the bookstore, which was closed, or take Civic Drive in one direction or the other.

I walked to the curb, intending to flag down whichever car came my way. I was now halfway between the library and city hall.

Bong, bong, bong, bong, bong, bong, bong, bong.

The city hall clock rang out the first eight notes of the Whittington chimes, marking the quarter hour. The melody I usually loved was startling this evening and nearly sent me to my knees. Five fifteen. It felt like midnight.

The SUV on my left, the one I thought of as the stalker vehicle, stopped, its driver perhaps also surprised by the loud chimes. I heard its engine growl, as if the driver had put the vehicle in PARK and then stepped on the accelerator. To intimidate me? It was working. It could be a problem with the car, I reasoned. Maybe one of the dashboard lights came on and the driver is testing something.

Another growl. I took another step away.

The first SUV in line on Springfield Boulevard moved in my direction. I crossed my fingers. I heard the toot of a horn, saw an arm wave at me out the window, and knew it was Mary Lou.

Whew. I raced toward her.

At the same time, the creepy SUV pulled away from the curb and squealed away, passing Mary Lou on the wrong side of the street and racing down Springfield Boulevard.

"What a jerk, huh?" Mary Lou said, indicating the stalker vehicle.

I buckled myself into the green Porter SUV, my heart racing.

"What's up, Mom? You're all out of breath."

"Take me to the hospital, please," I said.

* * *

Once Mary Lou realized I wanted to go to the hospital as a visitor and not a patient, she relaxed her shoulders, and we were on our way. I was embarrassed to tell her how frightened I'd been of what might have been an imaginary threat. Now that I was safe and warm in her car, listening to a Three Tenors CD, I thought of a couple of benign scenarios. The driver of the slow-moving SUV might have been trying to read a map (then why not park under a street-light?), or he might have been having a heart attack that I should have responded to (then how could he race away once I was out of reach?).

Maybe there were no benign scenarios after all.

"I brought you a peanut butter sandwich," Mary Lou said.

Thus, the extra time it had taken her to get to me. In the long run it worked out well since I was hungry and she'd arrived in the nick of time.

"How thoughtful."

"I had a snack myself as soon as I got home, so I'm fine, but I didn't know how long this latest errand would take."

I unwrapped the package and bit into eight-grain bread, creamy peanut butter, and homemade (by crafts group president Karen Striker) pear jelly. All was right with the world.

Except for Rhonda's and Zoe's part of it.

I briefed Mary Lou on the attack on Rhonda.

"All Lourdes could tell me was that 'the crazy lady' was knocked over, and the attacker hit her with something from the alley, then ran away. The ambulance came and took Rhonda to the hospital."

Had Lourdes mentioned a hooded sweatshirt or was that my overactive imagination again? I wondered now. Had she said, "the attacker ran away," or, "the attacker drove away in a silver SUV?"

I needed to calm my mind. A vigorous Italian aria by the late Luciano Pavarotti didn't help much.

"And you think Zoe was the perp—that's what they call them on those *Law and Orders* Richard says I watch all day—why? Because the timing is right?" Mary Lou asked, making it sound like flimsy reasoning on my part.

"Or one huge coincidence." I ticked off other reasons. "And she has a temper, and she was afraid that Rhonda would come after her. Maybe she decided to take the initiative."

"Or maybe it was Rhonda who attacked first in the alley and it was self-defense on Zoe's part. Or whoever's," Mary Lou suggested.

"Could be. Maybe Zoe is in the hospital now, apologizing to Rhonda for hurting her." My voice reeked with sarcasm. "But seriously, I wonder why I'm rushing to judgment against Zoe?" I asked.

"So Skip will be proved correct?"

Now that was an interesting rationale. For the whole week, I'd been hoping Skip and the LPPD were incorrect, because I wanted June to be happy and have her life back. It was possible that June's latest noncommunicative tone with me, and Zoe's walking out on me (though who could blame her for rushing out of a jail?) wasn't sitting right with me, and now I wanted my nephew vindicated.

Very silly, I realized. I doubted Skip himself thought that way.

I chewed the last bite of my peanut butter sandwich, pitying what the justice system would be like if I were an official part of it.

Mary Lou made a U-turn on Civic Drive and headed up Springfield Boulevard. The town's hospital, at the top of Lincoln Point's only hill, was a couple of miles north of where I lived.

"What did you tell Richard and Maddie?" I asked, as we passed my neighborhood on the left.

Mary Lou grinned. "It was tough. I couldn't say we needed some special time since we were together a lot of the day. So, I said we were going to stop off at the gym because we were thinking of joining."

"I'd never join a gym. Why now, on a Sunday evening? Are they even open on Sunday evenings? And why would you join one ten miles from your new neighborhood when there are probably ten better-equipped gyms in Palo Alto?" (I may have overreacted, but only because I wanted to protect Maddie especially from the knowledge that I was leaving her out of something she'd love to do.)

Mary Lou shrugged. "Okay, I'm not very good at improvising. They asked the same questions. I had to . . . uh . . . make up something else."

"What?"

Even in the dim, jerky light of a row of streetlamps we passed, I could see Mary Lou flush with embarrassment.

"I sort of hinted that there was someone there you wanted to meet."

I was confused. Who would I want to meet at a gym? A crafter? A student? A suspect? What would keep Richard and Maddie happy about not being with us?

"You mean, someone who wanted my advice? A former student?" I asked.

Mary Lou shrugged, fortunately able to avoid eye contact because she was driving. "Nuh-uh. More like a . . . guy."

"A guy? As in, I have trysts at the gym, or I'm going to pick up a guy?"

"I sort of implied that you were interested in expanding your base of friends."

I slapped my hands on my knees. "You told them I'm looking for a boyfriend. I don't know whether to congratulate you on your creativity or send you to your room without dinner."

But by now I was laughing and Mary Lou knew she'd gotten a pass.

Mary Lou parked in a lot next to a helicopter landing pad. In my many months of coming here during Ken's illness, I'd never seen a helicopter alight, but the markings were kept freshly painted, so I had to assume it was an active site. I pitied people who were a plane ride away when they needed emergency service as well as those who needed to be transported from one facility to another while in pain.

We walked to the ER entrance, located at the end of one of the five wings that came out radially from the center (where, of course, there was a statue of Abraham Lincoln, with anonymous children at his feet, as if he'd been a biblical leader).

As we entered the crowded waiting room I cringed at the condition some of our citizens were in this Sunday evening. I wasn't cut out for medical work and hated seeing even a little blood seep through a bandage. I wondered what I was doing here.

And someone else was questioning my presence, also.

"Why don't we just issue you a radio and put you on the on-call list?" Skip asked, coming up behind me.

"That would be very nice, thanks," said Mary Lou, who recovered more quickly than I did from seeing her cousin.

"I'm just visiting the sick," I said. "I'm thinking of volunteering. How do you think I'd look in candy stripes?"

That got a laugh, which was my goal.

"I'm just the driver," Mary Lou said.

Skip shot me a look, addressing Mary Lou. "I know what that's like."

"Now that we're here, let's talk," I said, pointing outside the waiting room to a small lounge area that was empty at the moment.

We took seats on wooden chairs with thinly upholstered, blue paisley covers that looked like the chairs in every medical waiting room I'd ever been in. Mary Lou and I looked to Skip with questions on our faces. He took the cue.

"Rhonda is pretty banged up but they're saying she'll be okay. It looks like whoever did it wasn't out to do away with her permanently—just wanted to make a point."

Mary Lou shuddered. "Nice way to make a point."

"She's sedated now and can't talk."

"Is she the one we're calling the crazy lady?" Mary Lou asked. "I can't believe I've been seeing her in the grocery store and all over town and she might be a killer herself."

"Is she the killer?" I asked Skip. "Is there any more evidence than there ever was about who killed Brad Goodman?" *Does the killer drive a silver or beige SUV?* I wanted to ask.

"We're a little farther along, but not much. Johnny Ortega, one of the shift supervisors at Willie's, ID'd her as the woman he's seen hanging around his store and in the alley behind the shop. We verified that the knives in the various objects around town were from Willie's, and he confirms that he's thrown out a few old ones."

"So that's the connection we . . . you needed."

"There's no problem connecting her to the mischief around town now. She had a key card in her pocket. We finally got a warrant and were able to search her motel room. She had a pile of Willie's knives—"

"And fruit?" Mary Lou asked. She wasn't smiling, but she drew one from Skip.

"No fruit. But from the number of knives she had stashed under her bed, some of which were new, she must have either broken in or posed as a customer and somehow stolen a bunch."

"Premeditation," Mary Lou said, leading me to believe she did watch television crime dramas when we weren't looking.

I thought about how I carried what could be called

luggage every time I left the house—either a very large purse or a purse and a tote. It would be no problem for me to scoop a dozen pieces of silverware or other sundries from Willie's counter into any of my carryalls, there to nestle among assorted crafts tools that didn't make it to my tool box.

Skip had been unusually forthcoming this evening. Because it was Sunday and technically his day off? Because for this case, more than others, he knew the solution would affect him personally and he wanted it over and done with? Or just because he was hungry and hoped to be invited to dinner at my house? He couldn't know there might not be a dinner tonight, depending on when Rhonda woke up.

I took advantage of the situation and pressed on. "It sounds like you've made a lot of progress. You must know for sure now that the woman's real name is Rhonda Edgerton Goodman, right?"

Skip nodded. "Yeah, we did learn that. One of her many drivers' licenses was in her real name."

"What's missing?" Mary Lou asked.

"We can't connect Willie's knives to the murder weapon, which was decidedly not a knife used to spread cream cheese on bagels. Goodman was stabbed with a serrated workshop knife, very sharp."

"Ouch," Mary Lou said.

"Neither can we say the knife used to slash the paintings was also the murder weapon."

Something Skip said prompted me to think back, and I pictured Rhonda with a leather briefcase, looking perhaps as sophisticated (and not crazy) as she had when she brushed by me on her way out of the jail's basement visiting area. I envisioned her dressed like a lawyer, posing as a customer, surreptitiously emptying the contents of Willie's white plastic container into her briefcase. Posing.

"Do you think Rhonda could have posed as Zoe and deliberately got herself on the security tape?" I asked Skip.

"She'd have to know that the paintings were right there where the camera would pick her up," Mary Lou said.

"She could have figured that out and moved the paintings," I suggested.

"Wouldn't she be flattered that she was the one Brad painted? If it was a good rendition, that is," Mary Lou asked.

Mary Lou had pulled a sketchbook from her own large canvas purse-tote and was multitasking. As we talked she worked with a piece of charcoal. I sensed a masterpiece in the making. She'd done a few caricatures of people in the waiting room across the narrow hall from us. She'd picked out the most prominent feature of each and captured them in an identifiable, whimsical way—a man with a bulbous nose who was wheezing; a little girl half asleep sucking her thumb; a man with heavy stubble and a head bandage. (Oops. Blood. I turned away.)

"If Rhonda recognized that Brad had painted her likeness, all the better for framing Zoe," I said.

We both looked at Skip, as if finally remembering who was the true investigator in the room.

"Don't mind me. But there is the unique jacket," he said.

"Rhonda seems to have unlimited resources," I said. "How difficult would it be to make a crude copy of a black jacket with rhinestones?"

"Easy for you to say."

"I take it you didn't find a tissue paper jacket in Rhonda's room?"

"Ha. Wouldn't that have been nice?"

Mary Lou began a sketch of a jacket with a large Z on the back. I wondered if she'd ever considered a career as a police sketch artist.

"Can you take another look at the tape? Or I could look at it," I suggested.

I got another I'm-annoyed look. "We can handle it, thanks."

"I just meant, I know fabric and crafts and all. And that's

what we're talking about. Putting rhinestones, or something that looks like rhinestones on fabric."

"It's just an analog videotape from an old VCR. It's not digital and it's not good quality. I don't think you're going to be able to tell whether the stones were stitched or glued for example. It's just not that good a picture."

"Still . . ."

"Just let her look and save us all some grief," Mary Lou said, wielding her charcoal now on small strokes to represent stitching on a leather jacket.

I gave my daughter-in-law a smile, but heard no promises from my nephew.

"Who do you think attacked Rhonda?" I asked. I'd come back to the tape viewing later, perhaps with a plate of cookies in hand.

"Who do *you* think attacked her?" Skip asked.

"Zoe" was out before I could pull myself together mentally.

"But Mom doesn't have any reason for that except that the attack occurred right after Zoe got released on bail," Mary Lou said. Her tone was neutral; I couldn't tell if she was supporting my rationale or not.

"Zoe has already been picked up, questioned, and let go," Skip said. I got the call about a half hour ago. Evidently they disturbed her bubble bath and she screamed at the guys since she hadn't had a bath for x number of days."

I hoped when all this was over, Zoe would schedule anger-management classes for herself. She should at least learn to control her temper when dealing with the police.

"Her alibi?"

"Zoe has an alibi to cover every minute of the time between her release and the attack on Rhonda." In a manner reminiscent of my friend Linda, Skip paused for dramatic effect. "She TM'd someone to pick her up from the station and was with that person until just before the knock on her bathroom door." I raised my eyebrows. "So to speak," Skip said.

"And the person . . ." But I took one look at his face and I knew who had given Zoe another airtight alibi. "June," I said.

His nod was slow, his expression sad.

I patted his hand and wished I had some cookies in my enormous tote.

The hospital cafeteria brought up more bad memories. Not only of bad coffee and ugly yellow walls, but of long nights with a book in front of me. I remembered having had to read the same page over and over because my concentration and energy, both mental and physical, were so low.

Tonight at least there was some good news as Skip and Mary Lou and I sat at a small round table, its top in a faux wood-grain design.

"If she's able to alibi Zoe, June's back in town, right?"

"Yeah, but I only know that from word of mouth from the guys who talked to Zoe."

"You haven't seen June or heard from her?"

Another slow nod.

I was stuck for something comforting to say. The sound of Mary Lou's cell phone broke the silence.

"It's Maddie," she said, reading the caller ID. "She hasn't put her new cell phone down since she got it." She clicked her phone on. "Hi, sweetie. Are you having fun?" A brief pause, then, "No? How come?"

We all knew how come. Because she was missing the action.

"We're just doing an errand," Mary Lou said into the phone. She rolled her eyes at us. Neither Skip nor I envied her task. "Why don't you call Devyn?" Pause. "I know I said not too many calls to L.A., but this is Sunday, and you have unlimited minutes." Pause. "Bye, sweetie. Put your dad on, okay?"

Less than a minute later, my cell phone rang. Maddie, of course. "Call me back, Grandma, so I can get a call," she said. "Then I won't call again. I promise, I promise."

I obliged my granddaughter with a call and then turned back to Mary Lou and Skip.

We were the only people in the hospital cafeteria who were laughing.

Chapter 20

Back in the ER waiting room, Rhonda's doctor reported that she wouldn't be awake before morning.

How many times had I heard that message from Ken's doctors?

"Go home and get some rest," they'd say, as if that were even remotely possible. But that had been a long time ago, more than two years, and I'd had many things to be grateful for since then. Once again, I implemented my plan to cut off my internal whining as soon as I could, each time accomplishing it a little more quickly than the last.

At about seven o'clock, Mary Lou, Skip, and I walked toward the exit, stepping on the large mat in front of the ER doors. The automatic glass doors opened for us and for the two people wanting to enter the ER from outdoors. We all stopped—the three of us, and the two newcomers, June Chinn and Zoe Howard.

June hugged each one of us in turn. She took a long time with Skip, causing the automatic doors to stay open and bringing complaints from the volunteer ladies at the information desk when the chilly February wind coursed through the hallway.

Zoe stood back, a slight smile on her pale face. I wanted to adopt her for a week and feed her right. Unless she was Rhonda's attacker, that is, and/or Brad Goodman's killer.

We backed up and commandeered the waiting area outside the ER again. (In fact, a woman and a teenager yielded to the mob front we presented and abandoned their paisley seats.) Mary Lou called Richard back and told him we'd be another little while.

Without our asking, Zoe volunteered her story. "I know it looks bad for me, but I did not attack Rhonda. I wouldn't have the strength, for one thing, and I wouldn't have known where to find her, for another."

I noticed that the observations "I wouldn't want to attack her" and "I'd have no reason to attack her" were not on Zoe's list of facts. I chalked that up to honesty.

June raised her right hand, as if she were under oath. "I promise you I am not lying when I say that I picked Zoe up at the jail and took her to her home, where I stayed until well after Rhonda was attacked."

One interpretation of June's grammar was that they had a hotline to Rhonda's attacker ("Call me when the attack is over," June might have said) but I knew it was just June's inadvertent obfuscation that made it seem that way.

The automatic doors opened and closed many times while we sat there. I saw enough crutches, slings, wheelchairs, oxygen tanks, and head bandages and heard enough wheezing, coughing, moaning, and sneezing to last awhile. But one pair of visitors caught my eye.

Richard and Maddie came through the doors. More exactly, Maddie skipped through and Richard walked in with his hands in surrender.

Maddie hugged me, then her mother, June, and Skip. She was smiling so broadly, she could hardly speak.

"Hi, everybody," she said.

"How in the world did you know we were here?" I asked.

Mary Lou snapped her fingers before anyone in her family could answer. "She heard the hospital noises in the background."

"That's right," Richard said. "Thanks to me, she recognizes even a muffled paging system or a code blue."

"What a detective!" Skip said, knowing what would make her blush.

"All she had to do was convince me to drive us here," Richard said.

Mary Lou grabbed her daughter around the waist and pulled her onto her lap. "Lord, I don't know what we're going to do when you're old enough to drive."

I shuddered at the thought.

Maddie reached around to her backpack. She extracted what looked like a crude photo album from one of the zipper pockets and walked up to Zoe. Nobody had thought of introducing them, but Maddie took matters into her own hands.

"You must be Zoe," she said. "I saw your picture in the paper. I'm sorry about your boyfriend."

"Thank you," Zoe said. The trace of awkwardness in her manner told me she didn't have much to do with children.

"I got some pictures of him off the Internet and made up a book in case I met you sometime. Dad said you were here, too, so I brought it for you," she said, handing over the album.

Zoe took the book, made of 8½-by-11 sheets of photo paper. Maddie had punched holes along one side of the sheaf and threaded ribbon (a selection I recognized from a roll of lavender with specks of gold that I kept in my ribbon drawer) through the holes to form a binding.

Crafts by Maddie. Not inspired by or forced on her by her grandmother. My heart swelled.

Zoe leafed through the photos, clearly touched by the gesture. We all strained to see. Some were headshots of

Brad, others group photos obviously taken from newspaper articles or trade magazines.

Now I could see what Maddie could produce when she had proper tools to work with.

I thought of all the times when she'd visited me and complained about my computer, which was a good three generations behind the state of the art. She was now using her own up-to-date system—with an enormous number of bits or bytes, a scanner, color printer, and a wide variety of papers—destined to reside eventually in her new room in Palo Alto.

Richard had also arranged for high-speed Internet access to be delivered (so to speak) to my house for six months.

"If you don't like it after that time, you can just cancel and go back to dial-up," he'd told me. He'd sounded as if I'd be turning in my Saturn Ion for a horse and buggy if I chose that option. In fact, I'd gotten used to the fast response and planned to keep up the subscription.

"When did you do this, sweetheart?" Mary Lou asked Maddie, flipping through the pages of photos and clippings.

"During the week, while you guys were, you know, doing errands." Her emphasis on the last word was not unexpected.

"This is really wonderful," Zoe said, her eyes tearing up.

Everyone present echoed the sentiment. We all held out our hands for a turn at looking at the album closely.

"I didn't mean to make you cry," Maddie said.

Zoe pulled her into a hug.

If you've never dealt with children, I thought, Maddie was a good one to start with.

The conversation broke into twos and threes. Maddie and June huddled for a while. I trusted June to explain to her little friend as well as she could why she'd left us with-

out a word. Skip and Zoe had a chat that involved many
hand gestures. Skip had made it clear that he was off duty,
or as off duty as a cop can be. As long as they're not hitting
each other, I mused.

Mary Lou, Richard, and I decided we might as well take
the party home and have some real food.

I clapped my hands, as I'd done in classrooms for more
than two decades.

"Is anyone hungry?" I asked.

I never would have predicted the dinner scene at my
home on Sunday evening. By eight o'clock, my house was
full of people seated around the living room and dining
room, plates of food on their laps. There were so many
things upside down about the picture. First, that I'd served
a buffet of leftovers to "company"; second, that the plates
were paper; and third, that the guests included a murder
suspect.

Of the cast members of the week, only Linda was missing. I was grateful, lest we get into a discussion of pineapples versus grapefruits again.

Richard and Skip were working on a smorgasbord of
pot roast and side dishes; Mary Lou and June found enough
Chinese take-out to satisfy them; Maddie, visibly delighted
to be back in the middle of things, had poured herself
a large glass of milk, the better to hide her microwaved
pizza.

Zoe had made herself a salad of butter lettuce, raw vegetables, croutons, and grated Parmesan cheese. "I need to
ease into eating real food," she said. "This is my first decent meal in a week."

"I'm glad I can accommodate you from my meager
pickings," I said, helping myself to pizza, the least popular
choice among those over eleven years old.

Light talk of the weather (more rain in store, but hope-
fully not on debate night) and guesses about who would be

this year's principal characters on Tuesday night (not Ryan, I was willing to bet, after I'd called his bluff and ruined his karma) lasted longer than I thought it would.

I knew once everyone had taken in enough food to quell their hunger, we'd have to get down to a more serious discussion. One of the guests, after all, had been charged with murdering her boyfriend. And another had disappeared for several days without telling *her* boyfriend. (The rest of us lived normal, boring lives, except for the occasional feeling of being stalked.)

Eventually, Zoe's voice rose above the chatter, as she cornered Skip. I doubted she meant to command the attention of the whole room.

"I don't know who would want to kill him. I don't know why you think I did," she said. "I know people who don't like me are bringing up all kinds of things. Like how I got fired from the school district. But I did not throw that eraser at a student. I threw it against the blackboard. In the opposite direction of the class, as a matter of fact. I had to get their attention somehow. Kids feel like substitute teachers are fair game for whatever bad behavior they want to indulge in."

I had no argument with that statement. And it wasn't hard to imagine that Jason might have been exaggerating. Skip gave Zoe a muffled reply then got up to refill drink glasses. I figured he'd worked out any department logistics about being in my home with a murder suspect.

I picked at my pizza (cheese topping only, since it had been ordered originally for Maddie on Chinese take-out night). It seemed ironic to me that with all her attempts at deception, Zoe looked and sounded more innocent to me each time I saw her.

I could hardly wait to get back to the hospital to talk to Rhonda. I was sure that the LPPD could hardly wait, also, to hear my opinion of each woman as a potential killer.

* * *

For the next hour, my house became the site of a group therapy session, or an Alcoholics Anonymous meeting, with all the outpourings, bonding, apologizing, explaining, and promises for the future.

June met me in the kitchen at one point. She put her arm around my shoulder. "I know I shouldn't have split like that, Gerry, but I was just so frantic."

"We missed you," I said.

"Same here, for sure. Skip has been so, so understanding, I can't believe it."

"I'm glad to hear it. Did you have a good talk in the car on the way over here?"

"Very good." She let out a long, pleasant sigh. "I'm very lucky he didn't blow me off. I should never have treated him that way."

"As long as you learned something."

"I did. And not just about me and Skip. I found out some things about Rhonda and Brad that I guess I really needed to hear."

"Oh?"

"It's almost a cliché, and Zoe didn't know anything about it. Rhonda put Brad through school, and when he started to make it in the art world, he also made it with a few younger artists, if you know what I mean."

"He cheated on her?"

June picked up a dishcloth and dried the few serving bowls I'd used for the buffet. "Uh-huh. And that was the opinion of his *friends*. I can hardly repeat what others who didn't like Brad said about him. I went to Chicago trying to find Rhonda and some proof that she was nuts enough to have killed Brad and I came away feeling a little sorry for her. And Zoe wasn't exactly an angel in all this. She pulled some tricks to discredit Rhonda at the real estate office where she worked."

"What you found out gives Rhonda even more motive, though, doesn't it?" I posed this question to myself as much as to June.

"I guess. Not that Brad deserved to be murdered. I don't mean that," June said. "I just feel bad for Rhonda now."

"I do, too," Zoe said, coming up behind with a load of paper plates and napkins. "And I feel really stupid myself, not knowing all this about my supposedly wonderful, faithful boyfriend."

I wondered if Zoe, though she wasn't younger than Brad, had been one of his liaisons during his marriage to Rhonda. It didn't seem appropriate to ask.

"Well, I'm just glad it all worked out that June is back, and just in time to post your bail, Zoe. Let's just hope now that—"

June stopped on her way to my trash compactor. "I didn't bail her out."

Zoe fumbled a glass (not paper) she was holding. "You didn't?"

"You thought I did?" June asked.

"Yes."

"No. You called me and I went to pick you up," June said.

"Yeah, and I assumed you'd posted my bail."

"I assumed you'd posted it."

And I assumed that whoever posted it was not yet through with Zoe Howard.

I walked toward the living room, calling as I went. "Skip!"

While Skip left messages with all his contacts to determine who'd posted Zoe's bail, we all speculated, unhampered by a lack of facts.

"Maybe Rhonda posted it so she could attack you, Zoe, and instead she got attacked." This from Mary Lou, who did a nice job of suggesting that if Zoe had attacked Rhonda in self-defense, this was the perfect time to confess.

The rest of us had more general questions. Skip had already told Zoe she had no chance of finding out herself on a Sunday night. She'd have to wait until morning.

"How come a person can walk in and post bail on a Sunday but you can't find out who it was on a Sunday?" I asked.

"You can always post bail at the jail, twenty-four/seven. But that doesn't mean the paperwork will be done and available," Skip said.

"Who could it have been?" was heard in many variations, as well as, "How much was it for?" and "Can anyone just walk in and post bail for someone without telling them?"

"Is that information available to the public?" Richard asked. "Or is it like a medical record?"

"It's a gray area," Skip said. "The press has a right to know but not necessarily a need to know. Whether the public has any rights in this regard is up in the air. There's nothing on the books and it's never been tested in Lincoln Point."

For some reason, my nephew gave me a look that said, "Don't you start."

Maddie left the room and came back with a printout of information on bail. We let her read some of it out loud.

"'You must be eighteen years old to post bail,'" she read, adding, "And you need an ID so I guess I can't do it yet." (I hoped she'd never have to.) She continued reading (at a very high level, I might add). "'If a defendant has no ties to the community where he has committed his crimes, or for any other reason, a judge can order that he be held without bail.' Hmmm. Judges are, like, in charge of a lot."

"Maybe you'd like to be a judge," Skip said to Maddie. "Stephen Douglas was a judge on the Illinois Supreme Court."

Either June had been tutoring Skip on Illinois history, or he really was into the spirit of debate season more than I remembered from previous years.

"Never mind," said Mary Lou, who, while law-abiding, couldn't quite let go of her antiestablishment roots.

Maddie wisely kept silent on the topic.

Skip's cell phone ring stopped all threads of conversation. If he wanted privacy, he was in the wrong house. We sat poised to listen and learn from his side of the call, but Skip was practiced in the art of the noncommittal.

"Yeah?" Pause. "Can you spell that?" Pause. "A two-for, huh? I really appreciate this, Jenny. I'll be right there."

I detected a slight twitching of June's eyebrows at the mention of a "Jenny."

Skip clicked off and smiled, playing his audience for all it was worth. It was the "two-for" reference that stuck in mind, and I intended to hold out for two pieces of news.

"The bail poster was a woman named Debra Ketough," he said, spelling it for us. "Now, I gotta go." He grabbed his jacket from the back of a chair.

"Who?" Zoe said.

"Oh, no. You can't go without telling us the second thing," I said.

"Who's that?" Mary Lou asked.

"I have no idea," Zoe said.

"Some stranger bailed you out?" June asked.

"Who said there was a second thing?" Skip asked me, zipping his all-weather jacket.

"Ketough. That's an unusual name," Mary Lou said, wiping off the end tables we'd used for our buffet. "Definitely not one of the ten people I know in Lincoln Point, all of whom are artists."

"I heard you say 'two-for'," I said. "Is Rhonda awake? Is that it?"

"I can Google her," Maddie said. She picked up a pencil and smoothed out one of the sheets she'd printed out with bail bond information. "Debra . . . can you spell it for me again?" I leaned over and wrote it down for her, then watched her disappear down the hallway.

"Who could she be?" Zoe asked. "I never heard of a Debra Ketough or Keting or whatever." She sounded flustered, as I would be if a stranger had had that much influence over my life at a critical stage. I'm sure she considered, as I did, that this Debra could be the killer.

Richard, who had the least amount of tolerance for this kind of uncontrolled scattered interchange, had turned away and put the television set on at very low volume. He'd found a channel showing the history of the typewriter.

"I never heard of a Debra Ketough," Zoe said.

"Well, that's what they told me," Skip said. "Is she from Chicago, maybe?"

"Someone you work with?" I asked. A fairly useless thought, since no matter how low the bail was, I couldn't imagine a casual work friend posting it, especially without creating some fanfare and informing the beneficiary.

Richard focused intently on the television screen. I saw a close-up of the row of number keys at the top of an old-fashioned black typewriter.

Ken and I always marveled at the concentration and interest Richard would show for the most obscure documentaries. The secret life of the American bison. A biography of a one-hundred-year-old African American woman who never left her West Virginia home. The evolution of the Barbie doll.

Today, I understood that he needed to distance himself from a situation he had no control over.

"I'm going to ride to the hospital with you," I said to Skip.

"Me, too, me, too," said the shortest one in our midst, just back from her research mission.

"It's bedtime for you, sweetie," Mary Lou said, poking Maddie in a playful way.

"And we need you to stay and work with June and Zoe to find out who this Debra is," I said.

"I tried. I couldn't find her. It's like she doesn't have an address anywhere, not in the whole state of California. Then I broadened my search and still couldn't find her. She must be from another country."

"Thanks for all the work," Skip said, ruffling her hair. I

wondered how long he could get away with that. Longer than either her parents or I could, I was sure.

"So can I come to the hospital?"

I leaned over and whispered in Maddie's ear. "I'll tell you everything when I tuck you in."

Maddie thrust her chin out. "Okay, okay."

"Who said *anyone* is coming with me?" Skip asked.

"I just need five minutes with her," I said.

"Suppose I call you in a half hour or so and let you know what's up."

I thrust my chin out, then realized that if it hadn't worked for an eleven-year-old, it probably wouldn't work for me. "Okay," I said.

Skip looked at June. "I'll see you later?"

She gave him a wonderful smile and a shy nod.

All was well again, I thought, until I caught Zoe's expression. She'd done very well at dinner and through the rest of the evening, with neither temper tantrums nor tears. Maybe that's why I felt so sorry for her. Now her lips quivered and her eyes were watery. She seemed to be barely holding it together, ready to go to one extreme or the other at the slightest nudge.

I knew what that was like.

My guests trickled out. It was as if, once Skip left, the party was over.

Zoe had tried to determine more about the woman who bailed her out, but as Skip had predicted, she couldn't get through to anyone at the courthouse or the jail. Frustrated, she left with June, planning to stay next door overnight. I didn't blame her. Under the circumstances, being bailed out wasn't necessarily a plus and I wouldn't have wanted to go home to an empty condo, either.

At some point in the evening, Zoe had learned about the slashed fruit at my home and at her neighbor's. (Richard had let it slip, thinking it was common knowledge.) That might also have contributed to Zoe's decision to stay where, unbeknownst to her or June, there had been a stabbed raccoon.

Chapter 21

Maddie and I left her father with a glass of wine, watching a program on the history of surgical instruments (this one was understandably interesting), and her mother with a cup of tea, at her desk catching up with correspondence for her Palo Alto art gallery.

"There is life for an artist after the Lincoln-Douglas debates, you know," she'd reminded us. "I have to prepare a mailing for our spring exhibit."

Maddie and I went to the room with the baseball afghan for our good-night session. I was hoping for an interruption by way of a phone call from Skip summoning me to Rhonda's bedside, but quiet time with my granddaughter was not a bad second choice.

"If someone is not a nice person, does that mean he deserves to be killed?" Maddie asked me.

"No, of course not. You know that."

"Yeah, yeah, but this artist was very mean to people."

"What makes you say that?"

"I saw a video on YouTube. It showed Brad Goodman

getting an award and he practically pushed that nice Mr. Villard out of the way."

"Mr. Villard? From the Rutledge Center?"

"Uh-huh. The man with the beard." Maddie was fading off to sleep. "I saw the TV lady on the video, too."

My eyes widened. The TV lady? We knew only one TV lady, Nan Browne. What was Nan Browne doing on a video with Ed Villard and Brad Goodman?

Ordinarily I wouldn't dream of trying to keep Maddie awake beyond her first yawn. But tonight I was merciless. I propped her up a bit from her supine position.

"Let's talk a little more about the video, sweetheart. You saw Ms. Browne with the artist who was killed? And Mr. Villard was there, too?"

"Uh-huh." Maddie slid down on threadbare soccer-design sheets (another of her father's legacies), yawning more deeply, eyes blinking. "You can see some of the Google images in the album I made for Zoe. And you can see Mr. Villard in the newspaper photos I cut out."

I detected a slight slurring of Maddie's esses. Why had she picked tonight to want to go to bed at a reasonable hour? I felt I was a candidate for the world's worst grandmother— leading my granddaughter into a crime scene, forgetting to pick her up at school, and now keeping her awake like some fourth-world minister of torture.

"Just a couple more minutes, sweetheart."

"I left out a lot of stuff that wasn't nice, though," Maddie said.

I wished I had Zoe's photo album. There had been too much going on at the hospital and then in the kitchen (even paper plates generated housekeeping chores) and living room at the time. I'd given the album only a cursory look, paying more attention to Maddie's crafts work than to the content. And now the book was next door, with Zoe and June.

I went to the bedroom window to see if there were still lights on in June's house. It was only nine thirty, after all.

Maddie's room was in the southeast corner of my property, however, and June's house was set back a little to the north, so I couldn't tell if anyone was up.

"Can you find those pictures again?" I asked Maddie, now almost asleep.

"Uh-huh. Tomorrow, okay?"

"It's very important."

Was I really going to do this?

What kind of grandmother pulls a little girl out of bed (at least it wasn't a school night), sits her in front of a computer, and puts her to work?

My kind.

Maddie valiantly woke herself up enough to show me how to go back to the Internet sites she'd visited. I was sure that little word from me about how this was going to help Uncle Skip was a great motivator. I draped a small daisy-chain quilt I'd made years ago over her shoulders. I wasn't entirely a monster, I told myself.

Maddie made bookmarks of the key places she'd used in her search, not only this evening but throughout the week, when we thought she was in here simply e-mailing all her old friends in Los Angeles. I watched her manipulate the mouse and keyboard, suppressing pangs of guilt until I felt I could manage on my own.

"You should get back into bed," I told her finally, half lifting her from the chair.

Her look of relief almost brought me to tears.

"You can stay in my room and work, Grandma. The computer doesn't make any noise." (I knew that much.)

"I promise I won't be very long, and I'll be very quiet."

This whole interchange seemed backward to me. Shouldn't my granddaughter be saying those things to me, and not vice versa?

"And don't worry, Grandma. You can't break anything."

(I was relieved to hear this.) "If you need me, just wake me up, okay?"

I gave Maddie a hug. "Thank you so much, sweetheart. You'll get a special treat tomorrow, okay?"

"Mmm," she managed.

When she didn't take this opportunity to make a deal, I knew she must be exhausted. I tucked her in, propped a pillow on the side of her bed to block the light from the monitor, and went back to her computer.

I pecked away at the keyboard, each click sounding like the clash of cymbals in the otherwise quiet room. I looked over a few times to where Maddie was sleeping a few feet away. Never a stir, so I kept going.

A page (did they call them pages when some of them went on and on?) came up of still photos of Brad Goodman—headshots, such as an actor might use. I knew Mary Lou had similar professional portraits of herself for art show brochures and other gallery publicity.

I got discouraged at seeing page after page of benign photographs and figured these were the ones Maddie had copied for Zoe's album.

I switched to the newspaper sites and had better luck. If finding juicy tidbits about a murder victim could be called luck. An article from an art newsletter produced in Santa Fe had the headline "Art Incident Delays Show." I read the opening paragraph.

> Up-and-coming artist Bradford Goodman filed a petition to the art commission today to exclude veteran artist Edward Villard from next week's Grand Illusions art show. Goodman claims that Villard submitted the same painting to a previous show, in violation of the current rules. Judges claim they need more time to investigate the accusation.

   The article, about eighteen months old, was one of many
on the topic through the next few days. I scanned them all,
getting few other details of the story. By the end of the
week, the allegations had proved false ("Mr. Goodman
apologizes profusely, regretting that he received incorrect
information about the talented Mr. Villard"), but the notice
exonerating Ed of misconduct got about one tenth the column space that the original story had gotten.

   I made a note to have Maddie print out copies for me in
the morning, since my printer was noisy and I didn't know
how to access hers.

   Buoyed by my new proficiency with the Internet, I followed a cheat sheet Maddie had prepared for me and ac-
cessed YouTube. I felt I'd shed a couple of decades and
could now call myself "cool."

   The video was very brief, not more than four minutes. It
captured another show, this one in a gallery in Carmel, not
too far from Lincoln Point (in miles, that is, not in charm,
where the oceanside town of Carmel had it all over LP).

   I watched a slightly jerky recording of Brad Goodman
at an awards reception. Maddie hadn't been exaggerating.
Brad, holding an award in the shape of a large palette, as
near as I could tell, pushed Ed away from the center of the
camera's focus and waved his trophy in the air. Not that I
was an expert in kinesics, but the motion made him look
more like a sports figure than a fine artist. Ed stepped awk-
wardly off the platform in what I was sure was an embarrassing moment for him.

   I played the video again, this time looking at people in
the background, in case this was where Maddie had seen
Nan Browne.

   The second time through, I saw Ed lumber off to the
right side of the screen with a nasty expression on his face.
The third time through I picked Nan Browne and her
daughter out of the crowd just behind the platform on the
left. Diana was holding a trophy of some kind also, smaller
than Brad's. Second place? Diana looked happy, but her

mother had an expression similar to Ed's and I suspected she also had a problem with Brad's winning.

I sat back in the desk chair, trying to recall my interactions with Ed Villard and Nan Browne. I was sure both of them had said they hadn't known Brad before he came to Lincoln point less than a year ago. Why would they hide such an innocuous relationship? Testy, yes, but still innocuous.

I knew the LPPD had interviewed all the artists who worked at Rutledge. Skip had said everyone had "alibied out." Since Brad's body had been found in the Channel 29 studio, I assumed their staff, including Nan Browne, would have been on the list as well. I wondered if "stars" like Nan needed as good an alibi as the common folk. I made a note to ask Skip what had come of his interview with her.

I decided to push my limits at the computer and try to find out who Debra Ketough was. I started by putting her name into Google. "I'm Googling," I said to myself, amazed at how I'd fallen in line not only with methods of research beyond 3-by-5 index cards, but with the new verbs computers had invented.

It took more than learning the jargon, however, and I had no luck finding Debra. What made me think I could do better at this than my granddaughter? Maddie was right. It was as though Debra Ketough didn't have an address, at least not one easily found. I quit before I was tempted to sign up for a paid subscription to a company that promised to find all my high school classmates.

"What are you doing up?" Mary Lou's voice startled me, and if she was prepared to scold her daughter as she peeked into the room, she also got a surprise.

"I'm digging into the art world," I whispered. "Want to help?"

"Let's work over tea," she said.

An excellent idea.

* * *

We moved to the atrium, cold enough for Mary Lou to turn on her space heater and sit for a few moments with her hands around a mug of hot chamomile. When I told her about Maddie's research results and my interpretation of the newspaper accounts, she took it in stride.

"I've been telling you this all along, Mom. There can be an intense competitive spirit in the art world. Whether it's all-consuming enough for murder, I don't know." Mary Lou shivered, from the chill and from the idea of murder among her own, I was sure.

"We should call Skip about this," I said. "It might be an avenue the LPPD hasn't thought of, considering it goes back to another time and another state."

"And there are a lot of other exhibits they could look into to see if there've been similar problems with how Brad conducted himself, who else he might have dissed, et cetera," Mary Lou said.

So many more potential suspects, also, reminding me again how I'd closed off the list at a small number of candidates, compared to what Skip and his colleagues had to think about. Not even Zoe could be eliminated from my presumptuous attempt at a list. From what June told me of Zoe in Chicago, her friend was equally capable of escalating a competition, not for recognition or advancement in a career, but to win Brad Goodman's attention.

Just as Mary Lou and I agreed that those of us who weren't the real police (she called us "virtual police") should go to bed, my phone rang.

The real cop was calling.

"I know it's late, Aunt Gerry, but if you want to come to the hospital to see Rhonda Edgerton, I can clear you."

Hmmm. Was I to believe that Skip was inviting me to the hospital at almost eleven o'clock at night to see a murder suspect/person of interest/assault victim? (It seemed Rhonda was all of the above.) I was amazed that he was offering me access to her.

"How come . . . ?" I stopped, not wanting to remind him that this was out of the ordinary.

I heard a resigned sigh from the other end of the line. "She asked for you," Skip said. "Are you free?"

"I'm reasonable," I said, already walking toward the coat closet.

I could hardly contain myself. I was finally going to meet Rhonda. She'd started out in my mind as a mere name uttered with scorn by June Chinn. She'd morphed at various times during the week into a woman with many names and personas, including one who was lashed out at by chief murder suspect Zoe Howard. She was a person who one minute carried herself like a lawyer—and the next, a crazy lady around town who may have slashed inanimate objects and an already-dead animal.

Now she wanted to see me. A brief moment of panic intruded on my excitement—what if Rhonda had snuck a weapon into her hospital room and was waiting to . . . ? I flicked away the thought.

With no traffic, I arrived at the hospital in record time and parked in a spot near the helicopter landing pad. Skip was waiting at the information desk to escort me through the sign-in area to the main hallway of patients' rooms.

Even at this late hour we dodged a steady stream of men and women pushing carts with meds and first-aid supplies. I averted my eyes from the open doors into the rooms. I knew too well how many would have spouses or parents on all-night vigils.

"What's new?" I asked Skip, as if we'd arranged a casual meeting for coffee at Willie's during the daylight hours.

"Not as much as I'd like." Skip was showing signs of a long week and a long day. "Rhonda is pretty banged up, but nothing life-threatening." He shrugged his shoulders and shook his head, looking helpless. "She didn't see her attacker."

"Not even to say if it was a male or a female?"

"Nuh-uh."

"I'm surprised she's not blaming Zoe, whether or not she knows for sure."

"Not yet, anyway. She says the attacker came up from behind and held something over her mouth to knock her out. She thinks she'd be dead or being tortured somewhere if Johnny hadn't come out into the alley."

"Are you going to charge her with anything?" Or Zoe? I was thinking.

"Not unless you want to press charges about a stolen and molested pineapple." I shook my head—I didn't think so. "As far as criminal activity, there was nothing in her motel room to connect her with any criminal activity more serious than using fake IDs. She had a lot of pamphlets and churchy literature on marriage in the room."

"No law against that."

"None that I know of." Skip pointed down the hall. "Her room's the last one on the right."

"No kidding?" I said. "The one with the cop at the door?"

I knew Skip was tired when he didn't bring out his oft-used adage—"Just because she's crazy doesn't mean she's not a killer."

Chapter 22

We entered Rhonda's hospital room, with me holding my breath for no clear reason. Here was yet another version of Rhonda Edgerton, in a hospital gown, blond hair pulled back, her face pasty. She looked neither crazy nor like a killer, but like a Lincoln Point oak that had been buffeted by a very strong wind. She was bruised, battered, and patched up here and there. No blood-leaking bandages, however, I was glad to see for both our sakes.

"Well, if it isn't the famous Geraldine Porter."

I felt my face redden. "Famous?"

Rhonda folded her arms across her chest, a motion that pulled along a tube/needle combination that was stuck in her hand.

"The woman without a life, so she has to rummage around in everyone else's."

That hurt, but I couldn't dispute it with hard facts. I hoped the sound I heard from Skip was not a snicker, but a simple clearing of his throat.

I gathered my wits and self-esteem. "How are you feeling, Rhonda?"

"How does it look?"

No small talk welcome, I gathered. "You sent for me?"

"I've been in town for a week or so, now, and the word is that you're the one who pays attention and may be able to help me get through to the"—she gave Skip a disparaging look—"small town cops here."

This time I knew Skip was not just clearing his throat. Lucky for all of us, his pager beeped. He looked at the display and said, "Gotta go." I had the feeling that he would have said that no matter who had summoned him, or that he might have pushed a button and summoned himself.

"We'll be fine," I said.

"I'll bet," he said and left the room.

As the now highest-ranking official (by family association) in the room, I pitched into the patient/suspect.

"What can you tell me about Brad, Rhonda? Who do you think wanted him out of the way? And try to think beyond Zoe, please."

Not bad, if I did think so myself. At least it seemed to work with Rhonda, who threw up her hands as far as they could go given the IV contraption attached to her.

"Are you kidding? There was so much competition among all the artists. I thought the real estate business was cutthroat, until I saw my husband's colleagues in action. It was all about who's chummy with whom, you know? For this shindig—your Abraham Lincoln thing—everyone had to submit a portfolio back in the fall, and only a few got chosen. I guess a lot of people were upset that Brad got two separate commissions since he hadn't been here that long."

"Do you think he was killed by another artist?"

"I don't know. But it wasn't Zoe, I know that now. There's nothing like being attacked yourself to give you a little perspective. We all loved Brad in our own demented way."

"We all . . . ?"

"I tried to kid myself for a long time, but Brad played the field even when we were engaged. If he were old and rich, he'd be called a womanizer, and I guess he was headed in that direction."

I saw my list of suspects growing by leaps and bounds. Not only artists across state lines, but rejected women left in Brad's dust.

"It must have been very difficult for you." (This was Geraldine Porter, the sympathetic one, as opposed to all those other, crass Lincoln Point cops.)

"It was, but I had my faith and I thought he would honor our vows. But when he left Chicago to be with Zoe, I knew it was over. Still, I had to give it one last shot. My church doesn't believe in divorce, and I thought if I could make him see that . . ."

"Did you have a lot of contact with Brad after the divorce?"

"I told you. There was no divorce."

In spite of her strong words, Rhonda's voice was weakening, understandable considering the hour and what she'd been through. I made an attempt to steer the narrative in the direction I wanted as I eked out the last of her energy.

"Tell me what happened the night he was killed."

She stiffened, tilting her head and raising her eyebrows. "I have no idea."

To strengthen my resolve, I pictured Rhonda with a couple of yards of inexpensive black fabric and a bag of crafts beads, poised to make a replica of Zoe's jacket. She didn't look the type to join our crafts group, I had to admit.

"We know you impersonated Zoe and slashed Brad's paintings. The police can do amazing things with videotape these days, Rhonda. And as for those pitiful stabbings"—here I made a disgusting sound as if I were observing a stabbed raccoon and an entire, wounded fruit store at that very moment—"we have all we need on that end, too. And that's just the beginning. There's the rest of the skulking around town that you've done."

With each figurative tick mark enumerating her activities, Rhonda's eyes grew wider, her lips tighter. I felt I was spot on.

What did it say about me that the one investigative technique I'd perfected was that of lying to suspects? First to Zoe in her jail cell, then to Ryan on his way to seek greatness as Stephen Douglas, and now to Rhonda, on her night of agony. I also remembered fudging the truth a bit with Nan Browne, leading her to believe I was a friendly reporter, ready to make her and her Channel 29 shows famous.

"I don't want to talk anymore," Rhonda said. She started to drift off (unless she was using her own investigative technique). In any case, I knew the interview was over.

The last words I heard as I turned to leave were, "He still loved me, you know. And I would never, never hurt him."

I left the room not much smarter than when I entered, but with a definite feeling that Rhonda did everything we thought she did, from the fake jacket to the last grapefruit, but she didn't kill the man she still considered her husband.

This left the distinct possibility that it was the killer who attacked her. But why? From my stellar interview, it was clear that she didn't know anything incriminating, so why bother?

It was close to midnight, and I decided to leave those questions for the morning.

I left the hospital and walked out toward the helicopter pad and my car.

I approached the row I'd parked in, keys at the ready. There were still quite a few cars in the lot, even at this hour. I figured that most belonged to the staff and the rest to the poor souls who were in the ER or staying all night with a loved one. I went down the first row where I thought I'd parked and found a late-model brown Nissan in the spot I thought had been mine.

Did I have the wrong row? I remembered exiting my car and looking directly down the hill at the Mary Todd Home, the assisted living facility where Linda worked. Maybe my car was one row over.

It had been a long time since I'd lost track of where I parked. I usually immediately memorized my spot, having learned the hard way after losing my car in the maze that was the San Francisco airport parking garage. That was easy to understand, however; this wasn't.

I tried two rows in either direction. No red Ion. My car was gone.

I walked back to the original spot, where I was sure I'd left it. I verified that (unless I'd lost my faculties) I'd parked in a legitimate spot, with no time or space restriction and no tow-away sign.

Though the lot was well lit, it now seemed spooky. I looked for a silver or beige SUV and saw too many to count. But none of them was blinking its lights at me, crawling toward me, or otherwise harassing me.

For the second time that day I found myself without my car, needing rescue. I fought back a frantic feeling and tried to convince myself that a stolen car was a small setback, unrelated to the frightening events of the week. People had their cars stolen every day.

There was nothing to be tense about—I still had my purse, my cell phone, and my wits. I took out my phone, undecided about whom to call. Did AAA respond to stolen car reports? Probably not. Should I claim family privilege and call Skip? Or wake Mary Lou and Richard, and, therefore, Maddie, to pick me up? I could call a cab. How about June or Zoe? (I felt they owed me.)

I really should have done what an ordinary citizen with no police connections would have done and called the general number for the LPPD.

I called Skip.

* * *

I asked Skip to pick me up at the emergency room entrance to the hospital, which was the closest to the section of the parking lot I'd used. I walked back and stood just inside the door. He arrived there in less than ten minutes, driven by June in her blue sedan. I took a moment from my own issues to delight in the fact that the two of them seemed to have worked out a way to be together, at least for now.

"Gerry, you poor thing. Are you freezing?" June asked. She'd brought a fleece throw and draped it around my shoulders, then pulled her own scarf up around her neck. "It's awfully cold right by these doors."

Overly solicitous, I thought, but sweet. "I'm sorry to have wakened you," I said.

"I was up. Zoe and I talked for a while, but then she decided to go home, and then Skip . . ." She trailed off, tucking the fleece shawl closer around me, as if I were a child.

"Thanks. But I'm really fine, you know. I just need to report my car stolen, or did you already do that, Skip?"

"But your car is in your driveway," June said. "We saw it there just now."

"It can't be," I said. "Unless car thieves are doing home delivery these days." I laughed at the suggestion.

"But—" June started.

"Let's just get you home," Skip said, interrupting. He waved his arm in the direction of the sidewalk.

June's car was parked illegally at the curb right in front of the automatic doors. The portable blue bubble light on the roof probably convinced any local security person riding around in a cart that a ticket wouldn't be effective.

I climbed into the backseat and started in on my story, unsolicited.

"I parked right near the helicopter pad. I know, because I remember where I was with respect to the Mary Todd. Then when I came out, my car was gone. In fact, shall we drive up there now and check out the spot? Maybe there's a tow-away sign that I missed."

"Let's just get you home," Skip said again, and June obliged.

I leaned back in the seat and closed my eyes for the short ride. I thought I'd never been so tired. So tired that maybe I was dreaming when June turned onto my street and I saw my own red Ion parked in the driveway, just as it would have been if I hadn't driven it to the hospital.

But I *had* driven it to the hospital.

"Aunt Gerry?" Skip said, in what was probably meant to be a comforting tone. "See, there's your car."

I blinked my eyes. My head hurt. The leafless trees that lined my street seemed to lean in toward the middle of the road, ready to pounce on me when I alighted the car. Their waving branches taunted me.

"Skip, you know I drove to the hospital. I left right after you called to say that Rhonda wanted to see me."

"I didn't actually see you drive up. I was waiting for you at the information desk, remember?"

I bit my lip to stop myself from raving at him in frustration. I had another idea. Maybe Rhonda was in on this little trick. She hadn't told me anything so dramatic that it couldn't have waited until she was out of the hospital. Or that she couldn't have put in a note or told the police directly. She'd simply told me she didn't kill her ex-husband. She must have sent for me in order to have someone steal my car and drive it home. Why? To discredit me? To dissuade me from investigating? Hers was not the kind of mind I understood.

Or it could have been one of Skip's pranks, now that he was in a good mood again, thanks to his reconciliation with June.

"This is a joke, isn't it?" I said to Skip, now leading me out of June's backseat the way he would a disabled person or a ninety-year-old. "You reported it stolen and your buddies came through immediately."

Skip's brow was furrowed into a worried look, as if his favorite aunt had lost her mind. I couldn't help feeling he was right.

The motion-sensor light on my house switched on as the three of us approached my vehicle. I felt like a character in a horror novel, expecting my car to turn on its ignition by itself and lunge at me. I saw myself tumbling down my driveway, then being run over by my vehicle, then lying in a heap in the gutter while my Ion's headlights winked.

"You didn't get a ride to the hospital or anything, did you, Gerry?" June asked.

"No, I did not." The protest was much too loud for the quiet street. "Of course not," I whispered.

We did a quick survey of the car. Skip opened the driver side door, which was unlocked. June and I walked around the outside, but neither of us saw anything unusual. No damage, nothing disturbed, either inside or out.

"Where are your keys?" Skip asked.

Finally, an easy question. I reached into my purse and produced them. Heaven only knows why I considered that a victory for me.

"Okay, then," he said, without telling me what that meant.

"Can you get someone over here to see if there are fingerprints on the door and the steering wheel?" I asked. "Other than yours and mine, I mean?"

"What are you thinking, Aunt Gerry? That someone stole your car and drove it home?"

"That's exactly what I'm thinking. Now, please, just humor me and get this printed." I turned on my heels. "I'm going to make some tea. You're welcome to join me."

"Don't you think you should just go in and get some rest?" June asked.

"No, I do not," I called over my shoulder.

It was my turn to storm out of a room. A driveway, that is.

* * *

I tiptoed (the storming attitude had been simply for the benefit of Skip and June) into the foyer and crossed the atrium to the middle bedroom, which I'd been using while my family lived with me. I was glad to note there was no sign that Maddie had heard the commotion. Her room was close to the driveway and I'd thought the light or noise might have awakened her. Possibly my keeping her up and busy until she was exhausted had helped in that regard.

I skipped the tea idea, since it was clear that Skip and June had refused my invitation. I went to bed and tossed around for a long time. I had fitful dreams in which my car was repossessed, since I'd proven myself unable to take care of it properly.

In another particularly clear image, a squad of crime-scene technicians crawled all over my driveway in search of a clue to the alleged crime. I joined them in my rose flannel nightgown and found a crate of fruit under the back bumper.

More than once I got out of bed (this part was not a dream), made my way to the crafts room between Maddie's bedroom and the foyer, and peered out the window, to be sure my car was still in my driveway.

It was. At least I thought it was.

Chapter 23

I looked in turn at Richard, Mary Lou, and Maddie, around the breakfast table with me on Monday morning. None of them, as far as I knew, was aware of the events of only a few hours ago. Unless Skip had called to alert them as to my mental state. In the back of my mind, I knew I should be grateful for all his and June's solicitousness, but in fact I was still a bit annoyed.

Between snatches of dream sequences and peeks out the window last night, I'd tried to think of ways to investigate what had happened to my car. I planned to check on any security cameras in the hospital parking lot, for one thing. Surely they'd aim one at the helicopter-landing pad. I wracked my brain to remember if I'd seen or said hello to anyone while I was near my car in the lot. No one came to mind.

I considered Brad Goodman's killer, whoever he or she may have been, to be the prime suspect in the auto theft. I came up with three motives. First, to drive me crazy slowly, using the *Gaslight* technique. Second, to make me appear untrustworthy mentally, therefore undermining my credibility with my nephew and the rest of the LPPD. Third, he did it just because he could.

I drank my cranberry juice and tried to focus on the wonderful family around me.

"I wish I had a holiday today," Richard said, lifting his heft from the table with great drama and a heavy sigh. "But some of us have to work."

Though all the important women in his life knew that Richard loved his profession and relished this new job, we humored him with a chorus of "poor Dad" in one variation or another.

"What are you guys going to do today?" Mary Lou asked as soon as Richard headed out.

"Finish the Lincoln-Douglas room box, for one thing," I said. "You?"

"I have to pick up my painting at Rutledge, then deliver it to city hall. Too bad we can't combine errands, but I have to leave in a few minutes."

It definitely was too bad, since I would have preferred not to drive my car today, for no reason that made sense.

"I wish we had school today," Maddie said.

"What?" Mary Lou asked. (I was too stunned to respond to Maddie.)

"It's Share Day on Mondays and I was going to play my DVD of me and Grandma on television. I hope they have it tomorrow and not wait until next Monday."

This was breaking news. Her parents and I had been assuming that since Lincoln Point had no school tomorrow (never on Abe's very birthday, no matter what day of the week it fell on) Maddie would resent having to go to her school in Palo Alto.

"Is Share Day what you used to call Show and Tell?" I asked.

"That's what the little kids still call it. We have Share Day."

"I see," Mary Lou said.

"I told Kyra and some other kids that I was going to show my DVD. Kyra and Danielle both have dollhouses, and I told them maybe I could stay later some day and go home with one of them and show them how to make some stuff for it. You know, like we do, Grandma."

I hardly dared acknowledge it—like a dream come true. Not only had Maddie made friends in her new school, but she'd done it through a shared interest in dollhouses.

I thought back. Kyra was the "not exactly" friend I'd seen Maddie with a couple of times when I picked her up. But Maddie hadn't been at school since Thursday afternoon, and she didn't know until Thursday night that she'd be on television. She'd missed school on Friday to do the show.

"When did you tell Kyra and the other kids about the show?" I asked her.

"I called them on my new cell phone yesterday. Did I tell you I was the last one to get a cell phone?"

Mary Lou and I looked at each other and probably had similar thoughts. Mine was—if we'd only known that one of the keys to Maddie's assimilation in her new school was a little red cell phone.

As much as I wanted to pursue the incident of the stolen (I had no doubt) car, I shifted my focus to the debate scene.

Except to make one phone call to the hospital before Maddie was ready to join me in the crafts room.

"Do you have a security system in the parking lot?" I asked the young-sounding woman who answered the phone.

"I'm not sure I can answer that question," she said.

"Because you don't know or because you're not supposed to?"

"I'm not sure."

I pictured a nervous candy striper.

"I just need to know if there's a camera in the parking lot by the helicopter-landing pad. I lost my purse there last night. (This device had failed me with the janitor at the Rutledge Center, but it was worth one more try.)

"I can transfer you to Lost and Found."

"No, I tried them. I need to see if the purse was there when I left last night, so if I could see any video that you have, that would be best." (I really needed a new bag of tricks.)

"Maybe you can come in and look?"

"Thanks," I said and hung up.

I'd have to give it more thought and come up with some other ruse. I should have called myself a consultant with the police or a major donor to the hospital's fund-raising efforts. I hadn't heard from Skip and doubted very much that he would be sympathetic to pursuing the matter.

"I'm ready. I'm ready," Maddie said, skipping into the crafts room.

I was glad one of us was.

We finished the room box in record time, adding bits of trash on the grass and a tiny, red knitted scarf over a chair on the platform, along with the famous stovepipe hat that had been featured on television recently.

"It's great," Maddie said, snapping a photograph of the completed scene. "I'm going to show Kyra and the kids tomorrow. I can hardly wait."

"What if you had to wait until you finished a roll of film with, say, thirty-six pictures, then had to take it to the drugstore, fill out a form, and finally pick up your photos a week or ten days later?"

"Huh?"

"Never mind." It was nice to have something to smile about.

The crafts area where we'd worked was in the room with the window onto my driveway. I peeked out twice during our session. My car was there, its headlights reflecting the sun, seeming to mock me.

With Maddie's help getting tissue paper of the right colors, I packed the scene in one of the shipping boxes I kept on hand for such deliveries. We filled my tote with snacks in case we ended up in a desert with no food or water. I couldn't avoid it any longer. I had to get in my car again and drive it.

But not without cleaning it first. There was no chance it would be printed, I knew. I could hear Skip in my mind, reminding me how long it would take to get results because of the backup at the lab, and how unlikely there would be any prints of value in the first place.

I took a spray container of cleaning solution and an old terrycloth rag to the driveway and wiped down the front doors and the handles of my car, plus the steering wheel, dashboard, and instrument panels.

"How come you're cleaning the car, Grandma?"

The real reasons weren't fit for a child's ears. Because I felt my car had been violated—*I* had been violated. The steering wheel was sticky; the gearshift clammy. The seats seemed contaminated with an eerie, unknown substance.

"Because you don't want our little room box to get dirty?" Maddie asked.

"You've got it exactly right," I said.

I was a tentative driver at first. I could have sworn my accelerator had a different feel, and the seat belt (I'd forgotten to clean it) seemed to have been stretched too far the last time it was used. But the lemony scent of my cleaning solution gave the car a whole new smell and I could pretend the vehicle had never been out of my control.

Not only that, I sat up straighter, with new confidence. If it was this easy to get my car back, I could get hold of the case and get our lives back, also.

Maddie was always the perfect driving companion, distracting me from what was stressing me out. Today, as we drove down Springfield Boulevard, she gave a standard running commentary. "The shoe repair shop is having a sale on slippers," she said, followed immediately by, "Sadie's is just opening up. Yum, yum," and, "Look at the cute Abraham Lincoln bobble-heads in the Toy Box window."

I thought she'd make a great DJ; but, then, I thought she'd make a great anything.

"We should be through with this errand by noon," I said. "Shall we make a Sadie's stop then?"

"Yum, yum," she said again, which I took as a "yes."

"I tried to find that Debra Ketough again this morning," Maddie said.

In the busyness of Sunday night, I'd forgotten about Zoe Howard's mysterious bail-poster. Today, a holiday, would probably be as difficult a day as Sunday as far as Zoe's getting any information out of the justice system. Maybe Maddie did better.

"Any luck?" I asked her.

"Nuh-uh. Where can she be living? It's like this lady doesn't have an address."

Doesn't have an address? A light went on, fortunately not the dome light of my car, on its own—I was having enough trouble adjusting to its personality since it had been stolen.

Maybe Debra Ketough *was* a lady who didn't have an address. What if someone with a sinister motive, like framing Zoe for attacking Rhonda, enlisted a homeless person to post bail? All he or she would have to do is provide some fake ID (which, according to Skip was easy to do) and give the indigent person cash for the bond, plus some incentive. He could, therefore, time both Zoe's release and Rhonda's attack.

A prosecutor could make the case that Zoe killed Brad and then attacked his ex-wife, all over a painting that provoked her rage.

"Maddie, you're a genius."

"I know, I know," she said. She paused. Out of the corner of my eye I saw her quizzical expression. "What did I do?"

I blew her a kiss and pulled over in front of the high school. "I have to call Uncle Skip," I said.

He picked up right away. "Is this about your car, Aunt Gerry? We're short-staffed today so it's unlikely anything will get done on it."

"Too many actors in the crew?"

"What makes you say that?" Skip seemed to be reacting to what he perceived as an insult.

"I meant that so many of our male population are trying out for Lincoln or Douglas."

"Yeah, well, with one thing and another, we don't have the manpower to get your car printed."

"Never mind. I cleaned it up anyway. That's not why I called."

I detected a worried gasp. Not audible, except to aunts. "Shoot," he said.

"I had a thought about the woman who posted Zoe's bail." I felt Maddie tug at my pants. I looked up and found her wide-eyed, pointing to her own chest. "After stellar research on the part of your youngest cousin."

"I'm listening," he said.

"What if she's a homeless person and that's why you don't have an address?"

"And why would a homeless woman bail out a stranger?"

I told Skip my theory of a double frame for Zoe, first for Brad Goodman's murder, and then to finish up loose ends, for the attack on her rival, Brad's ex-wife.

"Interesting."

I loved that word—one of my favorites from my nephew, since it always meant that he really was interested, unlike Richard who used the word to indicate that he was bored.

"Can you look into homeless shelters?" I asked him.

"Not easy to do. They're a transient population. And that might not even be her name."

"Do you have a better lead?"

"No," he said in a near whisper.

"What was that?"

"No, Aunt Gerry." Louder this time. "Okay, I'll get back to you."

"Did I help? Did I help?" Maddie asked.

"You certainly did. I never would have thought of looking for a person without an address if it weren't for you."

Maddie kicked her feet in front of her, her "delighted" tell.

Some days I had to remind myself to enjoy these moments with her and not get too wrapped up in the fact that eventually she'd be crossing her legs in a ladylike manner, taking a long time to get ready for an outing, and changing her socks without coaxing.

I loved her this way, and I was sure I'd love her at every phase.

The civic center was sparsely populated today. Mr. Fiddler was playing to the mostly deserted steps. The tune was something patriotic that I couldn't identify—a Sousa march? Our artist, wearing an attractive scarf and a warmer coat than usual, I was glad to see, was redrawing Abraham Lincoln on the first wide step. The mime was absent today, perhaps out getting some exercise. I gave Maddie change for the two receptacles and waited while she talked a bit to each entertainer. I noticed she pulled extra coins from her own pocket.

I made a note to talk to her parents about an increase in her allowance. What made me think I had to worry about her compassion for people who were less fortunate than she was?

Inside the city hall foyer, Maddie saw the mural and her mother's painting in place for the first time.

"Wow, wow," she said, to the delight of Mary Lou who came out from the doors to the assembly hall in front of us.

"You like?" she asked her daughter and was rewarded with a big hug.

As an extra thrill, I saw that a special place had been reserved for the room box Maddie and I (and, okay, my crafter friend, Linda Reed) had worked on. Our outdoor debate scene would be on a stand next to Mary Lou's painting of the Galesburg site.

"It's nice, isn't it?" Another artist heard from—Ed Villard. "You must come inside and see my Harriet Lane portrait," he said, in the most pleasantly animated tone I'd ever heard from him. I noticed that he didn't mention Brad Goodman's painting of James Buchanan, however.

"Speaking of the portraits and their artists," I said, "I was surprised to learn that you and Brad Goodman go back a few years."

"Oh?"

"Yes, I must have misunderstood when you said you met him only when he came to Lincoln Point."

"We may have traveled the same circuits, but"—he gestured behind me—"ah, here's your sweet granddaughter."

Smooth move, I thought, making a note to ask Nan Browne the same question and compare reactions.

Maddie had stretched her neck as far back as possible to get a good view of the mural. "Wow, this is cool. Where's your part, Mr. Villard?"

Ed picked her up in a swooping motion that startled me, though Maddie seemed unperturbed. "Way up there on the left," he said.

"It's very nice. Thanks," she said, slipping to the floor.

I wasn't enough of an art critic to know how good Ed's section of the mural was, compared to those of the younger artists. I'd have to ask Mary Lou about it later, if it still mattered to me.

"Do you know the lady who draws on the steps?" Maddie asked Ed.

The old—older, that is—artist stiffened. "What makes you ask that?"

Maddie shrugged. " 'Cause she's an artist like you."

"I don't think so," Ed said in a mocking tone. "A has-been, if anything."

I wondered why he seemed insulted and what had happened to his good mood. Maybe we didn't respond with enough enthusiasm to his invitation to see his Harriet Lane.

"I've heard the guys talk about the woman with the chalk," Mary Lou said. "The word is that she used to be a working artist but fell on hard times."

"Translation: booze and drugs," Ed said.

"It can happen to anyone," Mary Lou said. I pictured her organizing a march for down-and-out artists very soon.

"Tomorrow is her last day here," Maddie said.

"Whose?" I asked.

"The lady with the chalk."

"How do you know that?" Ed asked, beating me to the punch.

"She told me just now when I was talking to her. She wants to stay for the debate tomorrow night but then she's going back to live in Europe where she used to be famous."

"Poor thing. In her dreams," Mary Lou said.

A strange look came over Ed's face, as if he was envious of the attention being paid to an artist of less worth than him.

"Let's go in to see the portraits," I said, wanting to restore goodwill all around.

Ed looked at his watch. "You can check them out yourselves. I have to go."

Too late.

The rest of the holiday passed without incident, but with no satisfaction, either. I made a couple of feeble attempts to determine what had happened to my car, even going back to the scene of the crime to try to jog my memory of something or someone suspicious I might have seen.

I planned my trip and my phone calls around Maddie's and Mary Lou's schedules, since I had no desire to share my concerns with them. It was easy enough to sneak around. Maddie was distracted, watching her DVD again and again, rehearsing how she might narrate her Share Day presentation for Tuesday. Mary Lou had gallery business and last-minute details to take care of at the civic center. Even Richard had a lot on his mind that didn't concern me directly, having to revise a paper of his that was accepted to a major medical conference in the Midwest.

I excused myself right after dinner, claiming a headache. No one seemed to mind.

Better days were ahead, I told myself. After all, tomorrow was Abraham Lincoln's birthday.

Chapter 24

If I couldn't solve my own personal case, which (in line with my new movement toward more meaningful titles) I'd dubbed "The Red Rover," I could at least make myself useful in the matter of Brad Goodman's murder and the related case of Zoe Howard's anonymous bail-poster.

When all were accounted for—Richard on his way to Stanford and Mary Lou driving Maddie to Share Day at the Angelican Hills school—I set out to do some footwork.

There were two homeless shelters in town that I knew of, both in the neighborhoods south of the civic center. I drove to the first one and parked around the back. A CLOSED sign, nearly invisible among all the torn flyers and notices, was pasted to the window. I peered inside, around the dog-eared sheets of paper, and saw what looked like an abandoned kitchen.

I tried to remember which year I had helped serve a holiday meal here. Too long ago, and now it was too late.

I went back to my car and felt a wave of relief to see it

where I'd left it. My confidence that the theft had been a single, isolated incident rose a notch.

I had better luck with the second shelter, little more than a soup kitchen in an abandoned library branch that had closed several years ago from lack of funding. From the peeling paint and broken window shutters I gathered that funding was lacking for this establishment, also.

I knocked on the front door, and a few minutes later introduced myself to a stocky, middle-aged woman with an in-charge look. She wore an apron over a dark pants suit, low-heeled comfortable-looking shoes, and a hairnet. She carried the largest spatula I'd ever seen. She was either the administrator, the cook, or both.

"You people have already been here," she said, not inviting me in.

"Excuse me?"

"The police. You're with the police, aren't you?"

It seemed that Skip had had someone act on my idea of who might have posted Zoe's bail. But I hadn't used "Officer" or "Detective" before my name.

"What makes you think so?"

"You're not dressed like you're hungry, and the only other people who come here want information, and that's usually the police."

Fair enough.

"I'm looking for a Debra Ketough," I said. I stomped my feet a bit and pulled the sleeves of my jacket down, to indicate that perhaps I could step inside where it must be warmer. She didn't acknowledge the signal.

"Same as the others," she said. "I told them, nobody by that name comes around here. Not that I know of, anyway. We're not big on records here, you know. We just keep track of how many meals get eaten so we can get our piddling amount of money."

"Can I ask you a few questions?"

The woman heaved a sigh and raised the enormous wooden spatula to shoulder level. I was afraid she was going to hit me, but she merely scratched her head with the end of the handle.

"I'm really busy here. It's almost lunchtime and I'm expecting at least twenty people who haven't eaten since yesterday at this time."

"You serve only lunch?"

"That's all we can afford. We try to make it a substantial meal. Now, I have to go."

She started to close the door. I put my foot on the threshold to stall her effort, knowing she could have crushed my ankle if she chose. I knew her bad disposition was out of frustration with her meager resources.

"What if I stay and help?" I asked.

I didn't expect my offer to draw such a hearty laugh from this serious woman. "So you can feel good yourself?" she asked. "Or worse, badger them with questions? These people have been hassled enough by the system."

I wished I could contradict her. "Just one quick question, then. Has any of your regular diners acted differently in the last couple of days or said anything strange?"

Another loud laugh. "You mean other than the usual talk about rich uncles that are going to leave them a fortune? Or the trip they're going on tomorrow, to London or Rome or Paris? No. Now I really have to go."

I withdrew my foot, thanked her, and returned to my well-behaving car. There was no communicating with this woman.

I might as well get ready for the great February event and leave the debating to the professionals.

My afternoon chores included writing a check to the shelter. Alone in the house, I rummaged in my refrigerator for something not too old and dry. (A recollection of the oversize spatula had made me hungry.) In my haste, I knocked off one of Beverly and Nick's postcards from Hawaii. We'd stuck them all to the refrigerator door.

After three days of no mail, I missed hearing from the
newly formed couple. We'd agreed we wouldn't call since
this was supposed to be important bonding time for them.
I'd have to settle for reviewing the postcards we already
had. A particularly colorful card pictured a long view of a
Waikiki beach at sunset. The message was one I'd forgotten: *We're already planning our next vacation. This sum-
mer we'll be doing an art tour of Europe. Plan ahead and
join us in Paris! Love from B & N.*

My refrigerator motor kicked on and at the same time
something clicked in my head. Two other people were
planning a trip to Paris? One of the soup kitchen's diners,
(though the cook thought it was just a wild rambling) and
the sidewalk artist Maddie had chatted with (also considered a wild rambling).

What if the two were really the same person?

It was the only thing that made sense—our sidewalk
artist had been offered a trip, more like residence in Paris,
in exchange for delivering cash to the Lincoln Point jail. I
remembered the woman's upgraded coat and scarf. It all fit
together. She must be Debra Ketough.

The only question was who had paid her. The field was
wide open. I needed to talk to Debra Ketough herself.

Suddenly not hungry, I grabbed my purse and headed
out to find her.

The buzz was palpable in the civic center plaza as Lincoln Point citizens turned out for the great debate reenactment. The festivities started with informal picnics through
the day. Tailgate parties were in full swing when I arrived
around four o'clock, firework displays were being prepped,
and families had gathered around the park's barbecue
grills. I breathed in the heavy aromas of beef and a spicy
sauce and was hungry again. Only in California, Ken
would say, could you plan outdoor events in February. (He
dismissed other warm climates without apology.) Today's

weather was near sixty-five and sunny, a gift from Abe, we all thought.

I parked in the high school lot, checking all the signage. The otherwise restricted lot had always been fair game on debate day, but today I read every sign twice.

I crossed Civic Drive, scanning the crowd for Debra, convinced that this was our chalk artist's name. No luck. There were too many people between me and her favorite steps.

As I approached the steps, I still didn't see her in any of her usual spots, to the right or left of the center, thoughtfully never blocking anyone's access.

The fiddler and mime were on duty. I hoped at least one of them might help me locate their colleague. I started with the one who'd be more likely to talk.

"Have you seen Debra around today?" I asked him, right after depositing a twenty-dollar bill in his fiddle case. I hoped paying for information wasn't illegal.

He bent over, picked the twenty out of the pile of mostly ones, and put it in his vest pocket. "Who?" His voice was high-pitched and, up close, I realized he was much older than I thought. Typically, he'd been faceless to me all this time.

"The woman who does the chalk paintings."

"Is that her name?"

"What did you think it was?"

He shrugged shoulders. I wondered if I should drop another bill in the case, but he continued, free of further charge. "We call her Rainbow, 'cause of her chalk."

"Have you seen Rainbow today?"

"She's on her supper hour," he said, enjoying his own joke. "She's been talking about celebrating her last day. We've all heard that before, but this time she might be telling the truth. This morning, she brought me and Silverman here"—he pointed across the expanse of the steps to the mime—"some doughnuts."

"Do you think she'll be back later?" I shouted. A new

busload of people was dumped onto the plaza, this time
from the Mary Todd Home, according to the logo on the
side of the vehicle.

"I don't think she'd miss the most profitable night of the
year, no matter how much money she says she has. There's
still an hour to go before the debate starts and people tend
to be very generous when they're having fun. And even after the debate, the good citizens are on their way to parties
and they feel guilty when they see us, so . . ." He pointed to
his case.

I felt he had a good hold on the culture of Lincoln Point.

"Did Rainbow say where she got this money?" I started
to feel that I owed him another deposit. He was so much
more cooperative than the soup kitchen cook had been.
Maybe I should have offered her a twenty.

"She just said she did an errand for a guy and now she
was rich and was going to Paris tomorrow. Some errand,
huh?" He leaned into me and I smelled something on his
breath that wasn't doughnuts. "You got any errands for me?"
he asked with a pleasant laugh that made me wish I did.

"No, but thanks for talking to me," I said and turned to
leave. Then I swiveled back. "I'm Gerry. What's your
name?" I asked the fiddler.

"William." He smiled and tipped his hat. "Pleased to
meet you, Gerry."

"Pleased to meet you, too, William."

It was about time, I thought.

Now what? I couldn't very well wait on the steps for another hour until the debate started at five thirty. I spotted an
empty bench under the trees at the edge of the lawn and
headed for it. I pulled out my phone as I walked, planning
to call Skip with my latest theory about Debra Ketough. I
hoped he would enlist the LPPD to find her. I felt sure now
that she was in danger, that she was supposed to have left
town and taken the killer's secret with her. Whoever gave

her the money for a new lifestyle would not be happy to see that she was still here and advertising her newfound wealth.

"Fraternizing with the help, I see."

Ed Villard, dressed to the nines, had joined me in lock-step toward the bench. He seemed to be in a good mood again. I hoped he was getting high praise from the throngs who visited the city hall to see the special debate artwork.

"I wish we could do more for people like that," I said. "Did you know that one of the two shelters we had in town is now closed and that our chalk artist eats at a soup kitchen?" I didn't mention the theoretical nature of my pronouncement.

"God helps those, et cetera, et cetera," he said and waved to an admirer. "Excuse me. My public awaits."

I wished Mary Lou were with me to give him a good response.

I'd come to the end of the line for the moment.

I sat on the bench, phone in hand, undecided about what to do. I'd left a message for Skip, but hadn't tapped into the general population of the LPPD. I remembered Maddie's big day at school—Mary Lou would have taken her home by now. I called her new cell phone number.

"Hi, Grandma. I called you and your phone was off." She sounded breathless. "It was nuts, Grandma. Everybody clapped!"

"I'm so glad." I liked the new use of the word "nuts," also.

"And Friday I'm going to Kyra's house and make furniture. Is that okay?"

Before we clicked off, I listened to plans for at least five other "playdates" that Maddie had set up with her new friends in Palo Alto.

I knew her parents were rejoicing as I was.

At various times others joined me on the bench and we

struck up brief conversations. We talked about the format of the original debates and how it would never work these days. Historically, the entire debate took three hours (thus the early starting time), with the first candidate speaking for one hour without a break, the second for an hour and a half, and then the first one again with a half-hour rebuttal. The order of speakers was determined by a toss of a coin.

"No sound bites back then," an older gentleman commented.

One older couple engaged me in a discussion of the debate roles.

"Who do you think is Lincoln?" the woman asked me. "It's always the most exciting moment when he walks out on the stage."

"I want to know who got the Douglas role," the man said. "My son was trying out and I know he didn't get it because he's been moping around for a week."

"Apparently Douglas was very wealthy," the woman said. "He had lots more money to spend and traveled in great style on a special train with security and servants."

A wealthy Douglas with security guards? I'd forgotten about the major Douglas candidate, our own security guard Ryan Colson. He'd never called me back for our little chat about how he let Zoe into the artists' work area the night of Brad Goodman's murder. I supposed he realized he'd all but admitted to the infraction and would gain nothing by talking to me.

I wondered if he could have been the anonymous donor to Zoe's bail, but quickly dismissed the idea. He seemed too naïve to me to have executed the plan. He'd nearly fallen apart when Zoe caught him with a new honey. Also, he couldn't be rich enough on a guard's salary.

But someone was. Wealthy. I focused on the word. I'd heard it spoken of someone recently, besides the real Stephen Douglas. In my concentration, I feared I was rude to a little boy who tried to talk me into helping him feed a squirrel that had arrived at our feet.

It was time to search the crowd around the steps again for Debra. The last time I strolled over I thought I saw her in a bright red jacket, but it was just the popcorn vendor, bending over to scoop up spilled product.

I stood to leave the bench and felt something jab my ribs. At the same moment, I remembered who was being talked about as being wealthy. Ed Villard, the bearded man who now held a gun—or something round and hard—against my body.

"Act natural," Ed said into my ear.

"It's *naturally*," I said, easily the most ridiculous utterance of my week.

Chapter 25

Ed walked me away from the crowd toward the back lot of the library, which was closed today. I didn't know for sure if what I felt was a gun, but it didn't matter. He was a big man and could have taken me anywhere, even unarmed.

My heart raced. I thought of my family. I was supposed to meet Maddie and her parents in less than a half hour in the lobby by Mary Lou's painting and my room box. We'd planned to go into the hall and sit together.

I looked in vain for a way to signal a passerby, but they were all engrossed in each other and in their destination. Why couldn't they see how I was trembling?

The crowd thinned very quickly after the line of trees. Throughout the walk, Ed and I were strangely coupled as he held me close with his left arm, using his right arm to steady the weapon. Anyone who saw us might think we were on a date. Unless they heard his whispers, every three or four feet.

"Not a word. Understand?" came often. As did, "If you try anything, I'll shoot you and then anyone else at random."

"I understand," I said, over and over, as waves of fear rippled through my body.

"I knew you were trouble the first time I met you. I hoped I was wrong. I did everything I could to dissuade you," he said when we were nearly alone.

"You stole my car," I said, hardly aware I'd spoken out loud.

"Yes, your pitiful little car. I must admit it was childish, but I was flailing around at that point, trying to get your attention."

Why was I relieved that I hadn't imagined the car theft? Wouldn't it be better to be a bit off mentally, but alive?

"Why don't we talk . . ." I felt a cloth tight on my mouth. An acrid scent struck my nostrils. The trees, the library building, the darkening sky—all went out of focus as I felt my body being tipped onto the seat of a silver SUV.

"Lady, lady. Are you awake?" *Clack, clack, clack.*

The voice and the sounds echoed in a hollow chamber. My head throbbed, my body ached. It took a while for my eyes to focus. I was in the civic center, and then I wasn't.

"Lady, yoo-hoo, lady. Over here."

The loud voice seemed to invade my senses. Where was I? Where was the voice coming from?

The answers took shape, like the final result in a game of *Clue*. I was in the Rutledge Center artists' work area with Debra/Rainbow, who was yelling at me from across a couple of rows of empty workbenches. The clacking was the sound of her chair hitting the cement floor as she bounced her way toward me.

I was seated on a folding chair, my hands tied behind my back, my feet tied to the bottom rung of the chair. Though I couldn't see the details of her situation, I assumed Debra was in the same predicament.

"Where is he?" I asked, my speech slurred as if I'd been drugged.

"He brought me here and then he went to get you. Now he's back with his adoring fans."

"Are you the woman who posted bail money for Zoe Howard the other day?"

Clack, clack, clack.

"Yeah, that was me. He bought me a nice dinner and a new outfit. He said he'd take care of me if I just did that one errand. He gave me a lot of money and a plane ticket after I did it."

The room took a spin around me as I made an attempt to get up from the chair. No use.

"You okay?" Debra asked.

"Yes, as okay as I can be." I stretched my neck and arched my back as far as it would go. "Is Debra your real name?"

"Yeah. I admit it was nice to clean up my old expired driver's license and be a real person again. Even though the address on it is now an empty lot."

If I weren't so limp, I'd have hugged Debra and told her she was as real a person as anyone. I heard myself try to say something to that effect, but I was too sleepy to pay attention even to my own slurred words.

"Why didn't I leave town right away?" Debra asked, shaking her head. I imagined her trying to go back twenty-four hours and make different choices. "I've been asking myself that question over and over." She jerked her body, causing the chair to slip. She almost tipped over backward. "I had to take a chance to live in my own town like a normal person. Like buying doughnuts for my friends, you know."

The work area was dark and deserted, of course—all the artists and everyone else who worked in Rutledge Center were at city hall.

"What's he going to do to us?" I asked Debra. In the back of my mind, since she got here first, she was the knowledgeable one.

Debra moaned. "When he comes back, he's going to kill us. I just know. We have to get out of here. He told me the whole story, you know, Ed did. He called that artist a little twit. He lured him to the studio that night by promising to make him famous. He took a knife from the guy's own tool box figuring his girlfriend's prints would be on it. He told me everything. He has to kill us."

You've already said that, I screamed inside my head.

Debra swayed back and forth as she talked, her hands bound behind her. A sad sight. *Like me.* I couldn't recall ever feeling so depressed. If Ed told Debra all those details, he couldn't possibly just put her on a plane to Paris. Or send me back to my family and my life.

I wanted desperately to go to sleep. The room was dark, suggesting bedtime. I closed my eyes.

"Wake up, wake up. You can't fall asleep." *Clack, clack, clack.* "I was way over there when he brought me here." She tilted her head in the direction of the back of the hall. "But when I saw you, I starting pushing myself toward you. I thought we could untie each other if we can get close enough."

"I'm exhausted," I said. "And I can't move."

"You can't give up," she said. "You're the smart lady. You have to get us out of here."

My senses came alert when a creature flew high over our heads. I wouldn't let myself think about what it could be. I smelled the musty, dusty floors of the work area and felt the thick, scratchy ropes on my hands and feet.

If I was so smart, what was I doing here?

Debra wouldn't give up. Having had a longer time to overcome whatever Ed had drugged us with, she seemed to have enough energy for both of us. By the time I woke up again, she was in front of me, prodding my knees with hers. She'd crossed the entire expanse of the warehouse-like room, a couple of clacks at a time, lifting her body and inching forward.

If she could do that, with not much to live for except a

hot meal in a soup kitchen once a day, I could certainly do my part.

I assessed the situation. I couldn't see the ropes that bound me, but with some maneuvering, we got Debra's chair turned around and I could see hers. Ordinary rope, it seemed, but with a very tight knot.

"He might think we're still drugged," Debra said. "When he came back with you, I flopped my head down so he'd think I was knocked out."

"Good for you."

"When do you think he'll be back?" she asked.

"There's a cocktail party for the artists after the debate." A gathering I was invited to, as Mary Lou's guest. I wondered what my family were thinking. Had they gone into action to find me? They would know I wouldn't deliberately miss the event and not call them. "Maybe he'll stay for the party," I said.

"I'm sure he'll stay for that," Debra said. "He's so vain and hungry for fame."

"You seem to know him well."

"We go back. Ed doesn't miss an opportunity to tell me how I screwed up my life. Then he comes along and offers me a way to fix it. How stupid could I be?"

"You can't blame yourself. I'm sure he was convincing."

"Yeah, convincing. So how much time do we have?"

I couldn't see my watch, but the face of the old clock in the work area was dimly backlit. It read eight o'clock. The debate was almost over. Mary Lou, Richard, and Maddie, along with my friends and neighbors would be listening to Stephen Douglas in his final half-hour rebuttal.

"The debate will be over in a half hour. Then who knows how long he'll stay at the cocktail party."

"We have to get to work," Debra said.

With what? Ed had either kept my purse or destroyed it already. It was clear that Debra was empty-handed and the workbenches had been cleared of tools and supplies.

There must be something. "Okay, let's think about what we have to work with."

"He emptied all my pockets," Debra said.

As far as I remembered, Ed didn't do that with my pockets, unless it was while I was asleep. It was worth the effort to find out. My miniature tool kits were all in my purse, but now and then I dropped a small implement into my pocket for temporary storage.

Like this afternoon, when I used my small scissors to trim a tree in my debate scene? Had I dutifully returned the scissors to its case in my purse?

Lucky for us, I'd been lazy. Debra performed amazing contortions, digging into my sweater pocket and finally extracting the scissors. They were blunt nosed, and it might take forever to cut through rope with them, but it was our only chance.

We worked by the light of a single streetlight in the parking lot, aided slightly by a small nightlight on the wall next to us. It seemed to take hours for Debra to extract the scissors from my pocket, and then more hours for us to position ourselves so that she could work with them.

We decided using the blades like a saw would be best since the ends had safety tips, uselessly round. It would be tricky to hold the scissors open and saw, what with her hands being tied up behind her.

Tricky? Impossible, I thought, but I hated to be the one to give up.

At one point Debra dropped the scissors and endured what must have been excruciating pain as we cooperated to throw her and her chair down on the floor to retrieve them and then get her upright again. It was the first time I got a good look at her face and saw that it was badly scarred. Someone with as tough a life as Debra must have had didn't deserve this kind of end.

I checked the clock again. Five minutes to nine. Why didn't someone think to come looking for us? On the other hand, why would anyone look for me here, or Debra at all?

We heard a car pull up, saw its headlights through a sliver of unshaded window, and held our breath.

"Should we scream for help?" Debra asked, still looking to me to make decisions.

"No," I said. "If it's help, they'll come in anyway, and if it's Ed . . ."

"Then we should pretend to be knocked out. But I'm all the way over here, so he'll know . . ."

The car left before we had any more discussion. We blew out air in a long rush.

Debra had continued to work without stopping and now was ready for an announcement.

"I'm getting it, I'm getting it," she said. I felt a pang of sadness as she sounded like Maddie. "I got it!"

It all happened at once. My hands were free. I undid Debra's knot, which had loosened from all her work with the scissors. Once our feet were free, we ran to the door as quickly as our bruised and stiff limbs could take us.

We opened the door and saw Ed Villard, a startled look in his eyes. With great synchronization born of fright and adrenaline, Debra and I used our four newly freed hands to push him down the short flight of concrete steps. He hit hard, his head smashing into the metal railing at the bottom. We stepped over him and ran out to Hanks Road.

Just in time to be blinded by the lights from what seemed like the entire Lincoln Point motor pool.

The first cop to exit a car was Abraham Lincoln.

"Skip?" I asked. Was the drug kicking in again?

When my head cleared enough, I saw my nephew dressed as Abraham Lincoln. Without our knowing he was trying out, he'd gotten the role in the debate. How had I missed that? In my near stupor, I thought about all his recent recitations of Lincoln trivia and about the bow tie on his bulletin board. He'd said it was from the Mary Todd Ball. If I'd been paying attention at the time, I'd have remembered that he went to the ball in December as an early Pinkerton guard. He'd worn a uniform, with a dark shirt buttoned to the neck and a dark jacket, also buttoned high on the neck. No tie.

He grinned and said he forgave me for missing his great performance.

The paramedics were ready to whisk Debra off to the hospital for a checkup, and then to the shelter.

"We did good, didn't we?" she said to me.

"We certainly did, Debra," I said.

She smiled, revealing uneven, uncared-for teeth. "Debra. I guess I could be Debra again, huh?"

I hugged her and promised to visit her in the morning. I hoped I'd be able to do more than visit in the future, to help her become Debra again. I wondered if a good lawyer would be able to make a case for her getting the money Ed promised her.

I rode home in the Porter SUV, snug in the back with Maddie flung over me as far as she could and still stay belted. I brushed her curls back and felt her tears.

"I was so worried, Grandma."

"I missed you, too, sweetheart, but everything's fine now."

"Do you know it was Maddie who thought of the Rutledge Center?" Mary Lou said.

"Is that right?" I asked my brilliant granddaughter. I smoothed her hair and kissed her head.

"Uh-huh." Her voice was muffled, coming as it was

from a mouth buried deep in my sweater. She tightened her hug. I had a feeling she would have said more if she'd been willing to let go of me.

"We gave you an hour's grace, in case you had a flat tire or something, but by eight o'clock, every car was on the street looking for you," Richard said.

"Except for Skip," Mary Lou said. "He still can't believe he missed all the action."

"And I missed his action on the stage."

"Maddie made us call dispatch and route one car to the work area and one to the TV studio," Richard said.

"Wow, wow," I said.

Chapter 26

On Wednesday, we got our final postcard from Beverly and Nick. It read, "I'll bet things are quiet without us. We'll be back soon to stir up trouble!"

We all hoped not.

On Friday, I received a note from Ryan Colson with an apology for not following up with me (he didn't say about what) and a thank-you for not disclosing his meeting with his friend (he didn't say what kind of meeting or who the friend was).

On Saturday, I received a note from Zoe Howard thanking me for all I did to clear her of the charges and inviting me to dinner at a restaurant of my choice. I picked the Carnelian Room at the top of San Francisco's tallest building, where there were no prices on the menu. On second thought, I decided Bagels by Willie would suit me more.

I had no word from Rhonda Edgerton, or whatever she was calling herself now, but I assumed she was recovering peacefully at home in Chicago.

By Sunday, the Porters, except for me, were all packed

for their move to their new home in Palo Alto. Larger pieces of furniture had been put in storage, but the SUV and the convertible both were piled with odd sizes of luggage, boxes, and garment bags.

They'd be back for a family party on Tuesday, but for me, this was the farewell.

Skip and June were in my driveway for the send-off.

"Did you know Grandma's going to be on TV again?" Maddie asked Skip. "Mrs. Browne is going to interview her on Channel 29."

I heard a gasp from Skip. "On what topic?" he asked, sounding much too nervous for a matter this unimportant.

"My dollhouses and room boxes of course. She's trying to make up for lying to me about knowing Brad Goodman. I guess she feels the case would have been solved sooner if she'd been truthful."

"Oh, right."

"What did you think she'd be interviewing me about?"

Skip let out a long breath. "Nothing."

I peered at him, using my best mind-reading techniques, learned through years of dealing with adolescents who wanted to speak anything but the truth. "Ah. You thought it was going to be on my crime-solving skills."

"Nah." His smile said otherwise.

"What shall we do for our next room box?" Maddie asked as I leaned in to kiss her good-bye.

I knew that, like me, she wanted a specific task for her regular visits to Lincoln Point. I'd already consolidated some of my crafts boxes so she'd have more space in the corner bedroom. I thought how happy Ken would have been to see our granddaughter take over our son's room with such ease.

"How about a flower shop?" I suggested.

"Nah, nah. That's boring. I was thinking of a police station with an office like Uncle Skip's."

I knew that.

Gerry's Miniature Tips

MINIATURE TIPS FOR DRINKS

Miniature mugs and cups are easy to find, not only in crafts stores but in card shops and other "gifts and things" stores. They often are personalized, so this is a perfect way to add just the right touch to a scene you're giving as a present to a friend.

To make a mug of coffee, simply fill with brown paint.

To make a glass of wine, fill with red paint.

And so on!

MINIATURE TOP HAT

You can easily make a pattern for a top hat yourself. Start with four simple pieces: two cut in doughnut shape, one long rectangle, and one circle.

Use felt or other stiff fabric.

Glue the two doughnuts together fuzzy side out, if applicable. This will be the rim of the hat.

Curl the long rectangle into a cylinder for the body of the hat. Glue the cylinder to the rim. Glue the circle onto the cylinder to form the top.

These last steps are tricky. The easiest way to do them is to use a small puddle of glue. Dip one edge of the cylinder into the glue and place the gluey end on the rim. Hold the pieces together for up to a minute while the glue begins to set. Do the same with the other end of cylinder, placing the gluey end on the circular top. Hold the whole arrangement together (gently) until you're sure the pieces won't fall apart.

Gerry's Ginger Cookie Recipe

1 cup sugar (Gerry doesn't skimp on sugar!)
¾ cup butter, softened
¼ cup chopped crystallized ginger
¼ tsp. nutmeg
¼ cup molasses
1 egg
2⅓ cups flour
4 tsp. grated ginger root
2 tsp. baking soda
2 tsp. ground ginger
½ cup shortening
dash salt
extra sugar for rolling

Heat oven to 375°. Mix sugar, butter, crystallized ginger, nutmeg, molasses, and egg in large bowl. Stir in remaining ingredients, except extra sugar.

Shape dough into small balls (approximately one inch);

roll in extra sugar. Place a couple of inches apart on un-greased cookie sheet and flatten slightly.

Bake 5 to 8 minutes or until edges are set. Remove from cookie sheet and cool on wire rack.

Makes about 5 dozen cookies.

(No nutritional information is available. If you have to ask, you shouldn't eat them.)